D0126840

A PALM BEACH
WIFE

Also by Susannah Marren

Between the Tides

A PALM BEACH WIFE

SUSANNAH MARREN

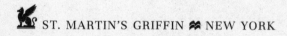

ST. MARTIN'S GRIFFIN ❧ NEW YORK

A PALM BEACH WIFE. Copyright © 2019 by Susan Shapiro Barash.
All rights reserved. Printed in the United States of America. For
information, address St. Martin's Press, 175 Fifth Avenue, New
York, N.Y. 10010.

www.stmartins.com

Library of Congress Cataloging-in-Publication Data

Names: Marren, Susannah, author.
Title: A Palm Beach wife / Susannah Marren.
Description: First edition. | New York, N.Y. : St. Martin's Griffin,
    2019.
Identifiers: LCCN 2018046840 | ISBN 9781250088918 (hardcover) |
    ISBN 9781250198402 (trade pbk.) | ISBN 9781250088925 (ebook)
Subjects: LCSH: Domestic fiction.
Classification: LCC PS3613.A76874 P35 2019 | DDC 813/.6—dc23
LC record available at https://lccn.loc.gov/2018046840

Our books may be purchased in bulk for promotional, educa-
tional, or business use. Please contact your local bookseller or
the Macmillan Corporate and Premium Sales Department at
1-800-221-7945, extension 5442, or by email at MacmillanSpecial
Markets@macmillan.com.

First Edition: April 2019

10 9 8 7 6 5 4 3 2 1

In memory of my mother

My candle burns at both ends:
It will not last the night:
But, ah my foes, and oh, my friends—
It gives a lovely light.

—EDNA ST. VINCENT MILLAY,
"First Fig" from *A Few Figs from Thistles*

ONE

The black-tie affair, to benefit animal activism, takes place in the Shelteere Museum. Chandeliers hang from the double-vaulted ceilings, illuminating the work of Hopper, Eakins, O'Keeffe. Coiffed and studied, women wear gowns glimmering in taffeta, satin, and jewel-encrusted silk, while men sport their mandatory tuxes. A sense of promise bounces around the salon. It's the first gala of the 2014/2015 season—anything is possible. No one has yet been excluded, shunned by a seating chart, or bewildered yet again at how clannish Palm Beach can be. Together, Faith and Edward Harrison whisk through the galleries, passages filled with guests—charmers, climbers, and interlopers.

"We should leave by ten," Edward says quietly to Faith.

"We've just gotten here," Faith says. Isn't he the one who likes to stay past midnight?

"Faith, Edward!" Neighbors, friends, and clients are gliding toward them.

Edward lifts his hand in a gallant wave. "By ten at the latest."

"Let's see how it goes." Faith smiles outwardly and waves along with her husband.

His hand is on her elbow in too tight a grip. Faith shakes her arm slightly for him to let go. Gamboling into the ballroom, she focuses on the festivities of the night ahead. What could be more critical than the kickoff Rose Ball for keeping count of exes and present wives, mistresses and lovers, stray friends? Who knows better the intricacies and hypocrisies than Faith, owner of Vintage Tales, the famed resale shop on Worth Avenue? Almost every woman at the Shelteere is a client—treated carefully and discreetly. "I make a living keeping women's secrets. I'm better than a shrink or a psychic," Faith likes to tell Edward.

The band plays "Moondance" by Van Morrison, selected when the charity wants to be less than stodgy, not quite adventurous. Together, Faith and Edward join those on the dance floor, Edward sidestepping as if it's a dance move, Faith slightly swaying to the lyrics, wishing she dared to twirl and dip toward the center. She lip-synchs her favorite lines, *"A fantabulous night to make romance"* . . . Edward puts his mouth to her ear.

"Listen to me." He is edgy, his voice sotto voce.

Couples collide briefly—the Norrics, the Carltons, the Finleys—and pull away deftly. A spinning disco ball lights the room, and Faith notices dark and bright spots across the dancers' shoulders. The band shifts to sing "Bette Davis Eyes," ramps the sound up a few decibels. Suddenly Edward stops and slouches, morphing from tall to muffled, slightly spasmodic.

"Are you all right, Edward? I can't hear you." Faith poses in a wifely, majestic mode.

As he leans nearer, Edward's lips brush her jawline. "I said we have—"

"Faith, at last," Mrs. A interrupts, leading her dashing young escort, supposedly Romanian, precariously close to the Harrisons. "You are impressive! How gorgeous you are."

Alicia Ainsworth, known only as Mrs. A, a ripened debutante, favors Faith. She takes in Faith's dress and jewels, upswept hair, and height in heels. Although Mrs. A might overlook one's social register or lack thereof, she is all about women at least five-seven and thin, mostly blondes (such as Faith), those who know paradise is a tricky game. "Perish the year-rounder," Mrs. A likes to say. "Anyone who lives north, west, or south might be in Palm Beach County but isn't in the same league as islanders." Mrs. A plays hard in season and leaves with her pack by May. It is she who taught Faith to divide her summers between Greenwich, Aspen, and the Hamptons. Occasionally Faith imagines what it would be like to have a mother such as Mrs. A, a taskmaster who believes that beauty and money are the criteria for friendship, love, and country club memberships.

To Mrs. A's left is her team of dowagers, women aged sixty or more. Faith calls them "the mighty" and secretly admires their tenacity. Short of a 104-degree fever, these women buy a ticket and fill the chairs.

As Mrs. A drifts off, Edward tugs Faith to his chest. "Faith, listen to me. . . . We have no . . ."

Faith gazes at him, hearing enough of what Edward is saying to wonder at how concerned he seems. "No" might mean no progress on the Maserati Quattroporte GTS that he is customizing. Or no time for next week's couples' golf tournament at Longreens. Or something more routine— no room left for more bougainvilleas meant to grace the front of the house.

"No what?" Faith speaks up against the cacophony of five hundred guests.

"No need for you to steal a husband," Priscilla, Faith's loyal client and former neighbor, comes close and announces. Priscilla's fiancé, Walter, hangs on to her. Shriveled and short, at the age of eighty-four Walter is a future husband on the wane, except for his great wealth and charity standing. Priscilla is part of a clique Faith labels "the aspirationals." In their mid-thirties to mid-forties, these women might be matriarchal in their own sphere, but rely on the men, husbands and fiancés, to provide "the life."

"Edward is *devoted*." Priscilla still speaks only to Faith. "And he *looks* good."

"Usually," Faith says. She admires his thick head of hair, which is neither transplanted nor yet gray, how he moves—toned and fit. At the moment he is squinting his sky-blue eyes. Perhaps looking for someone, perhaps toward the door.

Other women would not have stuck with Edward years ago when he was using, despite his sexiness, his polish, his potential. Only if you're flawed yourself, she thinks, would you sign on for an Edward. Only if you have your own past could you carry him to safety. Faith's commitment to Edward has paid off. Ever since Katherine was born, twenty-three years ago, he's been in recovery. His cocaine use and drinking are a long-ago memory. Today he is an ace tennis player, scratch golfer, lithe swimmer, dedicated to lifting weights. Edward and his partner, Henry Rochester, at their company, High Dune, are known as *the* boutique fund managers of Palm Beach. They manage bond funds for prospering clientele, risk-averse investors. And while most of the women choose not to work, Faith has spawned Vintage Tales. When Edward bought the building on the Avenue and gave her the shop, twenty years ago, he said, "All of it, Faith, proceeds . . . the building . . . are yours. The reward for saving me." She too owes him a debt—and loves him in a dedicated, wifely way.

Ten feet past Mrs. A and Priscilla's squadrons, Betina Gilles, consigner of Priscilla's evening clutch (rare turquoise and crystal, circa 1970, bought yesterday at Vintage Tales), stands with her husband, fresh out of prison for tax evasion. Among the hub Faith spots a woman whose Chanel crystal choker, circa 1982, was sold at the shop this morning by Katherine.

At the thought of it Faith scans the room without spotting her daughter, who should have arrived by now.

Paned floor-to-ceiling windows frame a dusky sky—not the usual starry South Florida night. Guests move in a cattle drive toward their assigned tables. Edward stops when he sees Henry Rochester, and together they become ensconced with a handful of men who are neither fit nor paunchy, neither friendly nor chilly. Were they at someone's home, their group activity would be lighting up

Cuban cigars. At the Shelteere they drone on about the market, golf scores, cars, and travels. Edward is oddly distracted, not talking but kicking his left heel with his right shoe. Faith realizes how off center he has been, and while the wives chat among themselves, she stands, watching him. The women, too, drone on about similar topics with a female twist—their conversations are more detailed and always include wardrobe. When Faith is adjacent to the women, she mini-smiles, her focus on Edward. If he turns toward her, she will rescue him, lead him toward the anteroom. If he doesn't, she will keep her eye on him anyway.

And ahead of her is Allison Rochester, lotioned and polished with her steely dimples, unaware of Faith's approach. On the wall behind her are portraits of fashionable, sophisticated women, painted by Sargent and Chase.

"Well, who wouldn't be busy, as the single chair. You know Faith's held on to it, solo, for the Arts and Media gig *for months*," Faith overhears Allison saying.

Margot and Lucas Damon, back in Palm Beach after five years in San Francisco, listen, rapt. Posturing as if on a date rather than fueling a ho-hum marriage, they nod at Allison while looking around. Lucas, whom Faith loved when she was twenty, the boyfriend who brought her to Palm Beach before ditching her, props himself close to his wife. As Faith watches him, the others fall away; only Lucas is in the room. His deliberate posture elongates him to a requisite six feet, and his untamed cowlick is slicked down by some sort of hair product. His limber runner's body is evident even in a tuxedo—as if he could do a steady six-minute-a-mile marathon and land at the finish line with the elite firsts. She hesitates at his eyes, dark eyes. Eyes that know you, that grasp the latitude instinctively. He's not a Palm Beach favorite, although no one is more a native than Lucas. Few would peg him a real estate developer with properties peppered throughout the country. Mostly he seems boyish, sensual—perhaps a creative type. Lucas purses his lips, big-screen style, glances at Faith and back at Allison. Or so she imagines. Margot links her arm in her husband's, and so Faith stands straighter, her cheekbones feel more angular.

"Mom?" Katherine taps her mother on the shoulder.

Faith spins around. "Sweetie—at last!" Faith and Katherine hug, genuinely, cautiously, to avoid makeup smears.

"Look, everyone came!" Katherine points toward her friends, who are off to the right, far from center, fringing the party in couples. "We're about to take a picture and post on Instagram."

Of the young men, Rhys, Katherine's longtime boyfriend, is slimmest, tallest. Still, his mouth is too narrow, and it's sheer luck that he pulls off a disarming grin. Katherine's wide smile, too wide at times, makes up for it, balancing them out. After a painful break during college, the last year in Palm Beach has brought them together. Several days ago Priscilla asked Faith if Katherine and Rhys will live together, then become engaged. Faith feigned disinterest, claiming Katherine is too young. Secretly she can't imagine a better catch, a finer young man.

Katherine's friends, young women of assorted heights, are wearing platform heels that add at least five inches. Another theme of the night is hair, buckets of it in an array of shades, pale blond, chestnut (that would be Katherine), red, mahogany, and raven. Some have it clipped up for the early evening, later to unleash it when the dance floor is packed and the songs a better beat.

"How these girls have evened out." Mrs. A appears. "Remember how some of them were little chubby things? I used to pray they'd improve—for everyone's sake."

Gathered at the Shelteere, the battle-weary daughters, having managed the pressure since fifth grade, signify a job well done. They've finessed a certain look, i.e., *pretty*. Too pretty as teenagers at the Academy, conjuring up trouble—jealous friends, boys who shied away, mothers who manipulated them off the invitation list. Over the years, the circle grew tighter, not wider, and the stakes were raised. Faith, like the other mothers, encouraged her daughter to be au courant, athletic and popular in lower school, adding beauty and brains by seventh grade. Pushed by their mothers toward the best colleges in the northeast, the caveat was that they would come home, sport a mild tan, marry well, and be on as many committees as time allows—factoring in tennis, golf, shopping, then lunch on the Avenue.

Tonight only the survivors prevail. Despite their hard-earned undergraduate degrees, some young women believe in a starter marriage as next on their agenda. And within three years, a first child, preferably a daughter, will be born. Yet not everyone is a fan, and among Katherine's dearest friends, Darby is getting her Ph.D. in quantum physics at MIT and Samantha is beginning Yale Law School in the fall. "I know you want me to work," Katherine said only this afternoon to Faith, "as long as it's at Vintage Tales. Or as a journalist at a local newspaper. Something within a ten-mile radius."

Faith had laughed it off before adding, "And not too stressful—a relaxed entrepreneur, if there is such a thing."

"Mom?" Katherine rubs her wrist. "Can we have a minute, the two of us, to talk?"

Faith turns to Mrs. A. "Will you excuse us . . ."

Passing a wall of Whistler's women, with their slender frames and nimble stances, Katherine leads her mother toward the ladies' room. In the sitting area they both look around carefully to make sure no one is listening. Katherine's frowning, a frown that young women can afford to have before they freeze their foreheads with Botox. Faith waits for her daughter to upset her with whatever it is she's about to announce.

"I'm okay." Katherine is still frowning and pulls out a long *o* on "okay." *Oooookay.*

"What does that mean?" Faith asks. If her daughter is about to complain about Rhys, Faith won't hear it. Rhys is a paragon of Palm Beach—with integrity to boot.

The door swings open, and Margot Damon stands before them. In the bright light radiating from the ceiling fixture, Margot is lit, like an aging actress.

"Why, it's the Harrison girls!" Margot speaks like one who has had too much Prosecco. Although her look is impeccable—Faith computes the entire ensemble: black silk pumps, a deep navy three-tiered gown, heavy gold-and-diamond earrings—Margot's breath precedes her.

"Hello, Margot." Faith smoothes the organza of her own gown. If this were a fashion critique she'd call them a tie.

"Am I interrupting something?" Margot asks.

"Oh no, nothing, not really," Katherine says.

"We're taking a powder room break," Faith says. "Primping . . ."

"Well, then, let me say what I'm sure you've heard. Lucas and I are moving home, not just visiting this time," Margot says.

Faith *has* heard.

"That's very nice, Mrs. Damon," Katherine says. "Isn't it, Mom? Mom?"

The weight of it, as if someone is standing on her chest. "Yes, what nice news," Faith says.

"Ah, yes, very exciting." Margot walks to the mirror and looks at them through the reflection. She straightens her diamond collar. "I'll serve on boards, some of your favorites, Faith, the Four Arts, the Book Festival, the Dance Guild, and the film committee at Longreens. Maybe we'll overlap at cards on Fridays and golf on Tuesday afternoons."

Katherine offers a small, gulping laugh. "My mom doesn't do cards or golf. She's at Vintage Tales mostly."

"Definitely, I'll stop by your store. Unload my Frey Wille bangles—they've become a little common." Margot takes a lipstick out and starts to apply it. Too red and heavy a shade. "I know some say they need more shelf space when they come to consign, but I hope, I suspect, the closets in our new house will hold my things. That won't be my excuse. We're looking to buy in the estate district."

"By all means, do consign your Frey Willes. They're very popular . . . they fly out of the shop."

"We should go; Dad's waiting for you. Rhys is waiting. . . ." Katherine stands up, and her Herve dress, short with the fit of a second skin, hikes up. She yanks it down. "Mom?"

Guiding Faith out, Katherine turns. "Good night, Mrs. Damon."

"Good night, darlin'. Good night, Faith."

"A mother-daughter duo that turns heads," Edward tells Faith when she sits beside him. Rhys comes around to Katherine, and they head to the dance floor neatly, succinctly. Katherine dips and twists, while Rhys focuses on getting it right, his dance steps more self-conscious. The crowd is rocking, some with their arms in the air as if cheering, others counting steps forward and back. Let out of their virtual cages to Barry White's "You're the First, the Last, My Everything."

"Shall we dance?" Edward pulls her toward the music, trots her out, twirls her steadily, and brings her in. *Handsome husband*, Mrs. A likes to say. Builder of the sanctuary, partner, father.

The song slows down, the band switches to Sinatra, "The Way You Look Tonight." Edward tugs her toward him, and she looks into his face. He smells of Lever soap and Tom's toothpaste, his skin too tan in the strobe lights. Again that surge of gratitude, *Edward/Katherine/Vintage Tales*. But he seems weary, almost collapsible. Leslie and Travis Lestat, longtime favorite neighbors, back away. Faith sees them dance toward the other side of the ballroom.

"Edward?" She pitches her body in slow motion. Some people are watching. Lucas might be among them.

"We have no money. We have lost everything, Faith."

A kind of dizziness—an imbalance—envelops her.

This time, with his third effort, Edward is heard. He repeats "everything" anyway.

Everything. "What do you mean? I don't understand."

He's too savvy; they confide in each other. He isn't telling her this. It can't be. His broad shoulders slump; he is a husband disintegrating at a black-tie affair. *Her husband.*

As they stand there, the song ends, the band takes a break. The covering DJ begins. He chooses something too current, too strident. People back off the dance floor, toward friends, the bar, the anteroom. She and Edward linger at the rim, almost posing. From the outside in, they might appear enchanted with each other, prolonging their legend and allure. Instead it's that Faith is too astonished to do her usual springy exit. She and Edward aren't close enough for their bodies to graze. Chiseled, they are like the statues in the Shelteere gardens.

The sleek Palm Beachers mill about, awaiting the band's return.

TWO

Three A.M. An uncommon dimness settles in. The library is murky, with only the gold-leaf lamp on low. A nebulous light comes through the slatted wooden blinds.

"Edward, what happened? Why wouldn't you have told me?" asks Faith. *No money, nothing left. We've lost everything.*

Since getting home before midnight, they have been at it. While undressing in their changing rooms, voices angling higher and angrier, words ricocheting off the walls. When women in the shop whisper, *don't go to bed mad, make-up sex is the only kind worth having, seduce your husband whenever necessary,* Faith hasn't listened closely. She never had to. Yet tonight Edward has resisted getting into their bed. And so she follows him into the library.

"I'm sorry. We *talk* about business, yours, mine. You tell me about finance and I tell you about the Chanel classics that sell like hotcakes."

His jaw twitches and he's eerily like the husbands who actually lug their wives' cherished possessions up the back stairs of Vintage Tales. The men are sorrowful, silenced, carrying what could fund the down payment on a modest home. Limited-edition handbags—a magenta crocodile "Carolyn" by Marc Jacobs, an LV patchwork, a rose Leiber evening clutch.

"I explained it. For hours now, I've been explaining it. We have lost our money . . . our personal money." Edward starts jerking his chin around, something he hasn't done since he was using.

"I invested in what I thought had great potential, high-risk emerging markets, energy stocks, start-ups. Henry called them questionable. I ended up putting good money after bad into them."

"I don't believe you. That you would make these decisions, that we wouldn't talk about it first. Talk about where the money goes."

He cracks his knuckles.

"I'm not sure that I completely understand." Faith looks at him, pacing. "Is it money from your work? What you have made at High Dune?"

Faith in turn has sent investors to High Dune. Cecelia Norric, a friend and one of her best consigners, convinced her husband, Alex, to move his money there. Only a week ago Faith and Edward were at the Norrics' home—a mini-palace on the A1A a half mile north of Mar-a-Lago—for a cocktails. Of course, the Norrics could withstand a loss—or so Faith imagines—yet the social damage to both couples would be enormous. Other investors at Faith's behest have gone to High Dune and are known *not* to be worth hundreds of millions of dollars. Demi Dexter, one of the few working wives in Palm Beach, a cosmetic dermatologist, came to High Dune with her own money. "I've got three kids at the Academy; I need a safeguard," she told Faith. Could Edward ruin other people . . . not only his own family?

"Edward, there are friends of mine, of ours, who are clients. I mean, the portfolios you've described . . . Is High Dune in trouble? What about Henry and Allison? Will they be talked about, cold-shouldered?" The room blurs. Even the idea that Allison Rochester could suffer upsets Faith.

"High Dune does well. No one who invests there will have a problem." Edward bends forward, his chin touching his chest. Suddenly he is not tall but battered, not handsome but insipid.

"I'm confused," Faith says. "We're in trouble, they aren't? So why not borrow against holdings? What about Henry? He should help. High Dune is yours together."

"Henry can't do anything for me. Not now. It's useless."

Barefoot, wearing her gray silk lace-trimmed night slip, Faith feels beyond naked, so raw her bones are exposed. Crossing her arms over her chest, she comes to where Edward stands beside the desk in his boxer shorts and a white polo shirt that reads LONGREENS with the club logo in olive green.

"I keep explaining, these are personal losses, not the firm's. *Our* net worth is gone—yours and mine."

Gone. "Did you do something illegal?" Her panic is rising. "Over how long, how long a period?"

Edward shrugs. "I don't know, it's been a process."

"A *process*, Edward? What is a process? High Dune survived the 2008 downturn. People around us were flipping out about the subprime mortgages, mortgage-backed securities. Madoff investors. Firms were failing and you were okay. Then, tonight, almost seven years later, you say we're in trouble? Doesn't High Dune have clients in a hundred-mile radius, happy clients?"

Edward nods. "All true."

"I don't understand. Maybe I was too busy working at my shop and being a Palm Beach lady—charities, parties, lunches." It has to be her fault too—they've been in it together for more than two decades, relying on each other. "What about Katherine! She's supposed to get engaged to Rhys, I'd say in a few months' time. Except if we're social pariahs, then Katherine is that too." Her daughter, who deserves to have all that Faith never had.

"I know. I know." Edward puts his face in his hands. "I took risks to be wealthier. For you, Faith."

"For *me*?"

"For you and Katherine. To have more. Here, in Palm Beach, to be at the top of the heap," Edward says.

His level of suffering must be unspeakable. The lines in his face run the length of his cheeks to the corners of his mouth. Lines that hardly show in the muted shades of Palm Beach—no more than they would on a Hollywood set.

Doesn't he know that "the heap" is miles high and unattainable? That he's put the reverse effect into gear?

The fear that they'll be demoted is aging her in a matter of hours. Expert for so long, isn't she the arbiter of recycling with grace—Vintage Tales her niche, setting her apart? Her heart is beating wildly. For the hundreds, maybe thousands of lunches, drinks, dinners at the Grill, Bice, the Colony—*public places*—and essential club events where Faith and Edward are respected, sanctioned—*private places*—an end to it would be crushing for them. Losing her place, most prominently as chair of the Arts and Media Ball, with myriad shunnings to follow. Overtly, covertly—from luncheons, golf, Pilates, parties, kaffee-klatsches. Tallying up those who would love to see her fail, her family fail, Faith braces herself for the salient question.

"How much money, how much are we talking about?"

"Thirty million dollars," he says.

Thirty million dollars. An amount that wasn't fathom-able, let alone known, where she grew up. Beyond what one strives for in Portsmouth, New Hampshire, Edward's hometown. Her husband might have vacationed in Palm Beach over Christmas as a child, but his father was a doctor, not a financier.

She starts pacing again, padding her bare feet against the area rug, the cool limestone coming through.

"I suffered investment losses, high-risk investments that *I* chose, that *I* thought were going to work."

"Your partnership at High Dune can be bought out, right? I doubt that's what you want. Still, with the amount you say is lost, Henry could, in theory, buy you out, right?"

"If there were something left to sell. Faith, I've bor-rowed against every interest I have in High Dune. In-cluding borrowing money from Henry. He's done what he can." His voice, usually robust, is withered. "I'm out of the company."

She has to sit down. Fumbling on the corner of the couch, she collapses, dumbstruck. Nausea overwhelms her. Faith swallows and looks upward as if she's a passenger in a car that's blundering forward.

"Faith, do you want water?"

"No, no." A moment passes. "Did you resign?" she asks.

"I had to," he sighs. "A forced resignation, with some dignity, I suppose. Based on Henry's worries . . . my financial stability was gone . . . the reputation of the firm."

Faith looks at the family photographs, organized by year and event, behind where Edward stands. She knows the order by heart: Katherine, age seven, between her parents at Wellington with her pony; Katherine, age fifteen, at Vintage Tales, by the bay window, looking down at the Avenue; Katherine, age seventeen, at her coming-out party at the Breakers Venetian Ballroom.

"Except for the local real estate holdings, you know—what you and Henry bought about ten years ago—that wasn't part of High Dune, was it?"

She recalls the two residential properties on Peruvian and three mixed-use buildings on Brazilian. Cash cows, Faith thought, and had convinced Edward to invest with Henry. This could be their life raft, a separate venture altogether.

Edward nods—she thinks he nods—but he doesn't reassure her.

"Faith, listen, I don't own my half anymore."

"Who does? Who owns it?" Now dizziness mixed with nausea.

"Henry owns the real estate—it's how I paid off the first debts; he bought me out. Then the losses, I borrowed against my share of High Dune. The deeper in debt, the more I wanted to fix it before you found—"

"No, no. That can't be the way you see it."

"Actually, I'm down to thirty."

"'Down to thirty'?" Faith asks.

She thinks of Heidi Lord, a cautionary tale. A mother of two small boys, third wife to billionaire widower Hays Lord, who was old enough to be her father, she ascended quickly. Welcomed at clubs, the private school junket, and the charity circuit, Heidi was favored, witty and fun, what Mrs. A calls "good company with a superb wardrobe." Then Hays suspiciously lost every cent—no one knew what happened to it, exactly. Within two weeks, Heidi, contagious, was rejected from every committee, tennis game, golf outing, and luncheon. Her little sons, slighted from the grade school birthday parties, had no playdates, and her nanny quit, only to reemerge as the nanny for one of the Finley sisters.

"Who cares if Heidi posted on Facebook how happy she is to relocate to Wisconsin," Priscilla had remarked while fingering Heidi's best goods consigned at Vintage Tales. A Medusa Versace shoulder bag with a gold handle clanked against the counter, an Edie Parker molten metallic with tags still on it, a classic Bottega woven leather in a pink or blue, brighter red Baccarat Fleurs de Psydélic earrings. "She had to be spooked, penniless. Elsewhere is nowhere," Priscilla had said. "You can't pack up for Greenwich or the city, forget the Hamptons. Maybe you'll land at another airport, but the nightmare follows you."

Is Edward about to join the foul ranks of those who wake up poor, sued, shredded, occasionally jail-bound, with only enemies left? Men who no longer stand up straight—why bother?

"What can we do to make this . . . ?" Her attempts at being a staunch supporter, for better or worse, keep kicking in.

"I'm searching for new investors. New clients. Lenders. I've been doing that every day."

The unreliability of Edward's actions, the secrets he keeps—it dawns on her that it goes beyond the real estate in town. He has to have taken a first mortgage on their vacation homes.

"Just promise me you haven't borrowed against the house here, in Palm Beach. Just promise me that you haven't forged my name somehow."

"No, not Palm Beach, Faith. I've borrowed against Colorado." Edward sighs.

"Well, that's something, isn't it? That will help us, won't it?" Faith, pseudo-serene, quickly embraces the idea that mortgages against their far-off properties have the heft to save them.

"The flat in London is easy, Edward. A luxury we can cast off. We can sell it, better yet than borrowing against it. We don't run into many people when we go. I'll tell anyone who asks that we're getting a house out in the country, an hour outside the city. Next year. And I don't care about skiing or summers in Aspen, so that's fine. Katherine won't care either. She hasn't been psyched to ski since she mastered the black-diamond trails two years ago."

"What these houses free up in terms of cash helps, but still we're short."

"Very short? Jesus, shit, Edward."

"Excuse me?"

They wait. "Are you very short?" Faith asks again.

"I borrowed at ten percent. And, if we can get top

dollar, the apartment in London is worth close to three million—the house in Aspen is worth maybe a million."

Ten percent. "I can't imagine this. I can't imagine what's happened." Faith stops herself, looks at her husband. "We should sell both. Or borrow against *both* London and Aspen."

"What will Katherine say about London? The two of you at the Saturday antique market at Camden Passage, or the V&A, looking at the Raphael cartoons?" Edward sighs.

"It doesn't matter. What matters is we fix this, that we're practical." She breathes deeply. "I'll talk to clients if you want. Women who have made major money, those with heavy-duty husbands or family money. I can ask them."

"Look, I appreciate this, but I'm not sure you should. I'm not sure you should bring in your customers. It might agitate things, put it out in the open when it's still quiet. I'm trying so hard to keep it quiet, Faith."

Leather-bound first editions, collected thoughtfully by Edward, frame him as he stands behind his desk. Defoe, Trollope, and Tolstoy. Thackeray. Doesn't Becky Sharp in *Vanity Fair* aspire to status and wealth? Dickens. Isn't Paul Dombey in *Dombey and Son* overextended with an export business that goes bankrupt?

Faith points to his library. "Wait, how about bankruptcy, personal bankruptcy? People do it, we hear stories, read about it in books."

"I want to avoid that kind of shame. If I declare bankruptcy, people will suffer. I can get us back on track without doing that."

"Who will suffer? I thought this is about personal losses." Faith's panic rises. "Wait, what about Mrs. A and

Patsy! They've followed you, asked you to treat them like family members. They're more than clients. Are they part of—"

"They're the only two. Mrs. A is in for a million and Patsy for five hundred. The only ones who I've placed in my portfolios."

Mrs. A and Patsy. "Oh, Edward, oh my God. What can we do?"

"That's why I'm asking a favor. For our family. I have four weeks to come up with close to twenty million dollars. That's enough to take me, take us, out of the hole."

"*Four weeks?* I don't understand, you're telling me with four weeks to go?"

"That's when I'll meet with creditors, and then three to six months afterward, I'll come up with the money. For that I'll need you to put your shop and building up as collateral for a loan. I won't default—I'll work around the clock, I'll—"

"Leave Vintage Tales out of it!" She's finally angry. "We're lucky it's in my name and Katherine's and not yours. It should be exempt, kept separate."

Unbending slightly, Edward walks the three steps to where she sits on the corner of the couch. A distorted shadow is cast by his body across the hardwood floor. Outside the wind whistles, South Florida–style, followed by more forceful rain.

"Faith, you have to do this for me. Four weeks from today. By the third week in December, at the latest, I'll have paid off enough. It will seem like none of this was real."

"And if you don't come up with enough for the meeting, I'd lose the building—and Vintage Tales?"

"I won't do that, Faith. I'll come up with the cash."

"Really, are you certain, Edward, based on what's going on—what has happened so far?"

"Four weeks, Faith."

But he's not promising anything, instead he's flattening her world. Her hands turn sticky, the kind of hands people hold for a second, then drop. Without some sleep, no concealer will cover the pouches under her eyes tomorrow, her chin will soften beyond what fillers can repair. There's little left to say. The room grays, the two of them rendered dull. Edward's losses versus Edward's allegiance. Her trust versus his deceit. Don't they come together, dovetail into each other and reconfigure as a different reality?

"I need a drink, Faith." Edward heads toward the living room.

She's on his heels—he hasn't had a drink in more than twenty years. The room becomes wavy. The hanging lanterns from the exterior of the house cast a bluish light on their Art Deco dry bar. He opens the top center drawer, about to select a bottle of scotch, or is it whiskey, when she reaches up, puts her arms around his shoulders.

"I need a drink too, this minute. I won't drink if you don't; I'll do it for you."

How strong he was at the Rose Ball only hours ago, her stranger/husband.

"Fair enough, Faith. No drinking," he says unconvincingly. She moves them both to the couch, away from the finely appointed bar with its mother-of-pearl inlay.

"I love you, Faith."

Edward places his right hand on her left thigh and she feels his calloused palm through the silk of her nightgown. From tennis—where he is ranked number two in singles at Longreens. His fingers are spread out and feel heavy. Without moving, she waits for him to figure out that in the moment he has no right to this familiarity. The morning peels away the night while the rain slashes at the windows. Without looking outside, Faith knows the pool terrace and tennis court are deluged. The day ahead is unknown, a life shaken out of a designer handbag into a trash bin. Edward removes his hand.

But Faith can't be merely accepting—she's come too far. Her mother's hopes from long ago, pinned to Faith, jounce her. The night her mother blew smoke rings at her while she planned Faith's exit strategy—how her daughter would shed her fate in a poor, sorry place, buried in the Pine Barrens.

She pulls away. "I'm tired . . . really tired."

"Faith . . ."

"I'm sorry." Faith holds her chin up. "Vintage Tales is my only hope. A kind of certainty for me. For Katherine."

"I know that." He's talking like a stranger again—part wheedling, part business. "So you'll think about it, right?"

"Oh, sure. I will," Faith says.

Despising Edward isn't an option. Others have hated husbands who fail; still Faith can only pray for his return.

THREE

W ow, I haven't seen anything like this ever. Who's viewed it so far?" Patsy Deller swooshes toward Faith, holding a lemon peau de soie evening clutch covered in opals and jade flowers. The mother of three daughters in their twenties, Patsy befriended Faith a year after Katherine was born. Her middle daughter, Abigail, has been Katherine's dear friend since preschool. Chic, placid, sincere, Patsy is Mrs. A's favorite neighbor.

"No one," Faith says. "You're the first."

"Look at the colors, sort of bursting inside the stones. I wish I'd had this last night at the Shelteere. Everyone was beyond dressed. Jazzed up, weren't they?" Squinting, Patsy holds up the bag. "Are these opals real?"

Handing Patsy a pair of reading glasses, Eve, the store manager, answers, "Oh yes, they're real."

"Does it have a tale? Some snippet of the Brothers Grimm?"

"Or 'Diamonds and Toads,' a French fairy tale by Charles Perrault?" Katherine says.

"What a title. I've never heard of it." Patsy holds the bag to her thigh.

"That's why I like it for this clutch—they're both obscure," Katherine says. "In 'Diamonds and Toads,' the younger daughter is kind to an old woman at the drinking well. She's rewarded for her kindness, and after the two meet, the daughter ends up with jewels, flowers, and precious metals that fall out of her mouth."

"The evening bag feels like flowers and jewels are tumbling from it," Eve says.

"Gosh, okay." Katherine seems pleased. "I don't want my tales to always be matchy-matchy—more about an idea, a sensation. These two fit."

Patsy stops in front of the mirrored armoire. "Before I buy it I want to make sure no else will have it. This isn't like a Chanel that gets sold and resold and—"

"One of a kind, Patsy. Part of an estate sale," Eve assures her.

Leave it to Eve, whom Faith has trusted ever since they met when they were twenty and modeling together on Worth Avenue. They worked for the independent shops that existed then—Martha's, Lillie Rubin, Sara Fredericks—hurriedly changing from one outfit to the next, mostly dresses and pants in pinks and greens, medleys of blue, or cashmere sweaters in every pastel imaginable, to glide down the Avenue. Trained to walk seductively past the doggy water fountains, through the whitewashed buildings and courtyards, they would pose in front of the art galleries and jewelers. Mostly they showed up at the restaurants, handing out bitsy cards that cited the designers and prices to the women diners. Allied by their common goals—the scavenger hunt for the right man and the "right life"—Faith and Eve became each other's confessor and confidante.

And until last night, Faith had come out ahead. She had corralled the husband and raised a peerless Palm Beach daughter. Eve, an early champion of Edward, lives on the fringe, twice divorced and childless, seemingly chipper. Her condo is civilized enough, with two large pools, tennis courts, and a sprawling gym. Whenever Faith visits, she does laps, marveling at how quiet it is, how few tenants are there. Still, by Palm Beach standards it's suboptimal, located across the Intracoastal in West Palm Beach, in a development called Sunrise Point. The units go on and on, inland, for acres. The mainland is the antithesis of the narrow island of Palm Beach.

"I like that. I want to be original." Snug in her tropical-print yoga pants and racer-back tank—straight from Pilates—Patsy is acrobatic and enthused. She parades around the shop with the clutch in her hand. "Faith?"

Although Faith tries to focus, mostly she's replaying her late-night, life-altering conversation with Edward.

"Faith?" Eve's tone reels her in. Patsy's interest in this individual clutch counts. Selling for a profit has never been more relevant.

"It's from the fifties. I think it's a winner, very delicate and chic," Faith says. "And perfect for this season."

"It's stunning. I can wear it to the Arts and Media Ball."

Patsy looks through the glass at Faith. "Still chairing it alone, aren't you?"

What has Patsy heard? Edward's impetuousness might lose Faith the prestige of single chairing a charity event in season. Not only was this a grueling achievement on Faith's part, but Edward's pledge—the check he would write for the cause—is what sealed it for her. "Few get to single chair more than once," Mrs. A had told Faith. "So run with it, make it your fantasy evening." Faith imagines the hapless Hindu wives of India—burned on the funeral pyres of their husbands. She'd read about the practice, *sati*—supposedly outlawed—in a book Katherine brought home during her sophomore year. Faith recalls the alternative for these poor widows—they were allowed to live only among other widows, shunned and exiled, heads shaven, dressed in white saris. Edward cannot cause her exile.

"Still chairing solo." Faith walks to the open casement window overlooking the Via and to her left Worth Avenue, to observe shoppers whirl along. Mostly women bundle through the twists of the Via. Three abreast, they are chic and determined to conclude their morning on the Avenue. Their voices rise; the scent of fresh-cut grass seeps into the shop before Faith closes the window. Vintage Tales has never felt more a refuge.

"I should totally buy this. For *your* black-tie fete. Everyone, snowbirds, travelers, will be there." Patsy studies the jade flowers.

Faith casts Eve a glance—the clutch hasn't yet been logged in as inventory, let alone tagged. An estate sale from Rhode Island. The ninety-four-year-old woman owned more unusual bags than Faith has ever seen. She isn't certain of the true value, but the sale will be useful.

"Excellent." Faith turns back to face Patsy, her Palm Beach smile breezy and socially bewitching.

"How much is it?"

Eve stares at Faith. "Would you like some water, Patsy, anyone? A coffee?"

"A water, flat, please," Patsy says.

"Faith? Let's check on the price. The bag is new." Eve motions to Faith to follow her upstairs.

In their scant kitchen behind the office, Eve starts arranging two glass bottles of Voss flat water. At Vintage Tales, few mistakes are made about which bottled water, flat or sparkling, to offer. An Excel sheet of each customer's preference is posted to the refrigerator—the ratio of bubbly to flat is three to one. Faith and Eve prefer tap water, while Katherine brings her own thermos—also filled with tap water—and is against any pretensions.

"We haven't priced that evening bag yet." Eve begins to look for the paperwork. "Let's see. It's from an estate sale we've bought for a lump sum. There's no consignment to split. I was thinking eight hundred or nine hundred. Around the price of that McQueen floral lace clutch we sold last week."

"Make it two thousand," Faith replies, looking away.

"Two thous—"

Eve opens the bottles and pours into a set of hand-painted glasses. Several of the more imaginative customers have admired these glasses. Faith bought them on sale at Anthropologie—which begs the question, what is actual beauty and what is trompe l'oeil? A kind of trilling laugh floats upward and then Katherine's slightly bored laugh in response.

"Yes, I'll tell her." Faith heads downstairs, ready to disseminate illusion. Patsy is still admiring the evening bag, swishing back and forth with it at her side. *Dear God*, Faith thinks, *it's just another ridiculously priced item—isn't it?*

"I can write this up for you." Faith looks Patsy in the eye. "It's two thousand dollars."

"Two thousand? That's sort of pricey." Patsy places the bag on the desk, stretches her shoulders.

"Antique bags, vintage bags are expensive. It's in excellent condition, perhaps worn only once or twice." Eve has come downstairs and places the tray of water glasses beside Katherine.

"I know, but we could send a child to preschool for the spring with that kind of money."

"You can do that anyway," Eve says.

"Preschool will cost more than that," Katherine says, sounding serious. "My friend Lilly—we went to the Academy together—is teaching at the toddler program at Trinity Church. You can't imagine what they charge for three days a week."

"I suspect you'll be sorry if you don't buy it," Faith says with her soft-sell voice.

"I know. But two thousand dollars? Do you think jewels and flowers will flow from my mouth when I carry it?"

Again Patsy walks to the mirrored armoire, holding the bag close to her hip with her right hand.

"Why not?" Eve says.

Patsy switches the bag to her left hand, spirals into her reflection. "Well, all right. I'll give you a check."

Eve immediately begins to wrap the bag in their

signature hand-painted shopping bag. Vintage Tales is inked in the Dakota font across the top with a rendering of a woman beneath.

Upstairs an hour later, consignment items are scattered onto the Estrella sofa—a lacy steel structure painted red that in truth isn't that comfortable. Enmeshed in their task, Eve and Katherine begin sorting through the latest goods. Across from the sofa is an Egg chair, covered in stretched indigo wool, where Eve has placed her iPad. Lifting it, she begins taking pictures, walking around the room to photograph every piece. The entire morning has been a blur to Faith. A round of clients have come and gone, raving about necklaces, designer bags, oval-faced watches, Katherine's tales, the danger of overbuying, the sheer thrill of buying. They've purchased mostly bangles, earrings, and shawls. Shopping an aphrodisiac, an esprit de corps, Vintage Tales a sorority of sorts. What more could Faith ask for in her new mission to sell high than a surge of customers who then head out, lured toward Renato's or Bice, Ta-boo or Café Boulud to savor their lunch. For some, a game of cards is scheduled for the afternoon; for others, more shopping is on the docket. Yet Faith is fitful, unable to concentrate.

"Will you join us?" Eve asks as she watches Faith pace. "Unless you've forgotten, it's late November. Any minute we'll hear clients coming in *after* their lunch with more shopping lists."

"Looking for exceptional things, intricate tales." Katherine starts flipping through her iPhone. "I'm ready!"

Ranging in age from early twenties to mid-forties, they are dressed for daytime in Palm Beach, costumed for an effect that neither exhilarates nor disappoints. Faith wears cropped khakis and a sleeveless blouse. Eve is slightly taller, blonder, more voluptuous, in stilettos and a sheath. Yoga devotees, they know aging is lethal on the island of Palm Beach, decrepit skin or rounding shoulders a curse. Lately Eve mostly talks about aging, decay. "I don't care if I look older," she laments at least once a day, "but I can't have jowls and I'm afraid of a face-lift." Faith always agrees, "Being your best weight, wearing the best clothes won't get us through our forties. We'll have to do more highlights and get fillers—half an hour at Dr. Zing, and for three months you're good as new."

Katherine wears fitted white jeans and heavy-rimmed tortoiseshell glasses, her dark hair pulled into a sloppy braid. A showstopper by virtue of being twenty-three, she doesn't care how she presents at Vintage Tales. Treading water would be her description if any of her childhood friends asked why she's working there. Not that they would, since they know how ardent she is about earning her MFA at Columbia, or Hunter, as a backup. She longs to be in New York; she wants to be a writer. Katherine made a reluctant promise to Faith to be home for a year. Because she's an only child and because she admires her mother, not because she'll earn a master's degree locally while working at the shop.

"Mom, are you looking with us? This estate is crazy, really cool."

"It's a lot of paste," Eve says. "Too much paste. Your mother seems to be into pricey at the moment."

"True," Faith says. "I'm seizing the day."

She ought to apprise Eve of her talk with Edward, the reveal and consequences. Instead she's almost disoriented, and very worried about Katherine. The flip side of having it all—having it all taken away. What can she do to protect her daughter?

After the downstairs bell chimes, Allison Rochester walks in. Her blond hair has no tinge, nor are her lenses tinted too deep a blue. Her skin is smooth, her manicure almost invisible. Her body language as precise as if she is a principal dancer and not part of the corps de ballet. Has Faith missed these details before today? Her Pucci sheath looks daytime—not made of the slippery, dressier fabric. Perhaps not purchased on the Avenue but in Bal Harbour or in Beverly Hills, since buyers differ from one place to the next. In what appears to be a visit to Faith alone, Allison carries a large Gucci shopping bag.

She looks around and speaks faintly in her southern drawl. "Ah've never consigned here before, so Ah brought a few things for you to choose from."

In her meet-and-greet role, Eve comes forward to take the shopping bag.

"We're okay, Eve. Allison and I will go up to the office together."

Upstairs the curio cabinet is open and Faith, out of habit, straightens the scarves inside.

"Those are *lovely*. They look brand new," Allison says.

"Popular designs," Faith says. "Especially the Chanel and Hermès. When the temperatures fall to the mid-sixties or low seventies and it's windy, women come in and want scarves."

"Like the past afternoon or two, it's been chilly," Allison says. "And a tough time for you, Ah suspect."

"I'm fine." A pang of trepidation. Faith wonders how much Allison knows. Isn't that why she's at the shop?

"Are you? Totally fine?" Allison asks. Faith can't read her expression—is it curiosity, acquired empathy?

"Well, not my finest day," Faith says.

She faces her quasi-rival. Allison isn't on the level of Lucas's mother, Rita Damon, or his wife, Margot, but a more middling, consistent competitor. Recalling that invitations seemed lukewarm, luncheons at Longreens and Mar-a-Lago, card games at Harbor Club, tennis and golf, ladies' days. The occasions where Allison sat at Rita Damon's table, with Margot in town. Fragments of conversation about why consignment wasn't quite a fit in Palm Beach. Enforced dinners with their husbands, Henry and Edward, filled with a pretense of friendship.

"Ah was at High Dune yesterday and saw Edward. He told me you are so busy at your shop. You never go, do you, never stop by the office?"

"Not really," Faith says. "Mostly I'm here, at Vintage Tales."

Settling into the white leather wingback chair, Allison positions her Dior Rihanna silver-and-gold-framed sunglasses on top of her head. Faith wonders again how much she knows.

"My, my. Looking around, Ah understand how objects become toxic. Especially if they remind you of a bleak event." Allison begins to unpack her shopping bag.

"Not only the association. Women *want* to sell things. They *need* the money."

"Everybody *needs* money. Just depends on how dire the situation is." Allison sighs. "That's all."

First she pulls out a Marc Jacobs mini-bag and then

empties the rest onto the coffee table. Another smallish purse, Prada in gathered off-white leather, a Valentino rock-stud bracelet, a Seaman Schepps onyx pendant, a midcentury set of gold link bracelets. "Voilà. Smaller than most of his collection, the Jacobs. It always reminds me of Daisy Laurent, who has the same one. She didn't invite me to her poolside luncheon at the Brazilian Court two years ago. She claims she *forgot*."

Faith waits a beat. "It happens."

Allison digs into the bottom of the bag. "Ah've brought a few other things too. These costume earrings were my aunt's." She opens up a dusty oblong jewelry box with gold-plated filigree clip-on earrings with Swarovski crystals.

"Ah've got the paperwork since they're Miriam Haskell. Her collection was handmade, they say."

"They're almost wistful—I think they're called 'paisleys.' Katherine would find a brooding tale . . ."

"Ah've got fine jewelry too. These are my grandmother's pearls. They're valuable."

Allison presents a double strand of pearls, probably six and a half graduating to seven millimeter, cream-colored with an old mine-cut diamond clasp.

Faith opens and closes it, safety locks it. While some customers might prefer ten millimeter, there is a Jackie O–ness about the pearls and the color that make them notable. Paired with the right client, they are a quick sale. "Don't you want to keep these? They're beautiful." She gives them to Allison.

"That they are. Ah remember my grandma wore them on her birthday, on Easter. And every Christmas." Allison puts the pearls in her right hand then her left, as if weighing the necklace.

"Keep these," Faith says.

"No, no, you sell them. Someone'll want to buy them, Faith. Besides, y'know, Henry's given me plenty o' pearls. South Sea, baroque, Mikimoto.

"Then from my great-aunt." Allison holds up a red Cartier faille evening purse in one hand and a Hayward tapestry clutch in the other. "Ah don't use these," she drawls, "but Ah admire them. Maybe they'll be bought right away."

She places what she's consigning into two neat piles, one for jewelry and one for evening bags. Faith ought to say something, but she's panicked. If Allison, who has been neither kind nor unkind, is showing such overt sympathy, she must know the worst. Is Edward unable to raise or borrow money, regardless of what he told Faith at dawn today? Is that it?

"Thank you, Allison. Everything is terrific, and some of it very 'vintagey.' If you're happy to part with these, we can sell them. The commission is a straight fifty-fifty split. Katherine will love conjouring the tales, especially for the romantic pieces. Eve and I will research the market values."

"Then let's get started." Allison takes out her compact, views her eyes and neck from several angles, shuts it. "Ah doubt anything will stay quiet for much longer. But right now, Ah'm probably the only person who knows, because of Henry, because of High Dune, that Edward hasn't delivered his pledge to Arts and Media for the soiree. Stenton Fields called Henry to chase it down."

Stenton Fields, head of the board of the Arts and Media Foundation. "Edward is definitely getting the money to Stenton." Her voice sounds high, her back stiffens.

"Oh my, Faith, Ah believe you." Allison puts on her sunglasses and lifts her Orange H Birkin bag, a signature shade regarded as a neutral, from the floor. She rises. "For your sake, let's hope that's the case. But if Edward can't pay the pledge right now, until he makes some money back—and you are no longer sole chair—Henry suggested—"

"Edward is . . ." Faith stops herself. If Allison is highlighting an unpaid pledge to Stenton Fields as decisive, Edward's straits might not be common knowledge yet.

"Ah could always co-chair the ball with you if you're going to be assigned someone. It ought to be me, y'know, partners' wives, an easy move, credible. We'll bring in more money if we co-chair, twist everybody's arms to get those checks." She smiles a Palm Beach smile. "Ah'll bring more for your shop on Tuesday, more evening bags."

Allison's generosity—wouldn't that mean she has been told by Henry? The measure of what has been taken and what is to come fills Faith with dread. Wouldn't it be prudent to give up chairing the Arts and Media Ball altogether? Co-chairing with Allison would prove as dicey, given what's ahead for her, for Edward.

"I should get back to other customers," Faith says.

Allison's hair swings like she's in a photo shoot; her carriage reminds Faith of equestrians out west at Wellington.

"By the way, Ah don't need to split that commission. You keep the proceeds on my stash one hundred percent."

"Thank you; we're fifty-fifty with consignors, that's how we work," Faith says.

"Ah know that. Except for today." Allison moves toward the staircase. "Such a shame about your husband, really."

FOUR

When Faith comes home through the garage door, Inez is at the kitchen window, gently watering two double white orchid plants. Carefully she pours a thimbleful of water over each leaf. "Four orchids in one's living room is the requisite number," Mrs. A taught Faith two decades ago. "At least four, and white is the preferred color."

"I'm really late," Faith says, racing through. "It's almost seven."

"The weather," Inez *tsk*s.

The sink is large enough to bathe a three-year-old child. Faith selected it when Katherine was one—knowing it would suffice for a few years. They were updating the interior of their 1922 original Marion Sims Wyeth house. Of the changes that she and Edward made, this was the only

one belonging to her alone. The rest of the restoration—
what Faith and Edward appreciated together—focused on
the Wyeth Spanish style and simple elegance. Faith knew
enough about Palm Beach to know Wyeth had designed
homes for illustrious residents: John Pillsbury, the Wool-
worths, and E. F. Hutton. By Palm Beach standards, it
is classic without being imposing. Tasteful, not ornate,
requisite five bedrooms, water views, contemporary art,
a minor Impressionist painting. Tonight their home feels
lessened, extinguished. It's nostalgic, as if the whoosh of
the central air (that she and Edward had installed), the
rich greens of the interior gardens, the stereo system set
up in every room and bathroom, playing mostly Carly Si-
mon songs or Rachmaninoff piano concertos, are being
snatched from her.

"Mrs. Harrison, Mr. Harrison is home."

Inez, who is intuitive, will suspect something. Beyond
her instincts, she and Faith are melded. They've run a
home together, and Inez has cared for Katherine since she
was born. For more than two decades, Faith has consid-
ered Inez a confidante and family member. It was Faith
who encouraged Inez's daughter, Isabella, who lives in
Miami, to go to nursing school. Once Faith's upset and
Edward's debacle becomes clear, Inez will worry. Not
only about her own security, but about Albert, her husband. The past ten years, Albert has also worked for the
Harrisons, as a driver and gardener. Faith can't let them be
hurt, without a source of income.

"He's been here," Inez adds. "For a while."

"That's odd, I thought he had a drinks date."

Inez reaches for a dishtowel. "Maybe his golf game was
rained out and that changed his plan."

Golf game. Wasn't Edward at a business lunch some-place north, meeting with lenders—promising lenders, first rounders? Faith's neck feels warm.

"I'm sorry." Faith pauses. "What time was that?"

Shrugging, Inez lifts the orchids from the sink. "I'm not sure. I'll put this on the first coffee table in the living room. Mr. Harrison is in the library."

Fumbling to place her zebra-print Scalamandré umbrella in the stand in their foyer, Faith slides open the carved wood door of the library. Edward is at the desk, reading his Kindle, engrossed in another war story. Some wives who come to Vintage Tales complain of husbands who channel-surf, devoted to their flat-screen TVs. Faith likes that Edward is a reader. He'll read two history books a week, mostly about past presidents, Woodrow Wilson, George Washington, John Adams. When they are home a few nights in a row, which doesn't happen in season, he'll read three.

"How was your day?" she asks. "Hectic?"

Edward looks up at Faith. "Unexpectedly pleasant. I ended up playing nine holes before the rain. Then a quick lunch and one round of bridge. The regular weekday group invited me to fill in for—"

"Weren't you driving up to Jupiter to meet with investors and seeing people who could help us? You said back-to-back meetings and then drinks at Brazilian Court. You said each contact is worth about five hundred to a million and that—"

"Now things are moved to Monday."

"Monday? That's five days away. You—we—only have four weeks before we lose everything." Faith pauses. "Wait, tell me, who canceled? The group from Jupiter, who are they?"

"You don't know them. They're not from Palm Beach." Edward speaks as if he needs to be patient with Faith. "Unfortunately, one of the guys had a work crisis."

"A crisis," Faith says. "I wish the others would have kept the plan."

"Faith, things are rescheduled."

The grandfather clock ticks, a sound that's never bothered her before. Awkwardly, she waits for Edward to keep up his explanation. He clears his throat twice; the clock sounds louder, discordant.

"Then Neil called around eleven looking for a fourth. I figured you never know who could be in the game, how it could play out."

"That's random—socializing. That works when you're cultivating new clients, not when there's a problem, an enormous problem. If you aren't in the office, you're not at work anymore, and you're not finding the people who could help, I'm afraid, Edward."

"I'm working on this. I've given you my word," Edward says. "I don't know what else I can—"

"It feels awful. Like we're posturing while you search for vague answers. Depending on people I don't know. Do they exist?"

"Are you insinuating that I'm some kind of shyster? I'm not Bernie Madoff, who had lunch with his clients while he stole their money. He was in tennis games with his clients, his *prey*."

"I'm not insinuating you're a Madoff. Except Mrs. A and Patsy—they trusted you, they *asked* you to put them into your favorite funds, your best investments. Mrs. A is important to me, a mentor. I have such respect for her. You know this. And Patsy is my *friend*. We can't harm them; they have to be paid back, soon." Faith's voice sounds shrill, pleading.

"Mrs. A is one of the wealthiest people we know. She could take this as a tax loss."

"That's not the point; it's about who you are, what's moral. Patsy isn't so wealthy. Besides, she might be divorcing."

Edward raises his eyebrows. "Really?"

"Shit, Edward, are you interested in gossiping with what we have to deal with?"

"No, no, I'm not," he says.

"We—you have to do the right thing. What about Katherine? She can't know any of this, we have to insulate her," Faith says. "I know she's old enough to be told, in theory, but she'd be devastated, heartbroken."

Wincing when he hears Katherine's name, Edward is humbled, humiliated, for a moment.

"Please tell me what's next on your list of who to call?" Faith asks.

"Listen, what happened is that things were postponed, not canceled. A Palm Beach day, a half-day dose."

A Palm Beach day, male version, includes golf, bridge, tennis, maybe a swim, lunch at a club, conversations about sports scores, the stock market, the real estate market. Sun on one's face, wind at one's back. She wants to scream at him: *How dare you, we need saviors, every day counts.* Instead she waits as he stands up and turns off his Kindle. He places it in the upper-right-hand corner of his burgundy tooled-leather desk, a partner's desk.

"Really, Faith, there's no need to be upset. I promise."

Edward convinces, assuages her. Hasn't she sought his support, depended on it, thrived on it? Edward, the sturdiest of men, a "three-tiered husband"—best friend, lover, and buffer—could be missing. As her partner in raising a child, he's been stellar, constantly present. If today is any indication, he could also be lost to Katherine.

"Edward, please . . . Listen, I'm afraid."

An anxiety sweeps through her, the kind she's felt at various points in her life. Palm Beach early on, grappling with the place, and when Katherine was born and totally dependent on her, before Inez came to the rescue. Edward's work demanded long hours of dedication, Vintage Tales was up and running and needed spoon-feeding. Yet nothing has felt this grievous since the night she left home, running away, decamping for the unknown.

"I said I'll take care of it." Edward walks to where she stands at the doorway and attempts to kiss her on the cheek. Stunning them both, Faith turns away.

"I'll go upstairs and change. In a flash."

Although unerring when she reappears—in a plum-and-lime Michael Kors sheath, a plum cashmere cardigan across her shoulders, Manolo pumps—it feels suddenly ludicrous. For the past twenty minutes, she's been in her walk-in closet, deliberating. The simpler clothes, day into dinner, lined up on the left side, seemed personified. As if these pieces of clothing could change her destiny or advise her. Was the Peter Pilotto pastel print daring her to zip up and be colorful? Would a Givenchy ruffled number whisper to her, *Be confident, feign that life is in order*? The tiered floral dress by Kamali, old enough to be valuable, might have cried out against being worn on an unhappy night. When she pinched a few skirts, Etro, Erdem, Moschino, that begged for her attention, she knew she had no interest in finding a top to match. The clothes felt scratchy, they evoked memories. Faith rounded up what her favorite dresses and cardigans are worth. Thousands and thousands of dollars. She ought to sell most of them. Not that Faith would deny how carefully she has collected and culled her wardrobe, but she would also admit, it's only a dress, only a handbag.

Edward looks at her and back to his iPhone. "We'll take my car. Katherine is texting. They've left her apartment and are on the road."

As if the calculability of Palm Beach life is not being threatened, Faith stops at the front hall mirror and applies the sheerest lipstick.

"Okay, I'm ready."

Whenever Faith walks through the two-hundred-foot-long lobby of the Breakers, she relishes how ornate it is. Although she's there often, especially in season when winter clients stay there or live nearby and belong to the Breakers Beach Club, she can't get over the Italian Renaissance design and gardens. She imagines the hotel in the 1930s, when socialites, stars, and locals partied in the Florentine Room.

Tonight Faith is in the very room, reinvented as a glamorous tapas bar. It is called HMF, after Henry Morrison

Flagler, turn-of-the-century industrialist who founded the Breakers. Faith scouts out the crowd, those who have been at it for decades in Palm Beach and those who have arrived for the season.

"People seem almost giddy," Faith says to Jean, the longtime maître d'.

"Seaside opulence, that's how it is for the next four months, Mrs. Harrison," Jean says as he collects four menus. "Shall we?"

With his shaven-head affect, he hurtles past the optimistic tourists to lead the Harrisons to their table.

"Every time I'm here I imagine the Vanderbilts and Rockefeller, J. P. Morgan and Andrew Carnegie, sitting in this room."

"That was another era, Mrs. Harrison," Jean says as they approach the "A Zone." "You'd have to believe me on that."

Once they are seated, Faith fluffs her hair then waves toward all four corners. As if there's a Nobel Peace Prize winner among them, a poet laureate, someone who will save the environment. Instead it's merely a Wednesday evening wedged between two galas as the season hits full throttle. Many diners are Faith's clients. A swooping wave at those who excel at positioning—meaning they're seated right beside her. And a swooping wave to those seated behind her—in the second part of the room. Instinctively they recognize an invisible divide—relegated to social Siberia.

Katherine rushes up to Faith. "Mom, this is crazy, so sorry we're late. Rhys is in line to park the car. There was traffic from the minute Rhys got to my apartment."

"I know. Utter madness." Faith is now nodding at others, having completed her waves.

Edward stands up and hugs Katherine. "Is this a minidress?" he asks.

"Dad!" Katherine looks at Faith and pulls at the hem of a lace miniskirt.

"She's stylish, Edward," Faith says. "Very stylish."

"Later on we'll go on to Cucina," Katherine says as Rhys approaches their table.

"Lovely," Faith says. "Isn't it, Edward? Cucina after ten o'clock."

Suddenly Edward gets a glazed expression on his face as Stenton Fields ambles over, undoubtedly to discuss the Arts and Media Ball. As the two men hail each other, Edward rises. They are equally tall, manicured, a pair of guardian lions protecting their turf. Male lovefest, Palm Beach–style. A handshake follows.

"Hey, hey, if it isn't the Harrisons. Faith, my sole chair of the ball," Stenton says. "You're quite a leader, Faith. I bet you've already roped in more than last year's total."

Faith smiles at Stenton although she feels like throwing up. She imagines Miranda, his wife, who is actually more social secretary than anything else, giving him the calendar. Informing him they're booked solid, lunch *and* dinner, including the Winter Ball, Civic Association, Night of Stars. Stenton will emphasize that Arts and Media is the pinnacle. The man probably walks around town explaining what the cause is, why higher art, community, sophistication, from pre-K to lifelong learners, matters. How the gala is for the new, very "green" campus, offering more film and music, theater. What a selling point, Faith knows. Were Edward not about to default on his donation, she would like Stenton. Edward's pledge is what keeps her as *the* chair of the ball.

"I ask, actually beseech, customers to come to the ball. And to take an ad in the journal," Faith says.

"I bet you do." Stenton shifts his focus to her husband. "When should we expect the rest of your pledge, Edward?"

Meaning Edward has paid very little to date. In fact, she doesn't know what Edward has promised versus paid. The going price for Faith to do the chairing solo, according to Mrs. A, is over two hundred thousand dollars. Faith needs her husband to lie, to stall Stenton.

"Tomorrow morning, Stenton." Edward is ultra-calm, confident.

"Your word is as good as gold."

The briefest relief, then the question: Could Edward be sincere and come through? Faith rises from her chair, nauseous, feeling gaslighted as she and Edward lock glances.

"The party will be magical, Stenton. The decor and mood. We have two bands volunteering half their proceeds. One is a Motown sound. We're lining up a surprise comedian—a woman. The goody bags are unlike any other."

"Promising to be storybook, eh?" Stenton says. "I treat the foundation like a child of my own."

"You won't be disappointed," Allison Rochester says as she and her husband stand behind Stenton. Does Henry hesitate before shaking Edward's hand? Allison air-kisses, twisting her neck as she solicits a fast hug from Faith.

"Thank you, Allison," Faith says.

Allison waves this away. "Well, it's true."

Katherine and Rhys, who have remained quiet and mannerly, nodding hellos from the table, rise from their chairs.

"Uncle Henry, how are the doubles games going with Dad?" Katherine asks.

"Not this week, Katherine," Edward says. "This week we're not partners at Longreens. Henry has tryouts for the nationals."

"I'm sure he'll miss you. Don't you carry each other?" Rhys asks.

"I'm not certain about that." Henry looks toward other tables rather than at Katherine and Rhys, as far from Edward and Faith as possible.

"Henry," Allison says. "There's no better partner than Edward to win; we know that's the goal."

"Well, you aren't signed up at the club for tomorrow, are you, Edward?" Henry says.

Katherine sees he is oddly quiet. "Dad, you are playing in the club tournament, aren't you?"

Henry turns to Faith. "Perhaps you know something about your husband's schedule that I don't."

"Oh no, Henry, alas, I know nothing more. Nothing to report. Let's sit down and order, shall we? I'm famished."

She opens the menu and glances at the tapas selection. Swordfish souvlaki, lamb sliders, crab dip. Deviled eggs for fifteen dollars, short ribs for twenty-five, chicken wraps for twenty add up since they're small plates. Everyone decides on at least three or four a person. For the first time in decades, Faith hesitates to order too much or too costly a dish.

Despite the late hour, valets at the Breakers car park toss keys to one another as if they pitch for the Miami Marlins. Fetching and parking cars for impatient guests and visitors, they sprint. Fourth in line, Faith and Edward wait to reclaim the Bentley without trading even a pleasantry. *I'm glad we came. Rhys is amiable. The menus are always satisfying.* Humid air pushes at Faith's face and hairline, and she feels the frizz starting. She hears the surf, the wind blows from the east. Streetlamps on the drive to the hotel ahead illuminate the starless sky. The line surges and they are up.

A dashing young valet opens Faith's passenger-side door and Edward settles into the driver's seat. In profile, his hunched shoulders show, he seems so worn, practically stale. What those who park the cars must trade in stories when the evenings finally end. Maybe while dinner is being served to guests they chat about a supposed universe where happiness abounds. During that lull, the attendants might whisper about which woman could be hot were she not forty-eight or older. Or what husband is a thug, a rich thug, inebriated when the couple arrived. Or who they bet will be flat-out too drunk to be behind the wheel on the way home. Sometimes they might discuss leftovers, what they will they be fed by the kitchen at intervals, after cocktail parties, dinner parties, and after-parties. Weddings provide the best in scraps, while cocktail parties, naturally, are the least impressive.

"Good night, Mrs. Harrison, nice to see you again," says Reds, the valet whom Faith knows from her sporadic card games on Thursday afternoons. His arms are taut; muscles ripple each time he moves—to hand over a set of keys, to close the door on the passengers.

"Why, thank you," Faith says, noticing his teeth are very white. *Are they natural?* she wonders, knowing she should be whitening hers again (for seven hundred dollars—which now sounds absurd) the first week in January. At least that was the plan. Reds shuts her door forcefully, offering another bright smile. Could he possibly use Whitestrips from CVS? Within seconds of Faith swinging her legs onto the amber colored leather, she puts down her visor and glances in the mirror. Under her eyes it has become smeary, like she's used too much of a cheap eyeliner. Behind her the Breakers grow farther and farther away, a castle disappearing fast. Edward has NPR on, but it's barely audible and doesn't fill their silence. As they turn onto the A1A, floodlights from the private homes show the waves rolling to the shoreline. The Bentley, the latest-model Continental sedan, cruises along, powerful coupe that it is. *How things should be.*

"Will you be able to get the check to Stenton?"

"I always have paid my pledges," Edward says.

"Right, but after what you said today . . . and if you don't pay it by tomorrow, I know someone else will take my place. Rita Damon, Margot Damon, now that she's back in town. Allison Rochester."

"I know that, Faith. I'll figure it out. You'll stay the single chair and I'll give them the money. I won't shame you, I simply won't have that."

Edward in line to do what plenty of husbands do in Palm Beach, pay their wives' way. She should be reassured; he seems convincing.

FIVE

The Pratesi Egyptian cotton sheets feel glossy against her bare legs and arms when she gets into bed an hour later. The full moon skirts the corners of the blackout shades and along the windowsills. The celadon walls and eggshell bedding, the palest pink throw, which breaks up the coolness, soothe Faith. She turns out her lamp and looks at him.

"Edward?" she whispers.

"Did I doze off?" He observes her mood. His head against the pillow, his messy hair make him seem young, earnest. He puts his hand on her waist, as he has for so many years—a reassuring come-on. Still, it isn't the same between them. A form of mind voodoo since Faith wants her husband to be untarnished. "What time is it?"

"Late." Faith veers closer to him. They are side by side

in their king-size bed. He wears only boxers. She places her right hand on the elastic waistband and slides it down. Edward's breathing is audible.

Tonight is tricky, they both know it. It can't be the usual married sex, the kind that grows more intimate with time. Any of what's gone on for years on end, she to him and he to her, feels absurd. Yet she needs some kind of attachment, solace.

Faith puts her head on his shoulder. "Thank you for what you did tonight. I can count on you after what you said. Please tell me what's happened, that the money's available."

"Shhh." He places his fingers over her lips. "I will tomorrow. Enough."

She starts the kissing and he puts his tongue into her mouth at once. Known kisses but more urgent than usual.

"Come here," he whispers. "Come to me."

Her hands on his chest, her fingers reach across the almost fleecy hairs.

Down to the hollow in his neck, she sniffs his skin. He draws her on top of him and yanks on the straps of her La Perla night slip. She helps him by contorting her body, the clothing slides to the end of the bed. Tenderly he runs his mouth over her breasts and thighs.

"You're like a lover," she whispers. "I can't tell if . . . if it's that you . . ."

"I want you," he sighs. "I want you."

It flits through her mind, comes, then goes, the question—why his yearning tonight, why hers. Instead of asking, she waits while he goes down on her. She's sighing, he keeps going. "Faith," he whispers.

Rolling on top, then inside her in one sleek motion is

acrobatic, romantic to Faith. Edward moves with all that he knows, and she moves back, in sync, reveling with him. He has to be everything—he can't fail her—she can't have it. She tugs at his shoulders and wraps her legs around his waist.

He feels so familiar and unfamiliar, as if the craving she remembers has resurfaced, laced with the intimacy of their shared lives. The kind of passion that flourishes with time. "Faith," he moans. "Faith."

She isn't able to go on. He stops too and says. "Kiss me."

Kisses have protected her historically, protected them. She feels parched, she doesn't kiss back.

"Kiss me, come with me." Edward lifts his left hand from the small of her back to stroke her. He's very gentle, patient. "Try."

"Not tonight." She can't hurl her body along.

Early morning brings a rancid taste of remorse; Faith senses this the moment she wakes up. The light around the edges of the blackout shades is an unwelcoming cantaloupe color, and Edward has already left. She reaches for her phone to read his text. *Left for meetings. More to come.* Faith is nearly weepy about Edward coming through. Opening the double doors to the master suite patio, Faith feels the chill in the air that guarantees a hectic day at Vintage Tales. During season, husband banter escalates— and few wives are revering. When someone is widowed, has recently divorced a husband, or is dumped herself, women whisper, *lucky you, no more service sex, no more untold dinners, hammering stone crabs, slurping clams on the*

half shell. Faith has been exempt, married to Edward, whom she loves. *There has to be one prince and you got him*, Eve has observed, in equal parts impressed and jealous. *Your handsome husband*, Mrs. A's recurrent chant.

Edward, keeper of the family. Faith is attracted to this even as an opaque layer of trepidation blankets her. She punches his name on her phone and it goes to his voice mail. She's about to text him when Eve's text interrupts. *My Durango's down, waiting for AAA. Will cab to VT after.* Faith answers, heading back inside, into her walk-in closet to get dressed. *I'll pick you up.*

The Flagler Memorial drawbridge is starting to go down and engines are revved for those in haste to get across, west to east and east to west, when Faith arrives. Upcoming holidays—people in motion, in a rush. Faith is surrounded, a Cadillac SUV in front of her and a Rolls to her right in the slow lane. Slow as molasses. Faith honks her horn as if she's from out of town. Vehicles cross.

"In two hundred feet, right turn onto North Flagler," her GPS oozes in an ersatz female voice into the quiet hum of her car. Switching it off, she makes a sharp left into Sunrise Point and parks close to the main building, where Eve is subletting. Several years ago, two clients at Vintage Tales, recent divorcées who had to sell their oceanfront homes in Palm Beach, rented at Sunrise Point. Not that they advertised their view of the Intracoastal from the wrong side—west to east. It was that Eve ran into them at the fitness center and everyone had to greet one another.

"We have the same layout, two bedrooms with a dining L; amenities are great," Eve told Faith at the time.

Today Faith tries to imagine walking through the Zen garden and flower beds to a Zumba class here. According to Eve, the women at Sunrise are as hell-bent on exercise as the women in Palm Beach. Only last month Eve announced that the complex had a new cleaning system for the pool. "You'll love it next time you come. It's not chlorinated anymore, but better. Except the water aerobics class has become mobbed."

Eve opens the passenger side of Faith's Mercedes sedan, tosses her Vintage Tales canvas bag onto the backseat. "Hey, ready?"

"Ready," Faith says.

Three hours until she's due at Mar-a-Lago, where women will embrace her, welcome her, maybe admire her, depending on what Edward does with his pledge. The identical women might feast on her loss.

She pulls out and stops to wait at the ongoing traffic. A brawny forty-something man walks by, squinting to see if it is Eve in the passenger seat. Eve waves.

"There's Cory," she says. "He's one of the guys who sublets."

"Where does he work?" Faith asks, more polite than curious.

"Right now? Well, he bartends. I think at CityPlace. The joke is he's become a bodybuilder and a surfer since he lost his job."

"What did he do?"

"I don't know. He's a good guy, maybe he was in sales. There are a few like Cory around," Eve says. "In great shape. Work isn't that important, they're just guys around here."

"He's kinda cute," Faith says. "Are you seeing him?"

"Not really, we're sort of sex-for-sex friends."

"Does that mean you are or aren't with him?" Faith thinks of how fit he is compared to most of her clients' husbands.

"Like having sex in college," Eve says. "No, better than that. When you're first single and sex is plain fun, no one is a boyfriend or husband. Like that."

"I hardly remember. Does that still happen a lot?" Faith follows the road but pays attention.

"Yeah, the drama of Sunrise Point. I bet it's the same with single women whether they live in a trailer park or an oceanfront mansion," Eve says.

"I believe that." Faith swerves onto Flagler, driving along the Intracoastal. "Except no one says much."

"Really? Are you sure you've been listening? To the ladies at the shop, or at the parties in season? Sometimes I look at them—who are they kidding? One false step, and Sunrise Point here they come." Eve opens the window halfway and lets the air rush in.

"I left the dog treats in my Durango," Eve says as Faith turns onto Worth Avenue. "A huge box—from Costco."

"We've got dog lovers coming in today." Faith eyes a parking spot in front of Brooks Brothers. If she parks immediately, it's hers. If she drives a quarter mile north to the Pooch, a dog spa and boutique, it will be taken by the time she returns. Dog cookies, prime parking—was this truly of consequence only yesterday?

"I'll go at lunch," Eve offers.

"No, I have Mar-a-Lago at noon. I was hoping you'd

cover for me. I better go now," Faith says. She envisions any of them, cockapoos, bichon frises or Yorkshire terriers, sojourning into Vintage Tales within the hour. Exceedingly small dogs, mostly playful and affectionate, sequestered in Louis Vuitton pet carry bags or Burberry satchels. "We should have biscuits and the water bowls out right away."

South County Road also has empty parking spots and an early-morning calm along the storefronts. When Faith finds the door of the Pooch locked, she knocks on the framed glass and peers into the darkened shop.

"Not open, are they?" a man's voice asks. Although she hasn't heard it in years, she has not forgotten the cadence.

"Not yet. Any minute." Faith looks at Lucas.

He's awfully close. She's able to stare at him through her sunglasses; he doesn't see her curiosity. There's the stubble of his shadow beard, a look Edward would never sport. Lucas's Adam's apple is as obvious as ever. Through his T-shirt she sees his flat stomach—so sexy to her. He has these small lines between his sideburns and his earlobes—he didn't have them before, when they were young and in Philadelphia together. He smells a little salty, like he's been on the water. She looks away from his face and realizes she's right. He's wearing Top-Siders and carrying a thermos.

"I just tied up my boat," he says.

He smells a little sweaty too. "A Hinckley?"

"Ah, a Hinckley. I suppose that's *the* boat. I didn't go the classic route, I bought a Sunseeker Sportfisher, going against the grain. A thirty-seven-footer so I could dock it on my own."

Docking it himself. What physical capability is

required—running back and forth, throwing the lines, securing the boat without crashing. She peers more closely at his forearms, waiting for a Popeye moment.

"Where are you moored?" Her question is rote. She could listen to his voice no matter what the topic.

"At the Australian Dock. I wanted to pick up a copy of *The Wall Street Journal*." He points two doors down. "At Classic Bookshop."

Lucas's proximity, that he remains beside her, also confounds Faith. Like when she lifts weights, forgetting to breathe, and Axel, the trainer whom she and Edward share, reminds her, *Faith, inhale, exhale.*

"I'm waiting to buy oatmeal peanut butter dog biscuits for clients who bring their dogs to Vintage Tales."

"Ah, delicious. I might try one," he laughs. "Margot would want them for Randy, her maltipoo."

Faith nods, half smiles. She pretends she hasn't heard Margot's name and skips any mention of her own familiarity with maltipoos. Instead she listens to his laugh.

"I wonder when she's opening up." Faith raps on the window to the right of the door.

Taking his iPhone out of his pocket, Lucas reads the time. "It's almost ten."

"There are shoppers on the Avenue by now. I ought to go," Faith says. Odd how upsetting this announcement is, their brief encounter about to end.

"The truth is I don't need a newspaper. I saw you when I was driving by, so I parked behind the bank. To talk to you."

"Really?" Is this happening today, of all days? Her tanking husband versus her old love who seems intact. A thought Faith might not have had before Edward's breaking news. Before that, given the occasion, she might not have yearned for Lucas. Would she?

"Do you happen to know it's been twenty-six years and three months since we met at Le Relais?" Lucas scratches his chin.

"Has it been that long?" Faith says. *Inhale, exhale.* That night there was no other person on earth; the room spun, paled. She had a gut-wrenching desire to know everything about him.

"I remember your date," Faith says. "I led her to your table and took the drink order, a bottle of Pouilly-Fuissé, before I sent over a server. Your 'friend' wore pearls and had on high heels. I saw her eating clams on the half shell."

"Oh, that." Lucas raises his right hand as if to wipe off a chalkboard.

"I watched you, Faith, moving around, seating people. You had on a minidress. It was black."

Startling them, the door to the Pooch opens. "Mrs. Harrison?" A woman about Faith's age, with a Havanese puppy in her arms, holds out a box. "Your office called with this order. I would have told you sooner, but I saw you were in a conversation. Eve—is that her name? from Vintage Tales—put it on a house charge."

"I had knocked. I didn't notice you were inside." Faith attempts to sound breezy.

"What a treat to have this treat." Lucas takes the box out of Faith's hand and examines it. "It's terrific."

He leads her toward the sidewalk. Shoppers have multiplied, beginning their day. They stroll by, flushed as humid air rolls in, bone-straight hair frizzing around their hairlines. No one Faith recognizes, thankfully.

He places his hand on her cheek, so quickly it's more a

flutter than a gesture. His touch radiates a kind of blaze within her; her entire being could fold into him. His chest against hers. His lips, salty, soft lips, would open her mouth. "Faith, I can't get you out of my mind."

"No, no, I'm sorry, please don't." She rushes to her car, not ten feet away.

"Faith, wait."

"You and Margot will have to come by for cocktails."

As she says it, she unlocks the door. Knowing how much she wanted to reach out and touch his neck as if he's still hers.

SIX

Mar-a-Lago is best for lunch this season, I can tell already." Mrs. A places her cool right hand onto Faith's wrist and stops her in the sprawling, splendid anteroom. "I hope you've booked for New Year's Eve. Everyone's planning to come; the key is to have a table near Melania and Donald."

"It is beautiful here, Mrs. A." Faith turns to Katherine, who artfully slinks behind her mother. "Isn't it Katherine?"

"Beautiful," Katherine agrees.

Mrs. A's guests have gathered not ten feet away. Arriving for lunch followed by cards, few dare to be seated before her. Mrs. A's hand remains on Faith's wrist.

"Faith, have you reserved? If not, I'll make a call . . ."

What would ordinarily seem a favor, a kind gesture, seems inquisitive, judgmental. "I'll check with Edward,

Mrs. A, but I believe we have. Thank you." She tries looking around, as if another guest will divert Mrs. A's attention.

"Shall we?" Mrs. A asks. Together they walk through the sumptuous surroundings to the al fresco Patio. Priscilla runs up to Faith, slightly disheveled, out of breath. "Do you know you and Edward made The List?"

"An honor, one that only a hundred people can claim." Cecelia says. "They are the most influential and dynamic Palm Beachers."

Cecelia and Margot Damon stand like two giraffes, craning their necks and grazing, elongated. Height as identity.

"Yes, and the focus is on Faith!" Priscilla holds up the page of *The Daily Sheet*, the local paper, half filled with a photograph of Faith and Edward, taken last March at the Masquerade Ball, held at Mar-a-Lago. A greenish tinge surrounds Faith's and Edward's faces, spoiling Faith's J. Mendel floral-print gown, her emerald-and-diamond necklace. In retrospect, it's foreboding. Faith only ponders what her husband knew that night, nine months ago. If the necklace she was wearing will be as valuable as she hopes and sell as quickly as she needs.

"See, it reads 'Palm Beach Royalty' beneath your picture." Priscilla raises her voice and half the room quiets down. She begins to read from *The Daily Sheet*. "Listen . . . it says, 'The Arts and Media Ball has become a gold standard. Right alongside the Restoration Ball, the Rose Ball, top-tier fund-raisers for diseases and medical centers. Faith Harrison, as solitary chair, has already raised a record amount for the cause, calling upon local merchants and Palm Beach society to purchase tables." She folds the paper, and women begin to speak among themselves again. "It also says you're the ambitious owner of Vintage Tales, in case you haven't read it yet," Priscilla says, swiveling to where Faith stands.

"I haven't. I usually read it first thing, but today got away from me," Faith says. Had she read it, she might have avoided the luncheon altogether.

"Oh, c'mon, Faith, everyone reads it the minute it arrives. We thought The List would be out sometime this week. What better timing than today?" Lara Mercer says, her tone unreadable.

"*Ambitious.* What a tough sell in Palm Beach—especially for women, no?" Margot says.

"It depends on your purpose, I suppose." Rita Damon nestles between Allison and Margot and does her notorious glower. "Beyond the charity circuit, ambition has other meanings."

Mrs. A simpers. "Rita, you must admit, Faith is *everywhere.*"

Intense whisperings float from each of Mrs. A's six tables as the women find their name cards and sit down. *Neither made the list, Margot Damon's missing and Rita too. Allison Rochester made it, Mrs. A, of course.* Faith can't breathe, and although she's beside Mrs. A, she can't smell her favorite perfume, Fracas, a heavy mixture of bergamot, mandarin, lilac, and gardenia.

"I knew you would rise to the top, my dear. With your magnificent husband, all the better," Mrs. A says.

Nothing is known. Faith, relieved, swallows. "That's so

kind of you, and I appreciate it," she says. She ought to check her phone, see what Edward has texted.

"How lovely that you have come on your mother's big day, Katherine. One where she's being recognized for her good deeds," Mrs. A says.

"I'm very proud of my mother, Mrs. A." Katherine takes her off-white cardigan, half silk, half cashmere, and ties it around her waist. How little her daughter knows, how crucial that she never learns about Edward. That the media attention today doesn't trip up the plan, that the payback happens swiftly.

"Lovely, my dear," Mrs. A says. "I must greet the others . . ."

She moves along the patio, stopping at each of her tables of four or six, where her guests show obeisance.

Curtis, the maître d', approaches Faith. What an outdoorsman he must be, despite his work inside the clubhouse. His neck is leathery—boating, fishing, surfing—without sunblock.

"Mrs. Harrison, the others haven't arrived. Will you be seated?" He points to an empty table set for four. Strewn along the way, Faith spots two Kelly bags, a Balenciaga, a Burberry Small Macken, and a Mizuki pearl-and-diamond cuff bracelet—each resold at her shop. The original owners won't acknowledge any previous ownership, nor do those carrying them let on they weren't bought at Hermès, Saks, or Neiman. Fungible items, who would pinpoint the purchase or sale. The fluidity of Vintage Tales.

"Thank you, Curtis," Faith says when he pushes in her chair.

Sunlight streams into the center of the patio. Katherine sits down and puts on her cherry-frame Ray-Bans. A throwback to their mother-daughter lunches of the past, at this very spot. Katherine makes a face and Faith laughs for the shortest second.

Women pause, ready to cautiously pour balsamic dressing on their semi-chopped chef salads, rejecting whole wheat rolls and Parmesan crisps. Gossip rises through space in whiffs and dense clouds. A first go-round: *husbands, lovers, arm candy, gardens/hedges, wardrobe/jewels.* A second go-round swooshes in at once: *lost weight, gained weight, hair too bright, only a mini-lift, cankles, stringy legs, poor posture, widowed, let out of a birdcage, grandson left Stanford, ballet tonight at Kravis.*

Faith imagines how her crisis would ratchet up the quality of their prattle, add an element of suspense and immediacy. Would she or wouldn't she survive, would be the log line.

"Maybe we should order, Katherine, since we have to get back." She glances at Curtis and a server behind him, speaking to both and to neither. "We'd like two kale Caesars without any meat. Chopped, please. And two mint iced teas."

"No fish or seafood either, thank you," Katherine says when Curtis comes to subtly remove her unopened menu.

"Well, that's better." Faith adjusts her chair underneath the table.

"As long as we can talk for a few minutes," Katherine says. "Please."

"Until someone comes and sits down." Faith positions her head in a practiced maneuver—focusing on Katherine without missing a beat. The women keep scurrying about, waving their copies of *The Daily Sheet*, heads craned while they scan The List. She might be the center of conversation, but Faith's presence isn't acknowledged.

"No one talks about the real world, no one cares, haven't you noticed?" Katherine becomes extremely pale. As pale as Faith feels.

"Are you all right, Katherine? I mean, we can talk about this, sure. People choose *not* to be absorbed by current maladies, climate change, tornadoes, political strife, tragedies of any sort, anything divisive. This is the jewel box of Palm Beach."

"You do that, Mom, you do. You have to be like them." Katherine's satiny skin, her cheekbones are mesmerizing. "Does anyone even know what the charities are actually doing—the ones they write these gigantic checks for?"

"Is that what you wanted to talk about today, here, with The List and my chairing? As Mrs. A's guests? I'm asking you not to find fault, to realize the variations. The causes are important; we have to help people who are less fortunate, offer them opportunities."

"We have to talk *now*," Katherine whispers, her voice has an urgency about it. "Not about this."

Something in Katherine's intonation alerts Faith to military attention, the despair in her daughter's face. "Okay, let's not say too much; sound travels. We'll talk later, we can rush out. Mrs. A knows we're not in a card game. We'll go back to Vintage Tales, upstairs in my office . . ."

"No, we can't. Eve's all over you there. It's about Rhys."

Faith forces herself to sit confidently, making certain no one is peering at them, second-guessing their body language, eavesdropping from a distance.

"I'm not sure I want to commit to Rhys." Katherine shakes her head. "Maybe I don't love him enough."

"Not love him enough?" Faith asks. "Why do you say that?"

"I'm really not sure. It's like I'm supposed to. Rhys is a prize." Katherine places her elbows on the table, realizes what she's done, drops them to her lap.

"Sweetie, Rhys, he's great. He's quiet, patient. He is *respectful*. You know that matters. And you've been together before—that's something. You *know* each other. He's enough older, three years older, that he seems mature."

"I know you really like him."

"It's true. But it's not up to me, Katherine. I see him as decent. Sure, he's had opportunities, privilege. But he seems to care about the world, especially since you just made a comment about how no one seems to. Didn't he want to join the Peace Corps for a while? I know he's a good son; that matters."

"Rhys is perfect for Palm Beach, if I stay and write my zany tales while he works with his dad on their health clubs around Florida. Ugly clubs that make them so much money. I don't know what to say about the Peace Corps, let's be honest. That was in passing. He loves it here. I'd like to live in New York, in Brooklyn or maybe downtown, go to Columbia for my master's. Where does Rhys fit in for that? I swear he recites the New York City crime rate to me almost daily and says he doesn't understand why people want to be there. He doesn't *have* to be at a poetry reading or an off-Broadway place. He doesn't love bookstores and museums."

Faith takes a mauve lipstick out of her Cademartori suede shoulder bag and counts to ten, purposely calm. "Well, plenty of Palm Beachers aren't against New York. They're from New York."

"I'm glad since you don't want me going to grad school in New York. Your New York friends, clients can convince you it's fine." Katherine readjusts her seat. "What makes you sure I'm such a Palm Beach girl?" She gestures with her index and middle fingers to convey quotation marks around *Palm Beach girl*.

"Not particularly, no, I don't want you to go. I understand why you want to, though." Faith applies a thin coat of lipstick, presses her lips together.

How can her daughter know that they're at a precipice? If Edward doesn't find the money to pay his debts and negotiate with his creditors, Katherine, like Faith, is embroiled in the disfavor that follows. Even her chances with Rhys could be sabotaged in Palm Beach, a throwback to the days when finding the right husband for a daughter was so consuming, one positioned the task ahead of any ethics. A few friends, including Noel Finley and Patsy, would eye Rhys immediately for their daughters. They are capable of such a maneuver. The winner-takes-all approach.

Their lunches are brought over, and both Faith and Katherine freeze as if they're mimes. They don't speak while the plates are arranged before them. More water is poured. Curtis hovers over the table and motions for the server to disappear. Faith and Katherine raise their forks and knives, wait fifteen seconds before continuing their conversation.

"Katherine, plenty of people revel in life here . . ." Faith pauses, looks around the room, back to Katherine. "Young people too."

"That doesn't make Rhys right for me. Or this place not provincial, that's part of it. Mom, you think people should marry their hometown boyfriend; you didn't do that—you want me to."

"You know where I'm from. How I got here," Faith says.

"What's that supposed to mean?" Katherine asks. "You're from suburban Philadelphia, Cherry Hill. An only child too. I'm sure the local boys were fine, suitable."

"They weren't; it wasn't like that," Faith says. "Of course there was a food chain, there were the boys everyone wanted."

"You didn't stay—you left. So you know, Mom, you didn't do it—you got away. I want to be in the city, to study there, be there. I could date some Bohemian guy in New York. A poet, a grad student. I don't know, an artist, a musician."

"Yes, you could. Not that it doesn't come with its own set of problems." Faith starts fanning herself with her right hand, squelching the urge to be insistent. "Before that happens, Katherine, if you care about Rhys, and it's about his wanting to be in Palm Beach, you should talk with him. How he feels about your going if you're accepted at Columbia, what you might do with a career in writing, that you want a career."

"He'll want me to come home to Florida." With her fork, Katherine begins to separate the quinoa from the kale on her plate, creating little piles on either side. She takes a small bite, puckers her mouth.

"A new chef," Faith says. "After so many years."

"I'm sorry?"

"The quinoa. Not really part of a Caesar recipe." Faith delicately arranges a forkful for herself.

"About Rhys, Mom, I think he'd be okay if I came back. He could tolerate time apart if he knew the end game is

Palm Beach. About my work and his, well, we'd have to hammer it out." Katherine's words sound rushed, uneasy. She's about to play with her food again and Faith signals to stop, it's rude. "I'd like more faraway, real-world experiences, and he wouldn't."

"Real world versus Palm Beach, I understand." Except Faith prefers Palm Beach and has worked long and hard at infiltrating it. Real-world images, the ones she hasn't shared with Katherine or Edward or conjured up for decades, clutter her mind. A memory of standing in a marshy meadow, swatting away mosquitos, in South Jersey, to sell wares—other people's junk. At dawn they'd unload the Toyota Tercel in the summer heat, affix their potted plants, flowers and seeds, Tupperware. Paperbacks sold on a scarred-up card table. Praying it would be a success because they needed the cash.

"Don't you want me to be happy?" The sunlight has shifted and the glare is reflecting off Katherine's sunglasses.

"Oh, I do, Katherine, more than you can imagine. I'm reminding you what it's like without Rhys—how you care about him, how you felt during that breakup a while back."

"Do you love Dad? Do you trust him?"

What a question, what timing. Faith sighs, polishes off her mint iced tea. A picture of Edward looms before her, from when he was younger, an old framed snapshot located on a desk among other photographs. "I have loved your father for twenty-four years, Katherine."

Faith pauses. Until three days ago, she would have relayed her marriage as a model to aspire to. She would have described Edward as her staunchest advocate.

"Mom? Anything else?" Katherine asks.

"Well, yes, this is what you might do." Faith suddenly feels purposeful. She almost whispers. "Stay with Rhys for a while."

"It's deceitful. You're telling me to deceive him."

"A tactic. Women do it every day. They reassure their partners, tell them what they want to hear. In Palm Beach, five times a day."

"I'll try. I will." Katherine sounds slightly persuaded and preliminarily defeated.

Faith straightens her spine. "We should get back to Vintage Tales."

Mrs. A rushes over. "Faith, you were stood up! The Grenier cousins canceled last minute. I didn't even realize until . . ."

"Oh, Mrs. A, please don't worry. Katherine and I have had a fine lunch." Faith puts on her Dior sunglasses to begin the slow-motion speed-walk across the patio.

A preoccupied hostess, Mrs. A is lured toward her other guests. Members of Mar-a-Lago, mostly women, dining on the patio, are also filtering out, to their next activity: tennis, massages, shopping on the Avenue.

"Will you think about what I said, sweetie? About Rhys. About your feelings for him?"

Katherine nods—a clue that she at least listened. If not more. Faith steers them along the perimeter. They walk past immense gleaming windows that face the golf course to the right and the ocean to the left. She discreetly glances at her phone. With four weeks minus the last forty-eight hours to raise the money, there has to be a text or a missed call from Edward. An update. Yet there is none.

SEVEN

As she careens across the al fresco Patio, Faith's Seaman Schepps rock crystal link bracelet glints in the sunlight. Katherine moves quickly to keep up. "Mom? Why are we racing?"

"I can't get through on my phone to Dad. I'm wondering if I should go to the entrance and try."

Mrs. A's entourage moves swiftly toward the "Little Ballroom" downstairs to begin their card games. Dissonant sounds, clients, friends, travel toward Faith as if spun out of a cannon. She resists covering her ears, instead bracing herself, cool and collected, as they stampede past her. *Excuse me, excuse us. A mini-vacation, he's away, that's why I'm divorced, divorcées choose, no one chooses.* They wave, rushing downstairs. *Again, congratulations, Faith.* Next Patsy, Priscilla, and Leslie catch up to Faith, each word they enunciate ricocheting off the walls. *Winter antiques show, Humane Society, at the Norton, Junior League, not seated at her table.*

"Did you say you're calling Edward? He's on the courts, playing singles or hitting with the pro. I saw him when I got here late, and I barely nodded," Leslie's voice booms, more an announcement than information meant for Faith.

"Are you sure, Mrs. Lestat? My father plays around eight in the morning at the Harbor Club or late afternoon, after work," Katherine says.

Faith looks around, worried anyone might hear. Edward is one of the few husbands who has an office in town and wouldn't be in a tennis game late morning or midday. As opposed to working in a satellite office or a home office, or flying back every two weeks for meetings. An exception in Edward's schedule might be made for a round of golf that includes business "friends." Otherwise he is known to be at High Dune for the bulk of his workdays. Respective clients' wives and several female clients are four deep at Mar-a-Lago today. They want him to be working.

"True, Katherine, Dad plays early or late in the day when he doesn't have a business conflict," Faith reassures those who are listening.

Another entourage files by, new members who Faith only knows from Vintage Tales. Young mothers in their green or blue Pucci prints and Jack Rogers sandals, texting and talking hurriedly, laughing or scowling. *I'd love to attend, a conflict that night, if we only could, a shame to miss your party.* Like the clown trick at the circus, they multiply down the stairs. Through the wide front windows the clouds cover the sun and a gray sky moves in. Everyone is in shadow until it passes.

"Has anyone seen Allison?" Faith asks. "I thought she'd be with Noel or . . ."

"She'll be here. Short of a trunk show for preorders, Valentino or Oscar, she's where the crowd is," Cecelia says. "We've got duplicate bridge in six minutes."

Unless, Faith shudders, something has happened at High Dune. Allison plays the dutiful-wife card, only a problem in her husband's life would supplant her schedule. If Edward has harmed High Dune, if his promise that the partnership is safe is wrong, Allison would be in hiding. That queasy flu-like feeling encircles Faith.

Katherine moves to the side of the banister as women disperse. "Eve just texted, she's trying you too. The shop is insane, and she wants to know about two green skin bags, one alligator and one—"

"All right, we'll get back. Please tell her I'll call from the car." Faith is looking down, ignoring Eve's text to her, searching for word from Edward. Allison's voice chirps across the reception area.

"Margot, Cecelia. Who knew Ah'd miss lunch altogether. Mrs. A knew Ah'd be late, oh my. But Ah'm ready for cards. Ah clearly chose the wrong day to have my roots touched up."

She does a benevolent, syrupy gaze at Katherine. An overcorrection of women who have only sons, no girls. "You wouldn't understand, honey, you're light-years from painting a hairline."

Allison looks toward Faith. "Faith. What a day for you! Ah read it all at the salon."

"Could we have a word, Allison?" Faith asks.

Katherine is already on her iPhone. "You go with Allison, Mom. I'm Ubering back to the shop."

"Katherine, we won't be long, I'm sure. If you wait I can drive you."

"Ah'd let her go, Faith." Allison shrugs with enough emphasis that her pink-and-green-combo Lilly Pulitzer shift, too short, rises at least two inches above her knees. With the confidence of a best dresser, she flashes the Dr. Ivy, dentist of note, smile. An extremely white smile.

A whippet, Katherine leaps toward the exit, through the living room with its gold ceiling and silk tapestries. The two women are left shoulder to shoulder, their eye level and stance precisely level.

"Let's move away." Allison looks around, beckons to Faith. "There has to be a quiet room somewhere, for a minute."

Overhead lights are low over the inlaid columns and chandeliers in the main dining room. Several staff members scamper about, closing down until the dinner hour. A sense of history and splendor sweeps over the room. Without diners, the room feels vast. Faith imagines Marjorie Merriweather Post, the original owner, who intended her mansion to have Spanish, Venetian, and Portuguese features.

Allison takes a copy of *The Palm Beach Times* out of her Birkin (deep pink with silver hardware) and begins to fan herself. "We'll sit here a moment, no one will mind."

Faith believes she hears the ding of a text and looks down at her cell, visible in her open bag. Nothing. Allison places the newspaper between them on the table, the page folded open to The List. Her eyebrows arch despite the Botox.

Allison tenses up and sighs. Faith sees the clumps of La Mer that haven't been patted into her neck.

"Ah'd say wherever there's cash for you and Katherine, find it. Hide it," Allison says. "Starting now."

Outside the sky has turned an almost sickly greige. Faith feels the toxic elements, close enough to suffocate her.

"I honestly believe that Edward will come through," she says.

Allison rallies herself, rises, puts her left hand around the handle of her Birkin. "No, no, you don't. You just wish it were so."

EIGHT

Breaking the speed limit after the Allison conversation is palliative, and Faith races along the A1A. The sky behind her reconfigures as if a tornado is brewing. In Palm Beach any unwelcome weather is an affront, too prosaic, too unpleasant for the islanders. Faith rounds the corner, noticing how lush her ficus trees, a necessary accoutrement, are. Despite that they are well tended to by Albert, Edward oversees these hedges that protect the house and provide a sound barrier. It isn't only that shielding oneself from neighbors is expected, it's about Edward's belief that their hedges are exemplary. When Patsy's ficuses suffered from a whitefly epidemic three years ago and were replaced with bonsai trees, the woman was in tears.

Rain beats against the house as Faith walks through

the living room into the sunroom. Standing at the double glass doors to the interior garden, she looks at more maze-like hedges. These are woven into the center, reminiscent of a miniature Hampton Court. In the pummeling rain the flower beds, filled with cabbage roses, appear melancholy. Edward, who oversees the garden as well, will be worried. For Faith, her house and her surroundings have never been more hallowed.

Inez pads into the sunroom, clearly surprised that Faith is home in the afternoon. At any hour, Inez has a kind of purity about her. Faith can't recall having ever seen her exhausted or untidy. Her skin is naturally firm, without the aid of micro-needling or Restylane.

"Mrs. Harrison? Is everything okay?" She stands with a bottle of Shout in one hand and Faith's favorite Agnès B. white T-shirt in the other. The smallest raspberry stain has been discovered.

"Okay, yes, Inez. I suppose. I realize you've never seen me home in the afternoon, unless I've had major bronchitis, a toothache." Faith laughs a high, false laugh that reminds her of a frantic client or someone upset in the locker room at Longreens.

"Is there something I can do? Would you like an espresso?" Inez hasn't moved.

"No, Inez, thank you. I have a plan, we have a plan. I've come home to compile a few things together."

"That's fine, Mrs. Harrison."

Although well trained to be discreet, Inez is dubious. She starts patting the hair on top of her head and tugging at the bun at the nape of her neck. She dabs at her light blue cotton dress, which is somewhere between a uniform and a plain poplin number, preparing for action. "A plan?"

"Let's go upstairs, Inez. We'll start there. I'll show you."

Together they climb the broad staircase, the part of the house Faith loves best. The stairs evoke the Brontë sisters and *Jane Austen*. Edward's favorite films, *Gentlemen Prefer Blondes*, *Titanic*, *The Artist*. "You have arrived when you have an important staircase," Mrs. A likes to say. If Faith has been skeptical about certain imprimaturs, signing on more for the ritual, the expectation, she has not taken a staircase for granted. She leads Inez into the sitting room adjacent to the master bedroom.

"We should pack up the silver picture frames, start in this room. And wrap them in old towels, beach towels, since I forgot bubble paper."

"Bubble paper?" Inez says. "Which frames, Mrs. Harrison?"

"All of them, Inez." Faith points and starts counting. "There are ten, including the mantel, the side tables, the dresser. When we take the pictures out, we'll put them in a big envelope." Faith walks to the desk and starts thrashing around in the bottom drawer. "Here, I've got an envelope."

Inez is frozen, immobilized. She keeps patting her head.

"We'll do it like this." Faith quickly opens the back of the first frame, a Christofle Perles, and whisks out a photograph taken at Katherine's graduation from the Academy five years ago. The sun is shining over Faith, Katherine (in the middle), and Edward, in a family halo.

"See?" Faith tosses the picture into the nine-by-fourteen manila envelope and starts on the next, a Buccellati shell-and-fish picture frame. Edward stands with the golf pro at the Harbor Club, having just won a tournament. Together they grin at the camera. Faith calculates it happened seven years ago. Edward not only looks younger, but lighter, as if he isn't carrying around a behemoth lie every single day. He hasn't looked well in months, Faith realizes; he's been haggard and his mouth too taut. How had she missed the evidence? A husband's demise, affair or illness—pro forma chatter at Vintage Tales. Reports from foreign lands as far as Faith was concerned. Until this week.

"This too, Mrs. Harrison?"

From the bleached wood writing table Inez lifts a baby picture of Katherine in a beaded frame from Betty McCarter on the Avenue. Katherine's initials are engraved at the bottom. Faith warps past her and selects two more sterling-silver frames from Betty McCarter, one braided, another woven around the edges, also engraved. A silversmith will erase the dates easily and the next owner will have her specific engravings, her own taglines for capturing the moment, embalming the love. With more potential, perhaps—isn't that always the promise when anything is resold?

"Yes, every one of them," Faith says.

She is staring at the next frame, an eight-by-ten Buccellati Vine Leaf, before she practically chucks it at Inez. Inez retrieves it in midair and hands it back to Faith. "I'm sorry, why are we doing this? What's wrong?"

Faith looks at the photograph. It's their wedding day, at the Breakers, in the Magnolia Room, the most intimate of event rooms. Forty-five guests were there that night; only Eve and a few other young women who modeled on Worth Avenue with Faith were on her guest list. "What about your family near Philadelphia? Aren't they coming?" Edward, who had paid for the wedding, had asked. "Oh, no one is left, really. There's no one to invite." Had Edward not been so smitten, he might have pressed her—wasn't there a family friend, a schoolmate, a third cousin? Then again, he had no family. His father had died when Edward was in eighth grade and his mother a year before he and Faith met. Why would he not accept her story? "Maybe we belong together because we're both only children, alone in the world," Edward said on their wedding night. What Faith felt was appreciation, as if Edward had signed a deed to keep her safe.

Faith and Edward stare straight into the camera. Faith wears a Vera Wang—who would dare anything else in 1990?—the simplest of the collection designed that year. She'd found it at a resale shop in Boca and was proud of the dress and her prowess. Her hair is full and long, darker with highlights, her face is remarkably angular. She and Edward are buoyant; they'll step right out of a spotless picture to greet their destiny. Today she is envious of her former self.

"Mrs. Harrison?" Inez is holding the baby pictures of Katherine that she's taken out of the frames. "Wasn't Katherine the cutest little . . ."

"Inez, you keep those. Or I'll have copies made. We'll get other frames, we'll reframe them."

Inez takes two and deposits one on the writing table. The corners are curled; the pictures show their age.

"Vintage Tales needs inventory, different inventory. I thought we'd begin with frames and some of the small figurines. Valuable, valuable *things*."

"Mrs. Harrison, these are *your* things. Don't you sell *other* people's things?"

Faith pauses. How far they've come together, Inez and

Faith. Inez, who pushed Katherine's Silver Cross baby carriage, when using such a carriage mattered, has been a palpable and impalpable presence. What will become of Inez and her husband, Albert, if Edward isn't solvent, and what would this home be without them?

"Maybe you should keep this one, in case one day you're sorry," Inez says.

"The photograph, sure. I'm unloading the frame, selling everything that I can." Faith points to a picture of herself and Eve that was tucked behind it. In identical straw fedoras, the two pose in front of a doggy fountain on Worth Avenue. Immense smiles fill their faces. "This one too."

Lifting the frame, Faith begins to open the back to take out the picture. "We have twelve, not ten frames. Look at these designs! Buccellati rose frames, Linenfold frames, Italian sterling-silver daisy frames." She hits the Safari button on her iPhone. "Let's see. Some frames are worth more than others."

Faith plows ahead. She moves her fingers over the screen for a quick assessment. Altogether the frames are worth twenty thousand dollars or more. An absurd amount for picture frames, for any person, in truth. Yet she'll resell them to clients who have money. To whom the cost is meaningless, and the frame a pretty possession. Didn't she once, until a few days ago, fit into this category?

"We've only started; there's a lot of inventory. We'll log out here and log in at the shop." Were she to sell eight rooms' worth of goods, she might raise enough money to pay Stenton Fields something. She'd save face, she would remain the sole chair of the Arts and Media Ball.

"Mrs. Harrison, what about Mr. Harrison? He isn't

going to like what we're doing." Inez has her hand over her mouth and she's sucking in the air.

"No, no, Inez. Please, stop." Faith sighs, waits.

Inez begins to cry aloud.

Faith takes a packet of tissues from a drawer for her.

"Did something go wrong?" Inez blows her nose.

"Really wrong. So, this—everything I'm selling, it's for us," Faith says.

With that, Faith abdicates the idea of securing her place in the social swirl; the proceeds have to stave off creditors. Stenton Fields becomes yesterday's snow in five seconds flat. She stares at a pair of crystal, marble, and bronze eighteenth-century lamps, purchased by Edward at a Sotheby's auction in New York on their tenth wedding anniversary. It is fitting they should go first, before she combs the other rooms, ransacking her home to preserve her family. "Start with these, although they aren't the most valuable."

"Mrs. Harrison, people will find empty spaces, empty tables in your home. There won't be lamps or pictures."

"For right now, we are in my sitting room, a separate part of the house."

"But Katherine, she comes over, and if she sees . . ."

Faith points to the entry table. "The Tiffany lamp—the Meyda Turning Leaf—that's worth quite a bit." Can she steer her shop toward serious collectors—will a woman who subscribes to retail therapy or lusts after a Birkin bag buy an antique lamp, or gold pen, silver picture frames at Vintage Tales?

Shaking her head, Inez refuses to touch the Tiffany lamp. "This will be noticed, Mrs. Harrison."

"I'll say it's being repaired."

"Katherine will know if you sell it at your store."

"I know. I'll have to tell her." Faith dreads the thought that she and Edward are failing their daughter. Privilege given and taken. "Thank God she's finished with college and she's not little, not a student at the Academy."

"They'll talk about her and about you anyway. Nobody cares what age you are, just if you have money," Inez says.

Katherine, who walks down the Avenue and buys what she wishes, who was raised in the estate section and has had a rarefied life.

"I'm really worried, Inez. I almost wish she were away and traveling and could miss the drama."

Inez clenches five frames to her chest, and Faith straightens the rest into a neat pile on the couch. She sighs. "Katherine will be fine. I know it."

The two women stand facing each other. What they share is unuttered. Faith holds her head a bit higher and taps the screen on her phone. She opens it to Notes and shifts gears as if she's taken a crash course in husbands who self-destruct, wives who prevail.

"Let's go downstairs and collect the Georg Jensen Acorn service for eighteen."

"Your silver settings, Mrs. Harrison? Those ladies, they'll say, where is this from, this picture frame, this soup ladle?"

"They can't prove it. Any more than a woman in my shop can claim her old Chanel silk evening bag. No one says that was my Ebel watch, there's my Rolex. Anyway, we won't be entertaining, Inez. Believe me."

Inez waits. She deserves something—a detail of Edward's extraordinary chaos, a modicum of comfort from Faith.

"Inez, you know I'm strong. Please, let's keep collecting things; that's what I'm best at anyway—selling. Sorting out what goes to my shop, what should be shipped to specialists."

"The tea set downstairs, Mrs. Harrison? Should I add that?"

"Yes, that's great, and the silver tray that it sits on."

After Inez leaves, Faith walks into her bedroom. She passes her custom tufted cream headboard, her favorite white-on-white Pratesi linens. She continues into her walk-in closet, where her dresses hang by designer, color coded, to the right. To the left are separates, blouses, jackets, cardigans, arranged similarly. Behind her buttery leather jackets—palomino, pale pink, teal blue, and black, is the safe. Pushing the jackets aside, Faith twists the combination and opens it up. From the shelf above her jackets she takes a fuchsia pashmina and spreads it on the floor. She begins lifting heavy wooden trays filled with velvet jewelry rolls and assorted jewelry boxes.

Her charm bracelets—including the first one Edward ever gave to Faith, a chunky gold chain with a square calendar charm, their wedding date highlighted by a ruby chip. A Chopard watch with a diamond bezel, very nineties, an Hermès day watch with an alligator band, classic. Each a gift to punctuate a birthday, anniversary, triumph. The long strand of nine-millimeter pearls from Mikimoto with a diamond clasp to double them, the drop earrings that dazzle in shades of topaz, from red to pink to deep gray. A pair of David Webb diamond, enamel, and gold earrings, Ippolita bangles. She glances at what is left, prized jewelry, deemed so by worth, sentimentality, and beauty. Perhaps in a future she never imagined, she'll sell this too. Her Cartier diamond gold necklace from France, her Tiffany "Bird on a Rock" pin circa mid-sixties, her Harry Winston diamond bracelet, her Verdura emerald cocktail ring. A despondency cuts into her fast packing, a loss she might never have known had Edward stayed on track. Why didn't he? Then the realization that she hasn't any answer; her husband, the one she loves, the one she trusts, is MIA.

An odd wind is howling through the bay window of the kitchen when Faith comes downstairs with her Max Mara shopping bag. The rain has lifted and she watches the trees totter.

"There might be a rainbow." Inez is covering a silver platter in a gray flannel cloth.

"Do you think so?" Faith turns to Inez. "Listen, whatever happens, you can count on me, on this job. You and Albert. Please don't worry, I won't let you be without. . . ."

Inez places the platter in a large Michael Kors shopping bag. "I know that, Mrs. Harrison."

Together, arms stuffed with goods, they walk through the kitchen door that leads to the garage. Inez gauges the open trunk. "We should divide things up, and whatever is left can go into the backseat."

Faith reverses her Mercedes out of the garage. After the rain, cards and teas, committee meetings, and massages, there is always shopping.

NINE

W here are these from, Faith?" Eve asks as she drags the sixth and final bag up the stairs, into the Vintage Tales office.

"An estate sale, a lead from Edward." Faith mops her brow. Although she rarely sweats, her blue print Lilly shift sticks to her thighs.

"Really?" Out of the Gucci shopping bag Eve spills boxes of jewelry onto the antique Louis XV desk. She opens them one at a time. "Who's the owner?"

Faith walks to the long mirror on the closet door, peers closely at her skin. Small welts are creeping along her jawline. An allergic reaction, anxiety hives, a liar's rash. She opens her Estée Lauder zodiac compact (given to her years ago by Mrs. A, who told her Leo is the finest of the twelve signs) and pats her temple.

"I honestly don't know. A client of Edward's, from Orlando. I'll ask." As she fabricates, the welts inflate and multiply.

"Look at this stuff! It could be an amazing stash." Eve takes a 10x loupe out of the drawer and puts it to her left eye. She begins to sort through the jewelry, opening the tight row of boxes. "Okay. First, this Bulgari women's watch, Serpenti, isn't that the name? And these H.Stern Genesis diamond earrings, I'd guess circa early 2000s. Wait, another watch. Piaget, an older model, maybe from the sixties, maybe pre-owned already? Faith, aren't you looking with me?"

"I checked it out." Faith puts on her sunglasses as if they're outdoors driving in a convertible, the sun beating down on them. She turns to Eve. "I know it's a good collection, classic and expensive. There's no costume jewelry in the mix. We should log them in and put them out quickly."

"Such beautiful jewelry, almost all mid-nineties. Usually an estate is more assorted. You'd find some precious seventies necklace, maybe a Masriera butterfly. Doesn't everyone have some travel jewelry? I thought we want a few affordable items too." She hesitates in front of the large shopping bags lined up on the floor. "What's in here? Leiber, Chanel? Let me guess—a Lady Dior from 1995?"

"No purses. Assorted things, picture frames, pens, gold and silver lamps. I figure with this collection Vintage Tales becomes one-stop shopping, and that's great for gifts. Buy a picture frame, a necklace, a designer bag under our roof. And we'll fetch high prices."

Eve gives her a puzzled look. "Lamps? What the fuck,

Faith?" She clangs her Tory Burch low-heel pumps impatiently on the floor.

"Well . . ." Faith presses open her inventory folder on her iPad and reads, *Line items, earrings, necklaces, shawls, scarves, bangles, purses, evening bags, clutches, chokers.* Next she hits the subcategories, *couture, costume, fine jewelry.* Eighty thousand dollars netted last month. "What a fabulous hobby your shop is—lucky you," Patsy has said on several occasions. Any vestige of Vintage Tales as a hobby is disintegrating. The revolving door for Faith's steady customers extends to new clients, more proceeds, higher sales. "I'd say we need more profit."

"Isn't this too decorative to sell here? It's for the *home.* They should sell online," Eve says.

Faith's iPhone bings. She takes off her sunglasses and reads out loud, "'Sold two Oscar challises with fringe, a sixties chain belt, drop-leaf earrings, signed, Tiffany, Chanel gold sun earrings.' See, Eve, we're so busy. Let's take a few things from this estate downstairs and try our luck."

Eve unpacks the large Buccellati picture frame. "Very elegant. This reminds me of your picture frame, the one you have in your sitting room."

Faith scratches the hive closest to her earlobe. "I'd say it's popular. I love that frame."

"I bet you do," Eve says.

Thumping of feet against the stairs as Katherine appears, rushed. "I'm grabbing a Kind bar and . . ." She looks around the office, gravitating to the jewelry. "What's this? I'd swear that watch is the same as yours, Mom."

"An estate that fell into our laps," Eve says. "We're unpacking now."

"Is that a lamp like the one in our house, in that bag? In that bag over there? See the top of it, the lampshade . . ."

"I thought so. These goods remind me of your mother," Eve says. "What a coincidence. The estate is from Orlando."

"I haven't seen anything that original yet in this grouping. Pretty and popular. I like the idea of selling picture frames, silver trays, becoming more gifty," Faith says.

"Okay, as long as I can match the tales." Katherine lifts a Paul Morelli gold-and-diamond hoop earring from the box. "What's this? Mom, it's eerie that this dead lady also has what Dad bought you a few years ago."

"I'll say," Eve says.

Katherine views the jewelry boxes, Graff, Paloma Picasso, Bulgari, that have not been opened. "The pricing is going to be high."

"We'll balance it out, add more costume, more bags, sweetie." Faith is so itchy, she resists scratching at her neck and earlobes.

The chimes ring. "I'll go back." Katherine dashes toward the staircase without the Kind bar.

Once Katherine leaves, Eve walks to the window, standing in Faith's favorite twelve square inches. "Maybe you can fool your daughter for a week or two about your personal things—she seems to have a lot on her mind. But we were roommates, decades ago. Six days a week we're together, selling other women's discards, beautiful discards, by sprinkling them with fairy dust. What the hell is going on? Something's going on."

The moment to divulge, to bank on Eve, has come. Faith joins her, looks out the window at the Avenue below. Mostly women, mostly shopping. Who else in Palm Beach is a shop owner married to a multimillionaire—isn't that Eve's recurring comment? Or *was* married to a multimillionaire. She might cry except that Eve is standing too close, waiting for the truth. Bells chime again, voices rise.

"This is *your* collection, Faith. Everything is yours. *Why?* Seriously? What could it be?"

"It shouldn't have happened. I mean, we . . . Edward's in trouble. Terrible trouble." Furrows dig in across her forehead, defying what's left of her three-month-old Botox application. She won't schedule the next appointment at Dr. Andrea Lattice's office—it's no longer in the budget.

"It's Edward, he lost our money," Faith whispers. "Everything."

Eve reaches for Faith's hand. "When?"

"I found out the night of the Rose Ball. I don't know when it began. There's less than a month to get as much money together as we can, make a deal with his creditors. I wouldn't know how to pay off all his debts, but I've got to raise money, Eve."

"Oh, dear God, Faith." Eve isn't quite believing it. "Edward wouldn't do something wrong, ever. . . . Are you positive that—"

"By now I should have heard that the first five hundred came in, or more. He should have let me know and the amount; that's only a start. I have to help, have to make more. I'm worried about Katherine too."

Faith imagines Katherine at fifteen, wholesome, playing tennis, swimming, writing for the *Academy Gazette*. Worried about a blemish, what to wear to a party at the

Breakers Beach Club, what authors to read, what music to download. Hopes pinned to a daughter—a Palm Beach daughter.

"I swear, I've never felt less safe," Faith says.

Wrapping her hand around Faith's wide gold-leaf bangle, Eve asks, "How about this, Gübelin, midcentury, isn't it? Didn't you once tell me it was Edward's mother's?"

Faith holds up her wrist; late daylight bounces off the bracelet. "Right, Edward's mother's. I never met her. I've worn it every day since I opened Vintage Tales."

"If we're selling high-end, we'll price it at ten thousand." Eve comes closer, without doing a sappy hug. Their arms touch.

"Someone will say something, notice my bare wrist, or recognize it's my bracelet. Every day it's on my wrist. . . ."

"We'll find some cheap, great-looking bangle to replace it. From a flea market. Who remembers anything for very long, Faith?"

"I'm early, aren't I? Katherine sent me straight upstairs." Mrs. A fusses about in search of a free space for her consignment. "My mother always said that being early is as rude as being late."

"Here, Mrs. A." Eve gestures toward the Finn Juhl easy chair, reupholstered in a deep yellow leather two weeks ago. "Put everything down. We've had quite an influx of estate jewelry today."

"I see. Am I interrupting?" Mrs. A asks. "The two of you seem so deep in . . ."

Eve and Faith lock glances. The desk remains cluttered with Faith's alleged estate goods.

"No, Mrs. A, we're happy that you've arrived." Faith fans herself with a Christie's auction catalog from her incoming mail pile. Since lunch at Mar-a-Lago, Mrs. A has not changed from her St. John's navy blue pantsuit. She remains polished while Faith, in the past three hours, feels she's been tossed to the shoreline during a nor'easter. Although ragged, she hasn't yet ventured into the eye-catching wardrobe closet to change.

"It's perfect timing." Eve pauses, then begins to sweep Faith's jewelry boxes into a shopping bag on the floor. Her long nails, painted shell pink, move like calypso dancers. The desk cleared, she gestures for Mrs. A to hand over her large Valentino shopping bag.

"Ah, yes, my 'gently worn' evening purses," Mrs. A sighs. "You know, my eldest daughter accused me of being a consignment maniac."

"I'm sorry?" Eve says.

"Well, she means I have no reason to sell. Buying is a pastime whether I'm at Neiman's or Vintage Tales. The selling is what she questions, I suppose. Rather than donating to charity. That's her take on what I do, why I bother."

"The fun, the game, isn't that it, Mrs. A?" Faith says. "No one believes you need closet space or money."

"Indeed. I like knowing that what I own is worth something. I like that it lives on once I tire of it. What could be simpler than bringing it to your shop. If that's a form of lunacy, it's better than most." She pats her nose with a lace handkerchief. Hastily she lays the bags, each in a flannel cover, across Faith's desk like a winning hand in gin rummy.

"Today I've brought a Judith Leiber slide-lock clutch, an Edie Parker zebra clutch, then this older dinner bag, a Pucci velvet print from the seventies." Mrs. A unwraps the first three and stands them upright. "And, let's see, a Fendi baguette, latest version, and a Louboutin cross-body. I'd be pleased for these to be sold."

"Ah, Mrs. A, this is what we need—great bags to add." Eve waits a beat. "Faith, weren't we talking about designer bags at holiday time?"

"Yes. About how strong inventory always brightens our day," Faith says.

"Although one can't predict a sale, these are crowd-pleasers. What's practically new will go at high prices," Eve says.

"Are they useful? Good. As I said, it's almost a diversion to buy and sell these bags," Mrs. A sighs. "Who can remember why it seems important to have these things— why we aspire to it. Why it catches your eye."

"A shopping mistake is another buyer's hope," Eve says.

"Then there are those miserable episodes, scenes, where you're carrying the bag or wearing the bangle. Then you sell to forget. There's plenty of that," Faith says. "Since we think that carrying the 'right purse' will improve our lives."

Chimes from the front door ring in succession, buyers and browsers file in. Eve almost hops to the stairway, her voice warbles upward as she vanishes. "If you'll excuse me, I ought to go down and help Katherine."

Alone with Mrs. A, the part of Faith that feels motherless wants to fall into her arms to be whisked away to a safe place. She imagines long lunches together, outside at Café Della Pace, between the fountains and gardens, sharing lobster salad and lemon-Parmesan angel hair. Faith would gently kick away the small lizards that leap over one's feet and ankles. Every second Saturday they would play golf in a women's multigenerational round at any of the clubs. There would be daily confessional phone calls—when Faith is closing up Vintage Tales and Mrs. A's massage is ending in the oversize anteroom to her master suite. How confessional—enough to reveal a husband's downfall?

"I love your necklace, Mrs. A," Faith says. "You know we're branching out to more fine jewelry."

"Are you?" Mrs. A raises her eyebrow and strokes her Van Cleef Alhambra necklace, the long version in pink gold. "I've had this since the eighties. My husband bought it for me at our favorite jeweler in Boston."

"It's stunning," Faith says.

"Fine jewelry, of course. It's unlikely I'll sell this, but ask me in good time. Some days, as much as I like it, I hate it."

"Excuse me?"

"You know—the association. My husband's affair, his business mistakes. My son, who seems to continue those traditions. How I've had to turn away."

"Oh, Mrs. A, I had no idea that . . ."

"I'm fine, absolutely fine. That's the point, isn't it? Whatever crosses me, I take care of it. I own my successes *and* my mistakes. What's the word I'm looking for? *Indefatigable.*"

Mrs. A assembles herself as if she's had enough and is

finally de-boarding her first-class seat on the plane. "Gracious, Faith. I almost forgot, I've saved the best for last.

"And these." She produces two medium-size Chanel shopping bags.

"More consignment, Mrs. A?"

"Since you're raising the bar with jewelry, the timing works." Mrs. A opens a flannel-wrapped purse for Faith.

Faith relishes the very feel and weight of it—a Blue Sapphire crocodile Chanel flap bag with ruthenium hardware. "How perfect. What could be more vogue, yet evergreen?"

Mrs. A reaches for the second shopping bag. "And here's another Chanel. A mini-classic . . . black crocodile. . . ."

"Why, they're both beautiful!" Faith appraises the bags longingly, as if she could still be part of a galaxy where this would make her day.

"I've done a little research, and blue Chanel is worth something like thirty thousand dollars," Mrs. A says. "You could sell it quickly." Mrs. A fondles the crocodile mini-classic. "I've never used this one, so I'd say close to fifteen thousand dollars. These sales are for you, my dear."

"Thank you, Mrs. A." Faith places the Blue Sapphire back in its cover. "They are special—you might want to mull it over before you consign. There are plenty of occasions when these would be—"

"Is that what you say to other clients, do you dissuade them from consigning their finest bags? You do not." Mrs. A smiles.

"A designer purse as an elixir." Faith, utterly exhausted, attempts a Palm Beach smile.

"How true. Well, good for you then, my dear. I have a

half hour before my mani-pedi at the Breakers, and with parking and traffic in season, I must be off."

Faith exchanges an air-kiss with Mrs. A as if it's another predictable afternoon at Vintage Tales. After she leaves, Faith checks for a text from Edward, knowing he's had no luck today.

TEN

L ate Sunday morning. A northern Parula, or is it a woodpecker, flies downward from the highest tree branch, buffeted by the wind. On the Intracoastal, mini whitecaps become waves as a Viking 60, a Fleming 65, and a Nordic Tugs 44 cruise along. A sunny but wintry day for December, one Faith would welcome were she not so preoccupied. She stands at the double entryway to the living room; Edward's back is to her. Through the window the light skips his shoulders and falls onto the limestone floor. He is at the far corner, kneeling at the wet bar, hunting around in the wine cabinet. He slams the door closed, rises, and roots through the liquor shelves, rushed, impatient. The very dread of it—the idea he is about to pour himself a drink. He wouldn't dare, would he?

Edward looks in the mirror and sees Faith's reflection. His oxford cloth shirt is a melon shade that he hardly wears. Although she usually likes how more of his neck shows when he wears a button-down shirt, today she looks away. Rosy, trim, elegant has been his persistent style, while today he looks ill.

"I thought I heard you," he says. "Did you get the family text from Katherine? She's coming now—for brunch, and bringing a friend, a new friend of hers. I thought maybe we'd offer Bloody Marys. I'm searching for the mix."

"I doubt Katherine wants a drink at noon on a Sunday. I don't know about her guest. I thought we'd have fresh-squeezed grapefruit juice. Inez is in the kitchen. . . ."

"We could offer the mix—it's spicy; people like it— and do Virgin Marys," Edward says. "If I can find the mixer."

"Edward, please," Faith says.

He begins to look under the bar. "I'm in recovery. I know what dedication is, my commitment, I know the routine."

"I do too, I've been there as your helpmate, your . . . your shield."

"I wasn't going to sneak a drink, Faith."

She steps away as Edward straightens, proceeds past the piano, toward the first sitting area.

"We can move outside and have brunch on the veranda." He surveys the Intracoastal and stares at the choppy water, dark enough to look brackish. "If we pull the table and chairs to the side of the house, up close, we'll be sheltered from the wind."

"Maybe not, Edward, it's below sixty-five degrees out. And very windy."

Katherine and Diana stand in the entryway. In a hundred milliseconds, Faith notices Diana's narrow jawline, the harmony of her face, and her long eyelashes.

"Thank you for inviting me!" Diana holds out her hand to Faith.

"Mom? Diana is about to shake your hand?" Katherine says.

"Welcome, Diana." Faith places her hand in Diana's. The sunlight streams through from the living room as Diana slowly lets go.

"I'm so happy to be in your home," Diana says, "Katherine's home."

"Well, my childhood home. I don't live here anymore, I live north a few miles with two friends from—"

"Hello, Diana. Welcome." Edward, almost jolly, comes toward them. "Shall we?"

He leads Diana past the soft beige of the walls, the white double orchids on the entry table of the wide foyer. Faith and Katherine follow them into the dining room. Diana's graceful, athletic walk, how she raises her right arm to put a plastic hair band in her hair, stop Faith cold.

Katherine and Diana sit next to each other at Faith's bleached-out cherrywood dining table.

"Everything looks so inviting," Diana says.

"My parents are always super proper," Katherine says.

"Every meal, you know, the white linen place mats and Wedgwood Wild Strawberry plates."

"Waterford juice glasses, Georg Jensen Acorn cutlery," Edward says. "That's your mother's favorite, Katherine. Yours too when you were in grade school. The table is set for you, and your guest, today."

"For breakfast, Dad?"

"It's lunchtime," Edward says.

"Unless you've been out as long as we were," Diana says. "Katherine and I, we were partying until the wee hours. . . ."

"Not exactly partying," Katherine says. "Diana, Rhys was there, Thomas, his cousin, and we were civilized."

"Very civilized, but protracted. We had such fun together," Diana says. "And here we are, with perfect place settings."

"Mom, aren't you going to say I was out too late? Or why you love Wedgwood?" Katherine is gaping at Faith, who seems fixated on how Katherine and Diana hold their heads so similarly.

"Well, we might have been less formal," Faith says. "But I, I am a beauty seeker. I appreciate a table setting that's . . ."

"Elegant, always elegant," Edward says. "That is how Faith presents."

"Katherine, did you always live in this house?" Diana watches Faith when she asks.

"I did, and I only put two of My Little Pony stickers on the windows. Except for that I was an ideal child, right, Mom?"

Carrying two Waterford crystal bowls, Inez emerges with raspberries in one hand and blueberries in the other. She places them on the sideboard, pauses. Faith does an imperceptible headshake, proving she's been at plenty of luncheons and dinners in Palm Beach, to indicate that nothing more is needed. Inez swings back through the kitchen door.

"How did you girls meet?" Edward asks.

"At Cucina," Diana says. "We were with groups of friends. We started talking. It was an unending evening."

"Diana and I got along from the start. We both love Proust and Kafka; we're both worried about the whales and global warming."

"And we have two friends in common. Katherine mentioned Rhys's older cousin, and Katherine's friend Jade and I take yoga together."

"These men, thirty- and forty-year-old men, real and phony, hung around Diana at Cucina that night," Katherine says. "Asking how you came to Palm Beach and why. Then you beat out the PB girls, catching guys like flies." Katherine laughs. Diana joins her, that laugh again.

"I believe it. That's what your mother did, Katherine. She came from out of town . . . with some turbid background . . . and every guy was interested." Edward sits up straighter, looking less peaked.

"Every guy?" Katherine asks as Inez reappears to set up the sideboard. Although she's discreet as she places the croissants and scones from Reynolds Bakery on South County Road, she is eavesdropping.

"Every guy I knew liked your mother." He winks at Faith—as if the old Edward is allowed to scoot in and out whenever he wants. Her face is frozen, immutable. How little he knows about how she got there, what she cast aside.

"I figure you had two major fans. One was Dad and then the Damon boys' father. You know . . . Lucas Damon," Katherine says. "When I was little I thought he liked you, Mom."

Liked her. Only yesterday afternoon Lucas was ambling down the Avenue in his tennis whites, ahead of Faith. She followed him as far as the Esplanade, admiring his legs, how he swung his arms in a rhythm. He turned in at the car park—she knew she had five minutes before the attendant brought his car to him, before he drove home to Margot. If she tapped Lucas on his shoulder, in his white Lacoste shirt, he'd spin around. He'd take her in his arms too quickly for her to consider Edward, passersby, the risks. *Every day is too long without you. Isn't this what you want, Faith?* he'd ask her. *Isn't this what we're waiting for?*

"I'm sure he did," Edward says. "He was a favorite, wasn't he?"

"He's on the list of old flames." Faith tries a smile. "We each have a few."

"True, I myself have a small stable. From high school, but mostly from Florida," Edward says.

"Diana's been in Florida for years," Katherine says.

"How long could it be? You look very young," Faith says.

"Do you think so, Mrs. Harrison?"

"Mrs. Harrison? Oh, Diana, please call me Faith and call Edward, Edward."

Faith reaches toward the breadbasket in the middle of the dining table. "Are you hungry, girls? Diana, do you eat scrambled eggs? Inez's lemon ricotta pancakes are delicious."

"I would like to try them." Diana grins at Faith.

"So Diana is seven years older," Katherine says. "That seems a lot, but it isn't. Mom, aren't you seven years older than Priscilla?"

"At least, depending on what age she is that day," Faith says. "Most of my friends are up to ten years older, ten years younger . . ."

"Where did you go to school, Diana?" Edward asks.

"The University of Miami—on a volleyball scholarship."

"Volleyball scholarship?" Katherine asks. "I didn't know that."

"It was great. Especially getting far away from home."

"Where are you from?" Faith asks.

"Mom, Dad! You're plying Diana with questions." Katherine turns to Diana. "Because you are un–Palm Beachy, no offense."

"I doubt you've heard of it. I'm from nowhere, a place no one knows, in southern New Jersey, called—"

"My mother's from New Jersey!" Katherine says. "Near Philadelphia. Is that more mid-state?"

"That she is. She had moved to Florida when I met her." Edward winks at Faith.

"That's sort of what I've done. The last eight years, since graduation. I worked at a bookstore and a costume jewelry store in Miami. Mostly I ran their social media campaigns, online advertising."

"Diana was engaged," Katherine says. "If she'd married the guy, she'd live in Minnesota. Or was it Indiana?"

"Indiana. It didn't work out. I wasn't sure, and in the end I couldn't do it."

"There are plenty of young men in Palm Beach. Eligible young men," Edward says.

"Dad! Ew!" Katherine says.

"Anyway, I stayed in Florida, single. I moved up the coast and got as far as Delray for my last job, and then Palm Beach." Diana pauses, looks at Faith.

"Do you have sisters, brothers?" Faith asks.

"No, no, I'm an only child."

"Me too," Katherine says.

"Faith is an only child. I am too," Edward says. "All these stylish only children. When I met your mother she knew so few people, she was—"

"Mom, you're grimacing," Katherine says.

"Am I? I don't think we need to rehash those years."

Inez, now pouring coffee for Edward, spills it onto his place mat and splashes it onto the back of his chair. "My, oh my. I'm sorry! Let me . . . Mr. Harrison."

"Inez, we should get a wet towel." Faith jumps up.

"I'll get it, Mom."

"No, please, excuse me, I'll get it, and a fresh mat, Katherine," Inez says.

"Thank you, that's fine." Faith pats the nape of her neck with her napkin. The room feels warm, stifling.

"Coming from somewhere else, you are so much a part of Palm Beach, Faith," Diana says. "I'm in awe of that."

"Thank you, Diana."

"Yeah, really, Mom, I guess it was your looks. That's important around here. When you get older, you keep looking good. So when you were young, it must have been some twist, being so pretty."

"Katherine, that isn't exactly fair," Edward says.

Inez returns with a clean linen place mat and napkin, silently rearranges Edward's place setting.

"Thank you, Inez." Faith looks around their dining

room and out the window toward the Intracoastal, imagining how lavish it must seem to Diana.

"Women come to Palm Beach from everywhere, with these bizarre accents too," Katherine says. "They're shoppers at Vintage Tales and have these made-up stories."

"Ah, bodies left in the bramble," Diana says.

"Not that dire," Faith says. The conversation should change course, the brunch should accelerate.

"No, seriously, some women think they were countesses or something," Katherine keeps going.

"Katherine, these women are clients. Haven't we taught you to be discreet?"

"That's what I've been taught," Diana says. "Working at shops for so long."

"You know, maybe we shouldn't judge harshly. Everyone has a story," Faith says. "Everyone gets to remodel in some way. Big or small."

"That's what my mother told me—don't judge anyone too quickly," Diana says. "She's the one who told me about Palm Beach and Vintage Tales. She knew about it."

"See, Faith, your shop is famous," Edward says.

"I'm flattered." Faith speaks only to Diana.

"She'd read about the shop. It was in *Vogue*, I think, maybe *Marie Claire*. She told me about your success, how awesome the shop is," Diana says.

Faith pushes her chair and stands. "Excuse me, I should check on the soufflé."

"Mom? Diana called your shop awesome."

"It is awesome," Edward says.

Inez swings through the door and places two platters on the sideboard, pointing to the silver Chippendale tray. "The soufflé is here, Mrs. Harrison."

"Let's begin." Faith takes Diana's plate. "Diana, will you eat asparagus?"

"Yes, thank you, Faith," Diana says.

"Diana's a vegetarian too," Katherine says. "Neither of us are vegans; we'll eat eggs, cheese."

"I eat everything," Edward says. "So if there is bacon today . . ."

"Diana came into Vintage Tales about a week ago," Katherine says.

"Did you?" Faith pauses. "Why was that?"

"For the same reason I came to Palm Beach: I was very curious."

"Mom, tell Diana how Eve thinks we should do online sales at the shop."

Faith takes Katherine's plate next and serves the exact same array as she has for Diana.

"You know, Eve and I were about to strategize, to figure out what needs to be done at the shop to make it more cutting-edge."

"'More cutting-edge,' Mom? That's gutsy, kind of," Katherine says. "Diana, I told Mom to post on Craigslist. Except she and Eve thought that sounded tacky and anti–Worth Avenue. I kept saying we needed to do it, find a freelancer."

"We're going to do it, Katherine. We need more help. The last week or two have been very busy." Faith glances at Edward. "I hadn't anticipated—"

"This seems serendipitous," Edward says as he butters his scone cheerily. "Faith, wouldn't Diana be a contender?"

"Right, Dad. Isn't Diana better than anyone you could have dreamed up?"

"This is embarassing. How could you know anything

about me?" Diana fans her smile at everyone. "If there had been an ad and I had answered, applied for a job, or if there is that process, I'd be thrilled."

"I suppose that's exactly it, isn't it?" Edward says. "You would have been the finalist, Diana, had you answered a Craigslist ad."

"There was no ad." Faith can't take her eyes off Diana.

"What would be the specifics?" Katherine turns to Diana. "Not everyone, especially my age, your age, wants to be on Worth Avenue. Or selling other people's precious previously owned shit—mostly to older ladies."

"Katherine, please," Edward says. "Vintage Tales is nurtured by your mother. Nurtured by her customers. You work there yourself. In any case, Diana, it's nice to know that you might want to help out. Season is very busy. Faith wants plenty of sales."

"I'm not denying Vintage Tales is resale; still, it's a boutique with a personality, a fastidious style," Faith says.

"Okay, Mom," Katherine says, "I didn't mean to call it shit. Diana should come, I would love to work with her. We can dream up mythic ideas for the shop."

"My wife isn't one to make a quick decision, Diana," Edward says.

"I understand," Diana says. "But Faith, I'd really like to try this. I'm good at social media, I did a few terrific campaigns, an indie bookshop in Lauderdale, the—"

"Tomorrow you could come by and meet Eve too! Mom, that is the best idea!" Katherine hasn't been this enthused since she was accepted at Smith and knew she was leaving home for four years. "It really is!"

"All right, we'll do it in the morning. Will that work for

you, Diana—are you able to take an hour from your present position to come by?"

"Yes, definitely," Diana says. "I'm between jobs, I can come anytime."

"Hey, let's get a picture of Diana and me. We'll Instagram it." Katherine turns to Diana. "I'm constantly posting. . . . Mom, can you do it?" Katherine gives Faith her phone.

"After brunch, Katherine," Edward says, with a piece of bacon in his hand.

"No, it'll take a second. We'll do a selfie."

Katherine and Diana put their faces close together while Katherine holds her iPhone at arm's length. The corners of their mouths raised, baring white teeth, both of them are somewhere between sexy and girlish.

"Okay, okay, I agree. It's a moment to have," Edward says, as if Katherine and Diana are infusing him with some kind of cheer. "Let's do the four of us. Inez can take it. Away from the light and the glare of the Intracoastal."

Inez returns to the dining room, carrying a fruit platter. Edward ushers them toward the far wall to pose in front of Faith's favorite painting by Molly Lamb. On the canvas families head to the ocean, threaded together by their happy afternoon.

"Ready?" Inez holds the iPhone.

Faith, Edward, Katherine, and Diana link their arms over one another while Inez takes multiples of the same shot—until she thinks she's gotten it right.

ELEVEN

After the girls have gone, optimism is drained from the room. Faith stands up. The last sip of her latte stirs up her stomach. Left alone, she and Edward are so husband and wife, so very married. For better or for worse—a hammering, hollow rhetoric.

"Well, Diana's interesting." Edward also stands. "Not many like that around. It seems she's from some foreign country."

"Miami, she said, since college. She's from a simpler world, that's probably it."

"She could be a good influence on Katherine. Another kind of young woman altogether, very earnest and smart too. Was she ever engaged or married?"

"I don't know, Edward, I've just spoken with her today. Once engaged, maybe. Katherine told us that." Faith feigns that she's an anthropologist while wishing Edward's decency had merit and meant good news. *Your handsome husband.* Mrs. A's frequent chant. *A generous man.* Edward today presents as if his reputation is deserving and pristine. No recently discovered money loss, no pending ruination. Faith knows he's temporarily buoyed by Katherine's visit; his problems haven't vaporized.

With a Jensen Blossom silver tray in her hand, Inez comes through the kitchen door, ready to clear the dining table. Only yesterday Faith googled the tray and found the resale value at more than sixteen thousand dollars. Inez places it on the sideboard beside the Koppel silver fruit bowl, also quite valuable, worth more than eighteen thousand dollars, new or resold. If not contenders for Vintage Tales, Faith will list them elsewhere.

"Brunch was delicious, Inez, especially the pancakes." Faith waves at the room. "We'll be leaving in a moment."

"Thank you, Mrs. Harrison." Inez's steps backward appear natural; she returns to the kitchen as if life is not altered and remains status quo.

Faith feels glued to the marble floor, immutable; Edward too looks stuck.

"Not to be a nag—the delay on the first five hundred, wasn't there going to be another call today to fix that? Isn't that why you skipped tennis this morning at Longreens?"

"I had James Finley cover for my game, to be available for the confirmation."

"And?" Faith walks toward Edward, who is almost cemented in place. A tall rush of air comes between them.

"It's not a go. " He is waxen. "Definitely they've reneged."

"Reneged. Oh my God, Edward, I'm so sorry. I feel awful for you . . . for all of it."

Edward glances at his phone, shakes his head.

"Listen, tomorrow is my next round of meetings with million-dollar lenders. I'd be borrowing at seven percent if I'm lucky, ten percent most likely."

"What lenders? Where are they, are they real?"

He half closes his eyelids as if they're at a performance of the Bolshoi Ballet at the Kravis Center. She's dragged him there and he's half asleep, half critical of what's going on. "I will save us as best I can. I've told you, promised you, that we'll get where we need to be." Edward sighs as if Faith is burdensome.

"As best you can, Edward? You *can't* do anything."

"I've treated you with respect, haven't I? Haven't I taken care of you and Katherine? On Tuesday I'll meet with someone whom Henry introduced me to ages ago."

"*Henry*? If you knew how Allison and Margot Damon are sharpening their claws. I feel it. As nice as Allison is, they want what's mine. I look at Katherine and am anxious how this will—"

"Faith, what's left as collateral, what we really need, as a team, to save *us*, is our—"

From the front hall, their eighteenth-century grand-father clock chimes. The way Faith startles, she seems unaccustomed to the sound.

"Is our house. I've looked into borrowing against the house," Edward continues. Their home.

"When we spoke at first about everything, we agreed the house was the last resort." As she beseeches Edward, the room almost disappears.

"That was five days ago, Faith. The hourglass is—"

"The house is in my name," she says calmly. "We decided that years ago when you were so worried about investors. Isn't it a precaution for us still?"

"It would help, you know. The sale could bring in at least ten million. What a chunk of money that would be toward my debt. Calm people down. We'd be able to set up the meeting to start the process. As scheduled, for the last week in December."

The obvious answer is menacing. If she names their home, she's crossed over, agreed to let it go. Vintage Tales would be next, despite her resistance. She adjusts her focus—woodpeckers are being tossed in the wind; the Intracoastal gets choppier.

"I knew this was coming, Edward; still, I cannot conceive where to go. Isn't there a window, a chance for you to try to raise the money?" *To keep our home separate from the fray?*

An unfinished conversation won't work today, Faith realizes as she stealthily moves behind Edward. Through the foyer, she follows him into the library. As he moves toward the interior bathroom, he fiddles with a set of earbuds. Although Faith has never opened a letter addressed to her husband, eavesdropped on his side of a phone call, or taken cash from his wallet left on the dresser, she is now as near as an interloper. He almost completely closes the door, tapping his foot to a song she isn't able to discern. It registers as a low drone, a constant buzz.

Reaching into his pocket, Edward takes out a small plastic bag and his American Express Centurion black card. After arranging a fine white powder into two neat, small lines on the marble vanity, he methodically rolls up a one-hundred-dollar bill into a narrow straw and half squats. Placing his face to the counter, he touches the bill to his nose, sucks in the air like a pro, about to dive in.

Faith shoves open the bathroom door and, leaning past Edward, she pushes the coke into the sink. She reaches for the right handle of the faucet and turns on the water.

"Where did you get it? Who gave this to you?"

"A client, a potential investor." His pupils are dilated and he smiles wider, a smile that has nothing to do with their present life.

"You're already high—you were high at brunch with Katherine! I don't fucking believe it, Edward!" she shouts.

"A temporary solution, a method to get through the days." He poises himself against the bathroom wall, dislocating their Henry Moore lithograph. Faith instinctively puts her hand up to straighten it. They are not five inches apart.

"After years, years and years of recovery, Edward, the Twelve Steps, your being *the* sobriety spokesperson in Palm Beach—a goddamn shining knight of a husband and father—how can this be? Do you want to be alone with your addiction? Because I won't stay for that; I'll work with you on your debt, okay, because I'm loyal. Not this. I can't, I won't."

"Faith, I promise . . ." He pauses, holding on to his credit card. "I promise. Listen, please."

"I don't want to hear anything you say to me. Not with less than four weeks left and you're doing drugs."

She walks out of the bathroom to the window behind the desk and looks out at the loggia. Albert is trimming the impeccably landscaped hedges of their front yard. Next he'll check the sprinkler system and water the hibiscus, flower beds, planted orchids with a handheld hose. The sun moves behind the clouds—it could be dusk for how gloomy the room is.

Two hours later, tennis at Longreens feels like a respite. Faith and Katherine move through the morass of courts, clay to the left, grass to the right. The waterway is deep blue, cumulous clouds puff up the sky. A resplendent Florida sun showcases tennis as a riveting activity of the afternoon. Mrs. A had warned her years ago that tennis is mandated. "We all play, Faith, darling. It is de rigueur. Until you are at least sixty-five."

Whiling away the afternoon after the unfathomable Edward scene, Faith has become an actress in her own life. The climate at a country club, mindless, unfettered, almost taunts her. If ever she dallied with the thought of being a lady of leisure, Edward's unraveling beats it out of her mind. Faith tries to process Edward's behavior. Mangled, darkness.

"Why are we here, Mom? I thought you'd want to be at Vintage Tales." Katherine spins her racquet and jaunts along beside Faith. "This isn't what you do unless Dad insists."

Faith wonders if she should confide that half the time someone fills in for her for the weekly women's game—and decides against it. Although she positions herself in most arenas from sports to culture with clever moves, she can't embrace tennis. Adequate on the court is how Faith is perceived—despite enough lessons to be better than that. Edward has played the circuit in Florida for the past ten years. *Your husband—such a fine singles player, you must love to watch him.* Edward, ready to snort cocaine in the library of their shared home.

"We had to come today. It was politic. Being on The List, chairing the Arts and Media gig, I *had* to show up, Katherine, this weekend," Faith says. "Mostly it's business."

"Had to? Vintage Tales is probably packed."

"Eve knows we'll be there afterward," Faith says.

Passing the first courts, the ping of one ball almost synchronizes with the ping of the next. As the following games are about to begin, men congregate, unpacking their tennis bags, opening new cans of Wilson balls. Each places his monogrammed towels, wristbands, and Adidas visors on the bench. Faith and Katherine turn the corner and arrive at the next batch of courts, unofficially called "the women's courts."

"If positioning counts, you should be happy. People are watching you," Katherine says.

Faith squints in the direction of several Vintage Tales customers, Noel Finley, Clarissa Barnes, and Cecelia Norric, warming up on the court while waiting for their fourth. Faith sweeps her arm into a running-for-office wave at her constituency.

Margot and Rita Damon are heading toward them, garbed in pure whites and Tretorn sneakers. Margot, like Faith, wears a Merve semi-pleated tennis skirt—equivalent to wearing a miniskirt in one's mid-forties. Rita's jiggling thighs, then her Lacoste skirt and matching collared shirt, manifest. They march toward the court, dyad of the day.

"Don't tell me this is our game," Faith says quietly.

"Yeah, I guess so. Your pro, your club." Katherine tugs her spun bucket hat down on her head. "They're coming closer."

Margot places her right hand on Faith's forearm when they say hello. "Faith, you look like you've eaten bad oysters."

"I'm fine," Faith says. In truth, she wishes she could leave the courts at once.

"Shall we?" Rita says to no one in particular as she walks onto the court ahead of the others.

"I'll hit with you, Mrs. Damon." Katherine walks to the opposite side.

Rita looks at Margot and Faith. "We'll hit, Katherine." Rita tosses her two balls. "Margot? Are you and Faith going to warm up?"

"You two play." Margot, of all people, stays with Faith. She presses a little harder on her forearm. "We'll sit on the bench for a minute. Have some water."

"It's raining." Rita holds up her arms to the first drops. They fall in small BB gun–like pellets, then harder and harder. Games on the adjacent courts come to a halt, players avoid the slippery courts. A godsend for Faith. She has to get out of Longreens.

Having pushed through the line into the clubhouse, Faith looks out the window at the drenched golf course. Members chatter away while the storm passes through.

Margot approaches her. "Faith, don't you love the decor? Look at these buttery blue leather couches, Emerson

Bentley wingbacks—what an improvement from the old pieces."

"I do like it. I was on the decorating committee. We wanted a midcentury redo."

"It totally works," Margot says.

Rita arrives on Faith's other side. "You hadn't moved back yet, Margot. Faith was the one to choose fabrics and pieces, persuading everyone to choose the Cappellini swivel chairs."

"Well, it's a wonderful room. Kudos to you," Margot says. Why is she being decent, friendly?

"A great result for a major time drain. To be honest."

"I'll bet. And a few mean girls, right?" Margot looks at Rita as she speaks.

"My mother would never say that about anyone," Katherine says as she appears. "Right, Mom?"

Continuous idle talk, remarks, much like the ones heard in any gathering, float toward them. *The daughter, married, the son—divorced? Dee Dee is failing, horrid. Lucinda's face-lift, a nameless surgeon, left her for a trainer, younger.* Then Faith captures remnants of praise. *At Vintage Tales, purses are the best, the jewelry, the daughter, her "tales," spooky how spot-on she is.*

"Is it true," Margot says, "that you're selling some high-end jewels at Vintage Tales?"

Coffee brews in the mellow, elegant locker room. A room without windows. Oak wood lockers flank every row, engraved with members' names and the year they joined Longreens. A large toiletry basket is set on the right-hand corner of the check-in desk. Tums, Pepto-Bismol, hair spray, hair shiner. A circumspect attendant is waiting to greet Faith. "Mrs. Harrison, what can I do for you?"

Opening the large bottle of Excedrin, Faith shakes out two tablets. "Water and coffee, please."

While the attendant pours, Faith checks her phone. Only a text from Eve, reporting how swamped they are. Not a word from Edward. She strips in seconds and chooses a steam shower farthest from the other stalls.

Margot, wrapped in a towel, comes to where Faith is slathering body lotion onto her legs. "No one's inside, Faith, we can speak."

What more would Margot have to say? "I have to rush, Katherine's already left in her car for the shop and—"

"I wanted to mention that your home is worth quite a sum. The market is very strong. I have a few customers—"

"I don't know what you mean, Margot. My home isn't for sale."

"Your home isn't *officially* on the market, I agree. Of course, surely, but perhaps a pocket listing? For anyone looking for a Spanish Mediterranean on the Intracoastal, views, five bedrooms, a Marion Sims Wyeth house."

"Margot, this makes no sense."

"I'm assuring you this is between us. I only sell high-end; I do it because I like to match buyers and sellers. Kind of what you do at your shop. One should always know the value of an asset."

Faith waits, tips her head like someone who knows the cool moves on the dance floor but prefers to be led. "I see. Thank you, Margot. It's always good to know, especially in Palm Beach."

"Especially in Palm Beach."

"You must be busy, moving back to town, selling real estate." Faith folds her wet tennis clothes into a plastic bag and zips her taupe Theory pants. "We'll reschedule tennis soon."

"Busy is good. Let me give you my card." Margot whips a card out of her green Goyard card holder. "You know, Allison and I are on your side."

Allison. With great purpose, Faith leaves, reconsidering why she ever needed to belong to Longreens in the first place. The rain thuds softly, moving in another direction.

TWELVE

I f these scarves could talk.' What better slogan for Vintage Tales?" Katherine holds up an Hermès Far- andole scarf of the famed butterfly motif, circa 1985. "We'll fill in the blanks. 'If these bags could talk, if these bangles could talk' . . . See? It works for everything."

Diana, hired to work at the shop six days ago, is pleased. Today her teeth, appearing not exactly even, nor with an overbite, remain bright white. Faith watches her pile her dirty-blond hair on top of her head. Sylphlike, fawn eyed, confident—more so than Katherine, whom Mrs. A has re- peatedly labeled "willowy." Diana is dedicated to a social media campaign for Vintage Tales.

"One of my roommates is from West Palm and raved about the tales that come with the purses and jewelry. In Palm Beach of all places," she told Eve at their brief interview. An interrogation, really—Faith was surprised by Eve's tone.

"Why is that?" Eve asked. "Not that we don't love Palm Beach. I question why someone young and single who needs work would seek it out."

"I read *The Daily Sheet*, so I admire Vintage Tales. I know about Faith Harrison," Diana said.

"Well, here is the real deal!" Eve curtsied in Faith's direction. "Look no further. And we are expanding—not physically, but we'll be selling more items, different inventory too. Not just designer bags . . ."

"We could use someone to do online sales, a Web site, Facebook, maybe Twitter," Faith said. "Instagram."

"*You* want someone to do online marketing? I thought you were not sure when I suggested it," Eve said.

"In season, with fresh ideas, maybe; we need it to increase sales, get the word out. You know I want to increase sales."

"You would have a larger presence and more clientele." Diana was confident. "That I know."

"More revenue." Faith looked at Eve. Edward's inability to come up with investors was beginning to frighten her. Excuses, canceled meetings, invisible backers.

"When would you like to start, Diana?" Faith asked.

"Whoa, Faith. Don't we need to get a few references? When I think of how we cross-examine every item before we tag it and sell it, the records we keep. Let's have a day or two to check," Eve said.

"Of course, I understand. That makes sense. I could be part-time or full-time, I could—"

"Eve is right, that's how I conduct business," Faith

agreed. "We're crazed and I'm relieved that you've come in. I know how my daughter feels about this."

That was when Diana offered to go downstairs and wait while Faith and Eve talked it over. Her enchanting spin as she left the upstairs office, part athlete, part naiad, was followed by laughter, Katherine's and Diana's, from below.

"We need her, we should hire her," Faith said. "I bet she'll find us another level of clientele, and the salary is worth it." Faith's rationale and persuasion were effective, yet beyond that, Diana was appealing, riveting to her. "Edward would say you have to spend to get."

"Right, he used to say that a lot," Eve said. "I'll crunch some numbers."

"One-stop shopping," Diana says. "That could be our second slogan."

"Depending on a person's to-do list, there could be other stores to visit," Eve says.

"Except for these Baccarat candlesticks and little strange lanterns and more turn-of-the-century compacts. Guilloché enamel compacts that we're not supposed to sell because they aren't allergy free. Right? I mean, who knows about the original powder puffs. Then all these silver frames, more lockets, watches, two Verdura cocktail rings," Katherine says.

"Two new estate sales FedExed to us, thanks to Diana and our Web presence," Faith says.

"More friends are coming to shop. Diana tells them at

night when we're out—high school friends, younger women around town, customers' teenage daughters come in. Diana is meeting everyone." Katherine is enthused, which is just short of miraculous. She and Diana glide from a beige display, python Leiber to off-white Chanel to a Prada cream leather clutch. Wearing their Pretty Ballerinas flats and J. Crew cotton shifts, they look as if they've gone shopping together for a daytime "working girl" Palm Beach uniform. If such a role exists.

"How about a tale of the Amazon women, when they ruled the earth. There was Queen Penthesilea—we could attach the tale to earrings—she was in the Trojan War. And Hippolyta. Her father was Ares; that might work for a beautiful Lalaounis necklace," Katherine says.

"I like it!" Diana says. "Wasn't there an Amazon warrior who fought with Telamon—in a battle against Heracles's troops?"

"Ainippe. That's who it was." Katherine is almost gleeful that Diana knows the myth.

"Yeah, Ainippe. I was raised on Greek myths."

"Aren't we esoteric?" Eve asks.

"That depends on the myth," Faith says. "We're setting a mood."

Eve places a platter of almond croissants on the coffee table and walks toward the Nespresso machine. "Lattes all around?"

Katherine unwraps a moonstone brooch. "Hey, Diana, from one of the sellers who e-mailed you . . . maybe it works?"

Diana nods. "Or another way to go, another kind of tale for this, from Upstate New York. A Victorian aquamarine-and-pearl choker. The stone almost twinkles, doesn't it?"

"Will anyone wear a choker?" Eve asks. "That's the problem with online customers, they aren't coming in. Who knows how they'll feel. Online retail is . . ."

Faith frowns. "I hate the word *retail*."

"Okay, Mom, fine. But you are in retail; you sell things. In a store."

"An upscale *shop*," Diana says. "An elegant, composed shop."

Eve taps her nail extensions against a glass saucer. "Online sales are a little like online dating. Meaning it's incalculable, with no checks and balances, no control. Here, at Vintage Tales, someone comes in, shops, convinced of their purchase. Paste, costume, David Webb, Cartier. They see, they pay, it's final."

"The more real jewelry we sell, the better it is. That's my concept," Faith says. "High prices."

"Some pieces are so expensive, though, Mom," Katherine says.

"Yes, but we're in Palm Beach in early December. Anytime, any month in season works to sell expensive things. It's always been a good idea." Eve comes close to Faith, pinches her elbow.

"We should do a mixed display, bags and jewelry." Katherine holds up another pin, an antique pearl cluster brooch.

"Two girls, cousins of Rhys's roommate from Deerfield, are stopping by this afternoon. They want cross-bodies by Céline and Dior, Chanel clip-on earrings—they're really into pre-owned," Katherine says.

"We met them last night at HMF, no, maybe it was at Echo afterward," Diana says.

"Ah, to be young," Eve says.

"I'm having the best time," Diana says. With her catchy looks and improved wardrobe, since she shops in Katherine's closet (Katherine, never a lender or borrower before, now open to sharing), one might not believe that Diana is living west of the bridge. With two roommates who bartend at Greg's Clam Bar in Lake Worth.

"Let's start pricing," Faith says, when a text comes in from Edward. *News delayed.* Since last Sunday when Edward and Faith argued over his using, she has been cool toward him. Except for a polite, distant hello, as if they are neighbors who cannot be avoided totally, but are not speaking. Every message sent by Edward seems a false promise, a sparse and unconvincing line about raising capital, how stalled it is.

Katherine walks to the window and looks out. The sun falls to the right of the Avenue as bells chime above the front door.

"Customers, Mom. It's ten o'clock."

By late morning Eve is carrying around fizzy and still water on a square silver tray. Of the dozen women in the shop in search of Christmas gifts, only a few are familiar. Diana's ads are taking off—a kind of outreach is the reward. Listening closely to each cluster of potential buyers, Faith is calculating what could be earned today when Leslie Lestat walks in with Priscilla. Since most recently she bought a Chanel classic double flap and consigned a gold Schlumberger circle rope bracelet, Faith perks up. Air-kisses are dispersed.

"We're late, parking is a nightmare," Priscilla says. "We'll end up at Ta-boo at the bar, if Leslie says yes to lunch. Have you ever seen her so woeful, Faith?"

Has Leslie lost weight? She's too thin, not a healthy thin. When she lifts her Gucci sunglasses, a fatigue is almost etched onto her skin and has settled into her jawline.

"Are you all right?" Faith dares ask the logical question avoided daily in Palm Beach. *Look the other way*, Mrs. A taught Faith. *Ask nothing, see little.*

"I'm fighting the flu." Leslie puts her sunglasses back on. "Since opening night at the Shelteere I've felt like this, flu-ish, vile. Even at Mar-a-Lago at Mrs. A's luncheon. For ten days."

"Twelve, to be exact." Faith would know. "Did you call Dr. Huber?"

"I have. He gave me sleeping pills. I'm not contagious." Sleeping pills? Faith should not have asked.

"I've brought a Birkin." Leslie rustles her Neiman Marcus shopping bag.

Each client becomes quiet, even the twenty-something twin sisters from Hobe Sound, whom Diana found at HMF. They freeze where they stand, admiring Schreiner fifties glass flower earrings, priced at one hundred and ninety dollars. Everyone waits, as if a knife thrower is about to perform.

"Take a look." Leslie carefully lifts her Malachite Birkin from the soft flannel Hermès covering. "See, it's palladium hardware. I have the paperwork, only a few years old. A gift from my husband. He ordered it months before it ever arrived; we were on a roster." Leslie is rattled, hesitant.

"Stunning," Priscilla exclaims. "A knockout."

"Useful too," an unknown customer weighs in. "I mean, it's a Birkin—you'd use it every day. Don't you think?"

"The bag is so unadulterated you could take it to Hermès," Mrs. A's friend says.

"I already did," Leslie admits. "They said it was ever so gently used. I explained I'd only worn it once. They said to bring it to Vintage Tales."

Faith touches the clasp. "Almost virginal."

"Why, you will have this sold in hours, my dear. This is your lucky day." Cecelia has just arrived, the scent of Eau des Merveilles Bleue preceding her. "Everyone appreciates these bags. They're coveted. Maybe there can be a 'Birkin Day.' I'm not in love with my Birkin—etoupe. I *know* it's a favorite color and thirty centimeters, silver hardware—what's wrong with me? I should sell it."

"Excellent," Eve says. "If you bring it today, we'll do a Birkin shelf."

Faith checks Leslie's reaction. She isn't presenting as a client who swaps out one luxury item for another on a relaxed Palm Beach afternoon. The importance of the money makes the room dense; the fun is drained away.

"Diana, can someone ring this up?" One twin holds up the flower earrings.

"Of course," Diana says. Trained on short notice, eager to know the drill, she takes out a small carved wooden box and puts the earrings inside, wraps the box in ice-blue tissue paper, and places it inside a miniature pastel painted bag. Eve runs the AmEx card while she seals the bag with a VT sticker. "Voilà." She gives it to the twin.

Faith takes the Birkin in its cover. "Let's go upstairs and do the paperwork, Leslie."

"And a fifties Schlumberger gold enamel bracelet." Leslie opens a Tiffany box. "It's signed."

Faith looks at the bangle and calculates it can be priced at more than forty thousand dollars. "Leslie, what you're consigning, the bag and the bracelet, are very valuable."

"I know. I really need to sell these. When will you put my bag out and this bracelet? When I called Eve this morning, she said the other Schlumberger bracelet, the one I brought in a few weeks ago, sold two days ago." Leslie sighs.

"It did. The check was mailed already."

"She said so. Then maybe these will sell fast too." Leslie looks around at Faith's inventory, piled higher than ever before. "You're swamped."

"We are, but what you've brought in is special."

"My girls are five, eight, and thirteen. They're going to have to leave the Academy. Everyone'll whisper about them, about us. You know Travis is going to trial in six months' time . . ."

"Trial? What happened?"

"Tax evasion, that's what Travis has done. He's ruined our lives, y'know. And meanwhile, until about a week ago, I acted like things are fine. You've got to sell these fast, Faith. Please. I keep thinking of my girls. How dare he. Piece a'shit." She covers her face and sobs, sounding like the Vimeo Faith and Katherine watched years ago of a crying hyena for Katherine's science report. "Hyenas are sad, not happy," Katherine had told Faith.

Through the slanted light from the windows that face north, Leslie is almost inverted. Her ballerina posture, her bearing, her sleek blond hair are blotted out. Instead she huddles and rounds her shoulders, her hair is ratty and flat. Leslie and Travis, both University of Pennsylvania BAs, he a Wharton MBA, rustle onto every dance floor. They are lauded, glossy, A-listed.

"Leslie, I'm so sorry." Faith puts her arms around her.

Leslie allows herself to be lulled for a second, then shakes out of Faith's embrace. "You know I loved him when we got married. We moved here from D.C., made a life, friends. The girls have been . . . I don't know . . . liked, invited places."

Really, Faith can't listen, can't tolerate what Leslie is detailing.

"I'm fucking forty years old. I should have known Travis had a problem, I should have helped him. I feel awful for him." Leslie starts pacing.

"Look, you can sell more goods here, if it helps. I'm expanding; we're selling sterling-silver frames, small vases, more fine jewelry. If you have to, there are places to sell clothes, even your furniture. Maybe online," Faith says. "Diana knows about it."

"How about my house—I've got to sell that. Margot Damon, you know she's a broker in town, having done it those years they were in California. Cecelia and Allison convinced me to give her the listing."

Margot. The listing. Jesus, no matter how dismal the hour, it can always get uglier, more tangled.

"You do want the house sold quickly, isn't that it? Margot knows her stuff," Faith says. *Always be generous to enemies; it costs you very little*: Mrs. A 101.

"We'll have to find something to rent, not expensive. We'll go west . . . north . . . I dunno. I love it here. The girls love it. It took me a long time to be *in* Palm Beach, to really be a part of it. I'm not sure you understand."

"Oh, no, I do, Leslie," Faith says.

"Be happy you have Edward for a husband." Leslie digs around for her iPhone in her Balenciaga motorcycle bag—one that Faith might sell to someone in her thirties. "What do you predict—how long, how many days? I need a check for the lawyers."

"About the Birkin. I have a buyer in mind. For top dollar—around sixty thousand dollars. Perhaps by tomorrow," Faith says.

"That's what I was praying for. I've done a little research."

Leslie texts, nods, pulls herself together, waves. "I have to go. I have a pickup for Taylor; she's at the Norrics'. Let me know, Faith. Thank you, thank you."

As she walks ahead, her Manolo double-strap sandals clack down the stairs. When she opens the door to the first floor, the chatter below floats upward, the way hot air rises.

With her iPad mini in hand, Katherine nears the Birkin five minutes later. "Hmmm. I have the tale for it, another type, a perfect tale. *A Doll's House* by Henrik Ibsen."

"Don't you think it's a sort of a downer?" Eve stands at the entryway to Faith's office.

"Sad, but Nora, the wife, gets to face her truth. Her husband's ready to disclaim her, and everything she's done has been for him. He's not worthy of her. Then she goes free. Well, she bolts, she leaves her family."

"My feeling is the bag will be sold quickly. I've already called a client, Missy Raleigh in South Beach. And Daisy Laurent in town. We won't be showcasing it," Faith says, ignoring the conversation. "So maybe this time, just this time, no tale is needed."

"Mom, the idea is to always have a tale."

"Diana can also sell the Birkin online. She's set it up, it's completely secure, priced at seventy thousand dollars," Eve says. "Holy moly, seventy thousand dollars."

Faith holds up the Schlumberger bracelet. "I bet this is worth forty to forty-five thousand."

"These prices are insane," Katherine says. "Who would pay that for a bag? For a bangle?"

"No, it's right, I looked it up. That's what the going rate is." Diana steps inside. "Talk about supply and demand; the buyers for the Birkin—that Birkin—they drive the price."

"It's obscene, isn't it, Mom?"

Obscene—hasn't Faith, despite her pursuits, known that it is? Eve and Diana, waiting for her answer to Katherine. "Well, not for the customer who has to have it. Who views it as a treasure. The thought being it makes you whole, content. If you can afford it." *Conspicuous consumption taken to the nth degree.*

"Mrs. A—she wouldn't want this spectacular Birkin, would she?" Eve presses.

"Mrs. A? I honestly don't know. I sort of doubt it. She has beautiful, costly things, still . . ." How certain is Faith that neither item would appeal to Mrs. A? Fairly sure, yet not able to vouch for her.

"If she doesn't have a bag that costs more than a year's tuition at Smith, I bet she has one or more that would pay for half a year," Eve says.

"It's how the world is, isn't it?" Diana says without looking up from her iPad mini. "I mean, I have three customers I'm about to contact."

"Let's see who commits first, Diana's Web contacts or tried-and-true clients. Leslie's already counting on the sale." Faith will come through for her, and for herself.

The downstairs bells chime. Eve and Katherine rush down the stairs.

THIRTEEN

Y ou seem upset." Diana remains in the office with Faith. She drapes herself over the curved section of the Egg chair. She wears three silver rings on her right hand; one has an amethyst in the center. "Is it because of Leslie?"

"It's very upsetting. Her husband, he's going to end up . . ." Faith pauses, decides not to be part of the gossip chain. "Let's say Leslie could be in for a rough time."

"So we'll make a push for her bracelet too," Diana says. "Sell it right away."

"Yes, she'll need the cash." Faith thinks of Edward. Leslie's sales are more significant for her than she might have anticipated.

"Ah, the wretched-husband syndrome. No wonder Katherine wants Ibsen's *A Doll's House*. Poor Nora, another long-suffering wife. Maybe it's too on the nose for Katherine to use."

Diana walks to the window. "How many years have you looked out at the shoppers and thought how they're so . . . I don't know . . . Palm Beachy?"

"A long time. Decades."

"Do you ever miss where you're from?" Diana parades around the office as if she is a clothes model. Hips forward, shoulders back. Mouth in a pseudo-smile.

"I'm sorry?" Faith says.

"Home. Do you ever think about . . . ?"

"No, not really. Philadelphia's a manageable city, livable, but I haven't missed it." Faith goes to the wall to switch on the overhead fan. Although it's more decorative than useful, she needs it; the room has become stuffy. The wings whir in a half-numbing, half-buzzy drone.

"You don't go back?" Diana asks.

"We go to New York, we ski, or we did when Katherine was younger. We spent time abroad on trips, summers we've rented in . . ." Faith says.

"What about South Jersey? Kendalton, the Pine Barrens?"

To steady herself, Faith sits on the Estrella sofa. Fear soaks into her being, thudding and foreboding. A hushed moment passes.

"May I sit too?" Diana asks.

"Please. Of course," Faith says.

Diana, looking somewhere between regal and fragile, sits across. The sun beats through the window, making a small pool of light on the bleached wooden planks filling the length of the room.

"I came to find you, you know. I had to find you, track

you down. I was so afraid, it was such a risk. I spent two weeks in the area, settling in, getting my courage up. That's why meeting Katherine first, unintentionally, was a sign. I'd already decided to try to work at Vintage Tales, to meet you, to know you a little."

"Diana, I want to explain, to tell you what happened . . . that . . ." Faith tries to speak.

"I told you my mother died recently," Diana says.

"I'm very sorry. That's so sad, I didn't know, I wasn't told."

"Right. I told Katherine. Not that she's so intrigued, but we talk, and she's described Palm Beach and Rhys. How you've been a working mother in this fishbowl of non-working mothers, nonworking women. How she knows you care about the place, the lifestyle. How you worry about her. I didn't say how I angled to get to Palm Beach."

"Katherine doesn't . . . ?" Faith swallows words. "Katherine hasn't any idea . . ." Her blood pressure rises. She is reprehensible, Diana has come to prove it, a trampling of Faith's very essence.

"No, she doesn't know," Diana says. "I tried to be careful, casual when I asked about you. She says you're an amazing mother, a popular lady." Diana inspects Faith. "Don't worry, I didn't tell her why. What I had learned."

"What you had learned?" The room is airless. Worse than a crowded coach seat in the back of an airplane. Worse than an elevator in Midtown in New York City that overcrowds and no one will relent. Why has Diana come with news, what is she after? "I'm not sure what you mean."

"My mother left me a letter with her will. It was about you. I suspect she wanted me to be in southern Florida all along. I'd gotten into other schools, better schools than the University of Miami. The last time she got sick—she'd been sick off and on for years—she started sending articles about Palm Beach. About Vintage Tales."

A long-suppressed memory. Faith feels it in her gut, moving toward her throat. She waits.

"Then that letter. You know what I mean, right?" Diana asks. "What I'm talking about?"

There's that kind of graying of the room, how it is before one faints. Faith coughs, squeezes her hands together to stop the sensation.

"Don't you wonder how my mother knew since there isn't open adoption in New Jersey? How my mom knew who you were?" Diana says.

Faith's memory of being sixteen, of giving birth, of her mother and grandmother, too young themselves when they gave birth to their own daughters, arranging the adoption. Assuring Faith she would be okay, that this was the best solution. She would let go of what had happened, what she had done. Escaping the Pines, beginning a life elsewhere. *A safe secret*, her mother had called it, *a second chance*.

"No, I don't wonder. I think I know." Faith begins to cry quietly. "There was a neighbor, Mrs. Barker, and she helped. She said she knew a couple in Chatsworth, a young couple who couldn't have children. Chatsworth was just far enough away, no one would figure it out. Mrs. Barker and my grandma went to church together. They didn't believe in abortion or sealed records. So she must have talked about it—although she wasn't supposed to name anyone. That must be how your mother knew."

"Why did you give me up? Why did you do whatever

they said to do? Didn't you want to be with me, your baby daughter?" Diana tries not to cry.

"I couldn't take care of you. I was a junior in high school, Diana. I wanted you to end up with someone who could give you a good life. And my mother and grandmother, they were convinced it was the right thing. I'm sure, I have looked it up, that this happens every day. This scenario— our scenario."

"Who was my birth father? What happened to him?" Diana begins to cry.

"Jimmy. He was my high school boyfriend. He was two years older. I loved him. I would have stayed in Kendalton if he hadn't died. I would have raised you. He and I would have been together—that's what I thought. Three weeks before you were born, he was in a trucking accident. He was driving. I was heartbroken, so frightened. That's how my mother and grandmother decided for me—and why I agreed. The minute you were born, I said, *I have a name for her*, and my mother said, *You can't name her, she's not yours*. Then they took you from me, I was screaming, begging them to stop." Faith covers her eyes.

"No one knows what you did, right? Nobody knows, not Edward, Katherine. Not Eve?" Diana asks.

"Nobody knows. I've walked around with this secret—a kind of lie—since you were born. The days it would eat at me and I would doubt myself, I remembered what my mother said about a safe secret. No one knows, no one judges a safe secret. Everybody's better off—that's what she kept saying to me. What would a pregnant sixteen-year-old girl with a dead boyfriend do? I hope you understand that part." Faith reaches across the coffee table and puts Diana's hand in hers.

"Our eyes are the same color. Exactly. Hazel turning to green in certain light. I noticed at the brunch at your house," Diana says. "We're the same height, we've got the same way of walking, we . . ."

"I confess, at that brunch, I thought, didn't dare think, that you and I are similar. You and Katherine are similar—your long necks, narrow chins, little pointy chins. We have the same wrists." Faith holds up her left arm. "See?"

Diana puts her right hand up against Faith's left hand like they're about to start a patty-cake routine. They stare at each other.

A terrifying sadness claws at Faith—fear, regret, remorse. "I don't know if you'll believe me, but not a day has passed that I haven't thought of you. Once, after Katherine was born, I almost told Edward. I saw how Katherine would be raised, I thought of Jimmy and the accident. I read articles on adopted children and their birth parents being reunited. I stayed quiet, I was silent, Diana, that's what I did." Faith is crying again.

"I would try to draw your face until I was about twelve," Diana says. "Over and over again, every night."

"Your adoptive mother and father, they were good to you, they took care of you, didn't they?" Faith can't imagine them. She has never wanted to.

"I had everything I needed. I mean, it wasn't this—it wasn't Palm Beach—but it was fine. South Jersey–style fine. My father died first. I think my mother knew I needed a mother once she got sick. She must have believed I needed to know, sending me to you."

"Clearly they did a fine job raising you," Faith says. "A great job. You are savvy and smart, kind. Beautiful."

"Beautiful. Thank you. Well, look at you, at Katherine." Diana pauses, wipes her tears. "My mother's name was Mary."

Mary. Wasn't Faith told that so long ago? Yet she doesn't want to hear much about Mary, as if Diana has been delivered today—under glass. As if her own proof of life beyond the day she abandoned her daughter is separate, justifiable.

"I was always imagining you didn't want me. Why, why not? I'd be tortured about it, couldn't figure it out."

"Oh, Diana, it's not true. Then I'd push aside my feelings, suppress them. I'd tell myself I had no choice but to find you a better way."

Enough days when Faith could not be distracted, the unrelenting weight of what she had done. Holidays, birthdays, Katherine's first day of kindergarten, her science fair prize, her high school prom.

"Let's think this through. We're together now," Faith says. "And here you'll stay. It's late in the game; still, I can 'adopt' you."

"Oh my God, I so want that. It would be meaningful," Diana says. "What about Katherine—she idolizes you."

"I'm not sure that she idolizes me, but we're close. To be honest, I'm concerned. I can't fathom the conversation—breaking this news to her. She might be devastated. She will be. It might be too much for her. . . ."

"I'm not sure what she'll say. I would imagine that she'll view it as if you made a mistake—how could you have done that and then kept a secret. A big secret, a shocking one," Diana says.

"She could be very hurt, angry with me. Maybe I've

always been afraid of that. The good news is she cares about you, Diana. Although she'll struggle anyway."

Faith looks at Diana. What will she do? She can neither hide Diana nor spring it on Katherine that in another life she left her daughter behind.

"How about the entire Palm Beach crowd? Your clients?" Diana asks.

"You know, that isn't my concern. This is about you and Katherine. Edward too. He'll have to know soon enough."

Diana squeezes Faith's hand and nods, exhales. "How about we keep it between us, for now. You can hide me for a while. What's another few days?"

As always, downstairs noises rise, the shop sounds inviting. The sunlight through the large windows facing south is almost obliterated. Faith and Diana remain sitting together.

"I have another question, one that's been on my mind since I came to your shop."

"Ask, ask me," Faith says.

"How'd you get away? How'd you leave Kendalton?"

"Ah, the great escape. If you think Chatsworth, Kendalton, the Pines were provincial—no, backward—when you grew up, it was ten times worse before then," Faith says.

"I get it," Diana says.

"A month after you were adopted, I was working at Cumberland Farms, heartsick. I'd dream of you, your small fingers, your little feet, the thatch of hair on the top of your head. I begged a woman who came in for a pack of cigarettes to take me with her; she was driving west to Cherry Hill."

"Cherry Hill—wow."

"It was something. It wasn't the Pines, where people whispered about me and Jimmy. Everyone knew what had happened. It was awful, another burden. Cherry Hill was an oasis. . . ."

"I loved that mall—the Cherry Hill Mall—when I was in high school. I thought it was, I dunno, sophisticated, close to Philadelphia, an escape."

"You're right, it was. Pure escape." Faith smiles ruefully.

Diana comes to where Faith is sitting, kneels and weeps. Faith puts her hand on her daughter's shoulder—against her finespun skin.

A text bings on Faith's phone on the side table. Diana lifts her head, reads the screen aloud. "From Eve: 'Are you coming down?'"

"Tell her not yet," Faith says.

"No, it's okay. I keep hearing the chimes at the front door. Maybe they need us. We'll pretend we were pricing more Birkins, comparing online with resale."

Both laugh for a second, stand, trace their hands across each other's face. They reach out and hold tightly.

"Sure, let's go," Faith says.

Why not—haven't the last thirty years been about pretending?

FOURTEEN

Cocktails, wardrobe, jewels, high levels of air-kissing as the Harrisons ease into Noel and James Finley's formal living room in their newly purchased Flagler mansion—acquired at close to twenty million. Earlier arrivals are exiting for the Norric or Barclay shindigs, but Faith and Edward, destined to party-hop the evening long, are late. Almost beyond fashionably late— Faith's fault since after speaking with Diana she could hardly pull herself together. What she yearned to do was remain with her lost daughter and celebrate. They would share thoughts for hours on end, the sheer joy of finding her, the relief of knowing she is whole and delightful after years of guessing and doubt. Instead Faith is showing up, as expected, camera ready for the night ahead.

"Faith?" Edward is searching for something. "Do you feel okay?"

Diana. She should have told him about her daughter from the start, she should have confessed to what she did three decades ago. He deserved to know, didn't he?

"Yes. I'm okay."

She wraps her geometric-print Loro Piana stole around her shoulders, realizing her last year's black dress by Prabal Gurung might be too understated. And realizing how little she cares. Never has a gathering felt less inviting, less festive. Glancing at the exquisite surroundings, she considers day-to-day life at this house, or anywhere nearby. The palette, the hues, the *quintessence*—that's what claws at her throat.

"Are you sure?" He has that "husband who protects" look about him—a gestalt that carried tremendous importance until now.

Faith nods. "We're here, we should start our hellos."

"Yeah?" He puts his hand on her wrist like he's feeling her pulse.

"I'm sure." Faith tugs the stole closer. "I think Henry and Ross Dexter are waving for you to join them."

Edward notices and drops Faith's wrist. "Maybe I'll follow you, see them first." He heads toward the satin lacquered grand piano in the symmetrical, white-on-white living room. As if it's just another night and he has not confessed to his wife, as if they are carefree and untroubled. Without debt. He senses her thought. "I might as well, right?"

A crunching crowd—gossip rising. "I'll move toward Noel," Faith decides.

Extreme lurching, greetings, *Faith, Faith*, clients gush, smile, hold up their latest Vintage Tales purchase, while others feign that they don't notice their sold Judith Leiber or Edie Parker evening bags. Faith smiles the smile, emanates demure, throaty sounds as she skims through. Only to swish past other factions of wives—a long-hair, sequined-dress brigade in stiletto Louboutins, sporting diamond, ruby, or emerald necklaces. To the right is a cluster of women with their "almost-husbands," rediscovered on Facebook or at a college reunion. *Faith, Faith*, the chant continues.

Long thin heels submerge into the soft sod and there is the buffeting of the Intracoastal against the bulkhead. Noel stands on the other side of her infinity pool, surrounded by guests. Her new labradoodle, named Coquet, is licking her hand. Another labradoodle, older, slower, lies at Noel's feet, almost forgotten. With the outside lanterns and shadows, Faith barely discerns Noel's guest, with whom she speaks. Until he rambles to her and smoothly comes to where she stands.

"Faith! All night I've been searching for you! Where's your husband? Don't tell me I've missed him," Noel says.

"He's inside." Faith is aware of Lucas listening, slowly assessing her. "Talking to Ross and Henry. Noel, your home is even more irresistible than at your luncheon in November."

"You're too kind," Noel says as she's tapped on the shoulder by one of her waitstaff, a wiry young man with a pencil mustache. He begins whispering in her ear, causing her to frown. Perhaps the salmon isn't cooked enough, overcooked? She excuses herself and Lucas edges beside Faith, puts his arm around her waist. A bold gesture were it not for the muted outdoor lighting. From the shoulders down it's pure speculation as to what's actually occurring.

"Faith, you're shivering." His skin is thermal, insulated.

"It's the wind, you know, at the start of the season." Searching for either of their spouses, Margot or Edward, she steps back.

"Meet me somewhere soon." Lucas speaks in a velvety voice, like a newscaster.

"I can't."

"Meet me—say yes."

Shadows on the wide, long lawn fall directly across them, a double shield of darkness.

"I can't." She desperately wants to.

"Why not?" Lucas asks.

"Because anything can go wrong." *Because enough is wrong, because being beside him is too tempting, too costly.*

"Tell me you love your husband and I'll go."

Stepping nearer to Lucas, Faith allows her bare arm to brush against his navy blazer, her bare leg is against his trousers. Not as a married couple, but as lovers, where every move one makes is a hankering for more.

She shakes her head—an unknowable answer.

"Tomorrow. Early. At seven. By the south end, the public beach, you know where I mean." He presses a cocktail napkin into her hand. "Here, I wrote down my cell. . . ."

With the next group spilling onto the limestone patio, he's gone. Faith pads the linen fabric, then places it in her vintage Gucci clutch. Black patent, a fashion dare since no one seems to be into patent bags, new or used, this season.

When Faith's iPhone alarm goes off at six the next morning, she is already standing at the window in her yoga pants and sneakers, a sweatshirt around her waist. As she turns it off, she tries to recall when she last had a decent night's sleep. Her head throbs; she ought to pop two Advil.

At the bottom of the staircase she finds Edward holding on to a portable handset, bleary-eyed.

"I've got a call with Zurich, then London. Where're you going? Isn't it too early to be out? It's goddamn dark outside."

"The Lake Trail, like most mornings. Except I have to be at work soon for a shipment—an estate's in."

"The trail at this hour?"

"Edward, please, promise me later today you'll let me know about the loans. I'll be waiting."

The call comes in. "Hello, hello, Fabian."

His greeting sounds self-possessed, like the Edward she knows. Her Edward.

A chill through Faith's heart. She ought to have texted Lucas, ought to have canceled. Instead she waves, blows a kiss to her husband, and races into the garage. How it's done, she supposes, once your desolation is greater than your moral code. When you're ready to hear what your old flame has to say and you envision what might have been.

Lucas is leaning against a bench at the public beach between Mar-a-Lago and Eau Spa when she gets there. The sky is filled with pink and magenta streaks; the sun is rising. In the gentle light, Lucas's face is unflawed, mildly

Clark Kent–esque. Today she finds the look both sexy and endearing. His straw hat reminds her of a picture she once saw of Ernest Hemingway. She smiles at Lucas's interpretation of incognito.

"Surreal, isn't it?" he asks.

Early risers, mostly fishermen, walk toward Benny's on the Beach for their pancake breakfast.

Faith nods. "Totally."

They stand without touching,

"Join me, Faith." Lucas leads her, pats the empty space on the bench for her to sit.

She collects her hair into a ponytail, runs her tongue across her front teeth. Nothing about him has to do with Palm Beach or the Avenue. Nothing about her either. As if they exist in a cubic prism—the lateral view belongs only to them. She slots in, they face the boardwalk jutting into the ocean, their shoulders close together.

"So many years apart. I'm still thinking of you," Lucas says.

"I don't remember the last time I sat next to you," Faith says. She's near enough to touch any part of his body.

"Decades." The voice again, a memory of telling a joke by batting an eye.

"A lifetime ago."

"Well, we've seen each other. Wasn't there one time at the Candy Kitchen in Bridgehampton, Margot sending daggers toward you? If looks could kill, they say." Lucas laughs.

"Margot. She and I are sort of friendly these days."

"Really? All that she wants is your title for the Arts and Media Ball," Lucas sighs.

"Not a bad idea," Faith says. A comment that pops out

of her mouth, filled with truth. Perhaps it was yesterday with Diana and last night with Edward's pretense that caused the tipping point.

"What?" How he gazes at her.

Uneasily, she turns to him. "Nothing."

Waves roll in, crashing into one another as if their rhythm is off. Part of her wants to strip off her clothes, instigate unmarried, untethered sex. She sniffs his skin as though it might save her life. She could breathe Lucas instead of oxygen.

After years of brief and tenuous thoughts, longings and no place to file anything. An affair of the mind that hasn't any home or port.

"I've missed you." Lucas's mouth at her ear. "Let's not wait another stretch like this—twenty-five years—to be together. I should never have let you go. I regret it—I've regretted it always. But now, now our kids are grown."

She blinks, remembering what Eve had said when Lucas broke it off with Faith. *He'll be sorry, really sorry. One day—a faraway day—he'll come begging.*

"Lucas," she says. "Maybe . . ." He places his forefinger on her lips, then over her forehead. She's made of carved alabaster, for his touch, unable to resist.

"Soon? Maybe?" He reaches over to kiss her. "Hey?"

"You don't want me, Lucas. Believe me."

She wishes this warning weren't true. He kisses her again and she opens her mouth. He tastes like licorice and tree resin; his lips are soft and strong.

The wind blows his hat and he tugs it back before it flies away. Faith pulls her hood over her head and stares at him. Is he being sincere, or is she too incredibly threadbare from what's gone on that she wouldn't know? How many years has she imbued Edward with qualities he may or may not have? Still, her husband needs help, and here she sits with Lucas. He hugs her and she sinks into him. A comfortable/strange caress. What kind of person is she?

"Something has happened with Edward. I want to tell you before you hear it on the tennis courts, at some golf match, a cocktail hour at Longreens," she begins.

"Let's not do that this morning. Can't we shut Edward out? And Margot out? Let's the two of us have our own little reunion." He puts his mouth close to her ear again. "Come with me, Faith, it's time. We've always been in love."

"I need to explain . . . first," Faith says.

"Explain what, Faith?" He's half listening, persuaded by their tête-à-tête, perhaps fascinated by her face so near to his—that they're in each other's company. He moves toward her ear again. She wants him to keep at it, but instead she stiffens, moves back.

"Lucas, we have to talk about Edward, if not the others. Today. Because he's in trouble."

He pauses almost politely as she shifts the conversation far from their interlude. A few more fishermen pass by on their way to the pier.

"Edward's lost our money. You'll know about it soon enough."

"How?" Lucas asks with a slight detachment, as if there's nothing original in her news.

"Bad investments, I suppose—personal investments. I'm understanding he was careless, imprudent. It's going to rumble through Palm Beach, people talking, whispering. Katherine has to be safe. I'm trying to help, to figure out what to do."

Lucas straightens up and looks at the shoreline, away from Faith.

"I brought you to Palm Beach. We were meant to be together. You and I . . ."

What might have been with Lucas, the life not shared. Has he missed her careful camouflage, threaded together over the years with great care? Rather he's searching for a reason, one he'll understand.

"Oh, Lucas, I don't know that, I don't know—I let that go. I had to."

The gulls caw overhead, cackling and dropping clamshells onto the boardwalk.

"A loan," Lucas says. "Would that help?"

"I'm sorry?"

"I'll loan you money, Faith. Name the amount."

"Why are you doing this, Lucas?"

"I owe you. I owe you for—"

"Please, please don't say this." She closes her eyes, wanting to touch his collarbone.

"You should take the check, Faith."

"I can't do that," she whispers.

He starts to kiss her. She kisses him back, wishing he'd invade her being. They would find a spot beneath the pier to make love, Lucas would be inside her. Whether they do or not, she's covered in Lucas anyway.

"Where have you been? It's almost eight—you're never back this late." Edward is pacing in the biscuit-and-fawn-colored living room. He stares at her so intently she looks away.

"Don't you have an eight o'clock singles at Longreens?" Not that he appears remotely well enough to be in a tennis match. His skin tone is off, he's agitated.

Inez walks in. Whether she hears Edward or not, she sees no evil. She places a small silver tray with a cup of espresso on the Chinese lacquered coffee table. Refolding the white hemstitch cocktail napkins, she is almost annoyed they might be wrinkled.

"Mrs. Harrison, I didn't know you were home." Inez clears her throat. "Will you be going to work, Mrs. Harrison, or shall I prepare something?"

"No, no, thank you, Inez," Faith says. "I'm going to shower and be off to the shop."

"Mr. Harrison, shall I . . ." Inez turns to Edward.

He throws his arms toward the ceiling. "That's fine, Inez, thank you."

Faith and Edward watch her leave, as if they're on stage and their next lines depend upon her exit.

He's jittery, apprehensive. Faith watches, remembering Edward from long ago, decades ago, when he was using. He's in recovery, he's promised, isn't that Faith's mantra? She waits for the sun to stream through the room, for her to see if his eyes are bloodshot. She can't tell. She thinks, hopes they are clear, as clear as when she left and he was on the phone with his possible investors.

"Where were you?" Edward asks.

Faith steps backward, rubs her neck. "When I left, you were on a call to borrow money. How did it go?"

He paces again, moving toward the windows that overlook the terrace and grounds. Albert is visible, clipping back the white hibiscus, trimming the hedges. Exactly as Edward likes it.

"Faith, where were you?" His voice has become a mixture, both jarring and plaintive.

"I keep believing you'll fix it, and it isn't happening. I keep thinking and hoping it will," Faith says.

"You know what? I'd prefer to be indigent than take favors," Edward says.

Images of Lucas tumble around in her head, a sensation of his palms across her thighs, against her waist. Since she left him at the pier she wonders when they'll next meet. If they'll meet. A hazy anguish begins.

"I'm not sure what you mean," Faith says.

"No?" His tone becomes eerily quiet.

"We're looking to borrow, we're looking for loans."

She comes to where her husband is contemplating the Intracoastal. Frothy waves hit the bulkhead. "Whatever you did, Faith, don't do it again," he says.

FIFTEEN

*A*nna Karenina earrings?" Faith asks. She, Katherine, and Eve are downstairs, rearranging shelves, color coordinating bags. "Weren't we worried that customers might not love the connotation?"

"Why not, Mom? *Anna Karenina* was written for Palm Beach," Katherine says.

"She jumped in front of a train," Faith says.

"After making some terrible decisions," Katherine says. "She was also someone whose life went wrong. Really the book is about women hog-tied by society. She didn't have many options."

"To me, Anna Karenina risks an awful lot for love. Isn't she a lucky wife? She's got money and beauty and a child—so what if her husband's boring," Eve says.

"She *loves* Vronsky. That's the rub," Faith says.

"Enough to bulldoze her marriage and be spurned by everyone who once respected her as an aristocratic wife," Katherine says.

"Why didn't she keep her husband and have Vronsky on the side?" Is Eve looking at Faith? She holds up the three-inch-long earring made of a leafy gold stencil with a heavy pearl dangle at the bottom. "They're gorgeous, whatever the tale."

"I'll focus on the romantic part. Because Anna wasn't only breaking rules, that I appreciate," Katherine says. "The problem is she abandoned her children. Annie, her daughter, was only a baby, so no one will like that."

Eve starts compiling receipts from the morning's sales. She holds up the stack and gives Faith a thumbs-up. "Excellent," she says, and begins computing them into her iPad.

Katherine is working quickly, her intensity and focus creating a sexy-librarian effect. In profile with her glasses on, she and Diana look very alike.

Soon enough she'll have to break the news to Katherine, without any measure for how upended she might be. As if neuropathy is setting in, Faith is unable to feel her extremities.

The door chimes and Diana walks in with Cecelia Norric and an unknown woman. They're deep in conversation about the three-dimensional structure of cumulous clouds over the ocean. Diana sounds informed—perhaps she is a science lover. In her red Ted Baker shift she is garden-fresh, her hair in a neat French braid.

"Hello, Faith." Diana comes toward Faith and kisses her on the cheek.

Eve looks up. "Aren't we friendly today?"

"We are!" Diana comes to where Eve stands and kisses her too. Next she walks to Katherine and does the same.

Katherine laughs. "Okay, Diana, I know you like working here. Though it's early in the morning for smooches. I'm writing up *Anna Karenina*, so . . ."

"I've come for a pickup," Cecelia announces.

As the unknown woman studies the armoire filled with bangles, David Yurman, Seaman Schepps, Chanel, Faith recognizes her from ubiquitous photos in *The Palm Beach Post*, *On the Avenue*, and *The Social Journal*. Nadia Sherman—hired straight from *South Beach Diary* to be the features writer for the *Palm Beach Confidential*. The rumor is she's invited to every country club fashion show, private party, and gala in season. Close to forty, ultrathin, and tall, with dark glossy hair, she balances in her blush suede stiletto sandals—Jimmy Choos—as if she's mastered the tightrope. Her shift, a pastel aqua print, DVF or J. McLaughlin from last winter, is becoming. If Palm Beach is her new beat, she'll have supporters and frenemies in a flash.

"Hello. I'm Faith Harrison." Faith takes a step toward Nadia.

"Of course you are. What a place! Everyone says it's a must now that I'm working at the *Confidential*. This stuff is gorgeous! How you must love it, love having created it. What taste—wherever did you train, Faith?" Nadia swivels her head.

Eve, laying out a Louis Vuitton monogram scarf, coughs, covers her mouth, looks at Faith. "Excuse me."

"Oh my God, Anya Hindmarch and Etro." Nadia fingers the purses cautiously, as if she's picking fruit, and moves on to evening clutches in champagne, beige, and cream.

"Chloé, Fendi, St. Laurent." She takes out her iPhone and takes pictures of both displays. "So many bags!"

Faith does introductions—Katherine, frantically whittling down *Anna Karenina* to an appealing log line, smiles, while Eve procures the cross-body ostrich Lanvin purse that Cecelia has come to collect, then nods, smiles. Diana, sitting at the desk with her laptop, looks up. "Well, we're reading your pieces, and we're fans—love that it's online too."

A very pregnant woman comes in with a very blond five-year-old daughter, or thereabouts, in tow. Noticing the Vuitton scarf, she says to Diana, "That might work; I need a Christmas gift for my mother-in-law."

"I'd say it's perfect for a mother-in-law." Diana holds it up. "We describe it as 'rare,' this particular scarf."

The woman strokes the silk while her daughter starts shouting, "Mommy, can we see—can we see?" The little girl points to the Art Deco Bakelite necklaces, showcased with two Trifari necklaces from the fifties. A result of Diana and Katherine's search for midcentury costume jewelry.

"Can we buy those?" Once more she points to the necklaces, swinging her arms so enthusiastically that she practically knocks over the Judith Leiber minaudière display on an end table.

"Please, Gretchen, please be careful or we'll have to go," the mother says. "Yes, I'd like to see that one." She points to the silver and black squares of Bakelite. "Not for your grandma."

"You know, I'm taking in this scene, Faith," Nadia says. "It's not on my calendar, still, can we chat for a few minutes about a possible feature on your shop?"

"That's cool, Mom," Katherine says. "Be sure to include how I'm working on tales and myths to match the jewelry and bags and shawls."

"I'll take the Bakelite," the pregnant woman says to Diana. "And the Vuitton scarf."

Cecelia comes close. "It is interesting. Surprisingly interesting, Faith."

"Why don't you and Nadia go upstairs?" Eve suggests.

"Shall we sit here?" Faith points to the Estrella sofa when she and Nadia get upstairs.

Nadia crosses her long, tan legs, stretches her toes, and starts tapping on her phone. "A piece about you and your family as the quintessential Palm Beach success story. How you both work in a town filled with play. Maybe a bit about the male playground syndrome."

Male playground syndrome. Nadia and Faith exchange the briefest glance, but neither reveals how it sounds.

"A cover piece—I'd interview people, do research. The works."

A cinch for Faith in the old days—when challenges were met with confidence and life was contained. Instead, today, Nadia Sherman's take on Faith would practically be an exposé. She would learn about Edward's losses quickly and eventually about Diana.

Without glancing at her phone, Faith texts Eve, *SOS.* A text bings seconds later. Faith looks at it as if nonchalant. "Nadia, you know, Eve is texting. This is a hellish week for us; your visit is unexpected . . ."

Eve's footsteps on the stairway, her mouth pursed,

indicating she's tightly wound. "Excuse me? I don't mean to interfere, it's that we—well, there's no time for an interview today. Clients are here to consign and customers to buy."

"Except what I'm willing to write ASAP would be a boon to your store, Faith." Nadia doesn't so much as acknowledge Eve's decision. "You must know, I'm getting calls from every merchant on the Avenue, begging me to write something for the January issue—out late December. Height of the season."

"I'm sorry, Nadia. I'm the gatekeeper, I guess." Eve shrugs as if she couldn't give a damn. "So an article is fine. Let's schedule it, that's best."

"Eve's probably right, Nadia." Faith saved by Eve's acting skills. "We'll get a proper date."

"I can't say when. I'm date stacking and have truckloads of invitations"—Nadia gestures—"a foot high."

"I'm sure you do. Faith has the same stash, maybe higher."

"Nadia, we will book it," Faith says.

Nadia rises and sweeps down the stairs. "Do you mind if I take a look at that Anya Hindmarch on my way out?"

"We always order a few different dishes," Katherine says the minute they're seated in the rattan chairs at Pizza Bellini. The patio is spilling over with assorted women, their designer bags placed on linen napkins on the ground, the small mosaic tables almost tipping from the weight of lemon chicken and portobello sandwiches.

"Mom, you must know everyone. Look, weren't those

four women sitting in the corner table at the shop?" She starts to point in their direction, remembers, stops.

"I see acquaintances." Faith keeps her sunglasses on to fight the glare and to be inconspicuous. "Most of my friends are at cards or tennis by now—Longreens or the Harbor Club. Mar-a-Lago. They shop earlier or later in the day."

"Yeah, fine, but over there"—Katherine moves her head over her right shoulder—"they're waving at you."

Faith lifts her hand graciously and waves, turns back to Katherine and Diana. A lobster salad and a misto salad arrive. "We'll share?" Faith asks as she begins dividing portions in three, serving Diana first, then Katherine. Faith and Katherine lift their forks and knives and deftly arrange their first bites. Diana detects their protocol and lifts her knife as well. Faith's cell vibrates through her blue coated-canvas Goyard bag—which she's planning to clean up and sell this week—against her leg. Dreading a text from Edward since they seem only to validate how poorly his meetings are going, she ignores it. Her girls sit before her—more veritable than a picture on a flat-screen—evenly, silkily tanned with self-tanning cream. Faith compares the length of their necks and slope of their shoulders. In the natural sunlight, she sees both fathers in her daughters' faces and bodies. Diana reminds her of Jimmy—that right-sided dimple, her ears flat against her head. And Katherine like Edward, soldier-straight, with a trenchant sense of what's ahead.

"Wow, it's really packed here," Diana says.

"The menu's great," Katherine says. "Especially the pizza."

"It is," Faith agrees. "I hardly manage lunch on the Avenue; I'm glad Eve suggested it."

"Suggested it? She's given us less than an hour." Katherine laughs. "Such a taskmaster."

"Yeah, but we're together," Diana says. "She stayed back at the shop."

"We're going to two parties tonight, Diana and I," Katherine says. "One's at the Rochesters' and one's at the Parkers'."

The Rochesters—verification that Katherine remains in the game. "How nice," Faith says. Her daughters, together. An unpredictable dream. One that has to be revealed to Katherine, soon. A dreaded, necessary admission.

"I told Katherine I'm too old. I'm thirty and everyone is under twenty-five."

"Would you rather be home alone? Or with your roommates in West Palm?" Katherine asks. "Besides, I bet the group'll be more mixed. People vacationing, visitors, cousins of cousins . . . Rhys says his friend's cousin is thirty-three. I hear he's cute, really smart. From Montreal. And he's bringing friends."

"Katherine, you're the best," Diana says while glancing at Faith. "First I shop in your closet and then I tag along . . ."

The server holds their pizza high above them. Faith begins rearranging the table, handing over the sugar bowl, the breadbasket, and olive oil to make room. Diana's scrutiny continues, yet this isn't the proper moment for a declaration—there has to be that.

"Ouch." Katherine starts swatting her ankles. "Oh God, the lizards. They're touching my toes . . . my ankles. Oh God."

Diana looks at the ground. "Yeah, I see them."

Katherine bends her legs onto the chair. "I can't stand it. I don't know how I forgot this. They're freaking me out completely."

"She's always been like that," Faith says. "In South Florida, there are plenty of lizards scurrying around."

"I can't. I have to go inside."

Diana takes her napkin from her lap and snaps it at the two lizards dancing around Katherine's feet. "They'll go now."

They watch the lizards scuttle off.

"That was valiant, Diana," Faith says.

"So gross. Thanks, Diana." Katherine is looking at the patio.

"This is nothing," Diana says. "Where I grew up there were frogs and turtles everywhere. The frogs were disgusting."

"I like turtles, not frogs. Where?" Katherine asks. "I mean, where exactly?"

"What will you wear tonight?" Faith asks, divvying up the pizza slices.

"Seductive, chic. Dresses probably," Katherine says.

"We're wearing Birkin bags. Nothing more!" Diana says.

All three laugh. Diana bats her eyelashes. "Maybe we'll add dresses. Katherine is teaching me. She's so very chic; her wardrobe is amazing."

Faith's cell rings. *Edward.* Backing away from the tables, Faith motions that she has to take the call and heads toward the stucco exterior of the restaurant. Before she focuses on his voice, which has become gravelly, he says, "Meet you at the shop," and hangs up abruptly. She would

be more displeased were she not watching her two capti-
vating daughters.

Rushing to the front door when Faith returns, Eve whispers, "I'm sorry, why is Edward claiming he needs *our*
office for a meeting? Isn't he supposed to be at his own
meetings or in some golf game?"

Whether he hears Eve or not, Edward, at the desk with
several small Vintage Tales notepads in front of him, smiles
disarmingly at both women. He's dressed in a kelly green
polo shirt with a yellow cashmere sweater across his
shoulders, sockless, in loafers. Not his navy blazer and
button-down shirt—his uniform for workdays. He holds
several pens toward the light from the window. "Hey, hey,
Faith. There's a Parker, a Tiffany—sort of slim, isn't it, a
Montblanc—some say those are masculine pens." He's
restless, uneasy. The idea of it, that he could be using,
could be high, forms in Faith's consciousness. She needs
to push it away—using the same technique Diana used on
the lizards at Pizza Bellini.

"Edward, it's probably better to choose pens from
the drawer," Faith says. "Everyday pens—we don't pass
around our better pens. These were gifts from clients,
mostly."

"Where's Diana?" Eve asks. "She and I are working on
social media upstairs in an hour, posting some of Katherine's tales—snippets—then looking for fresh clients."

"They're walking back; they decided they wanted ge-
lato after we'd finished lunch." Faith, turning to Edward,
can't recall the last time he visited her shop. "So Eve and

Diana can be in the back upstairs, and you can use the sitting area for your meeting."

"No, no, I'll actually need the entire space upstairs," Edward says.

Katherine and Diana walk in. "Dad? Are you okay?"

"Hello, Katherine, Diana. Yes, yes, I'm fine. What can I say—I missed your mother? Golf is postponed to tomorrow. High Dune is swarming with the accountants. I can't conduct 'business' at a club, so I'm trying this out, I'm going to meet with investors upstairs. We need peace, a private place." He's sniffling.

"Dad, I don't quite get it," Katherine says.

"We should go upstairs, get things ready," Faith says. "Before your meeting begins, Edward."

Faith closes the door to the office. "There's no meeting, is there, and you've already blown today's chances, right?"

An awkward quiet in the room, a sense of hopelessness while Edward starts drumming his thumbs together.

"Listen, we have to do more. Have to see . . ."

His voice, language. She looks at his face, searching for powder, residue. She can't accuse him, yet it's so apparent.

"I had to come today, to ask you." He speaks in a grotesque cultlike way. "I'm asking out of your loyalty to me— you have the shop. I've given you—"

"What have you done, Edward, or what is it you're about to do?"

"Sell the house. Our Palm Beach house." He isn't in motion, he stands like a crossing guard. Edward has become immediately sobered, somber.

"Sell it? Margot Damon has been all over that. Through Allison. It's our last resort, remember? A new owner walking through the garden, the hibiscus. Someone walking up the stairway, deciding the hedges aren't trimmed properly, the pool is murky, the outdoor furniture covered in a thin film of salt air. The location, that's what I love most, the flower beds. It's our *home*. Why don't we borrow against it first? Because once it's sold, we both know, it's gone. For me, it's worse than a death."

How about me, what about Katherine? Faith wants to screech. Instead she leads him to the exact spot where Nadia Sherman sat trying to get the story on the Harrison family, not four hours ago. They sit.

"You'll help me, won't you?" His body against hers. Not in that very married loop but in a sloshy, messy tangle. He is barely able to sit up.

"You know, in the past week, I've been watching those women who come into the shop, the ones who think that nothing bad could ever happen to them. Or to their kids or their goddamn rich husbands. Nothing bad *has* ever happened."

"Sure, welcome to Palm Beach," Edward says.

"When I really listen and watch carefully, there aren't many of them. There are lots of pretenders. They're good at it—three such women were in the shop on Tuesday. And they have an ironclad plan B. So what if there's talk, gossip, nastiness—they know everyone reconfigures." Faith waves in front of Edward's face as if he's a toddler and he can't follow along.

"I'm apologizing, Faith." There's such sadness in his presentation.

"This whole scene, what you've thrown in my lap,

Edward, is surreal. I'm finally, incredibly pissed. I do backflips for you; you snort cocaine for you."

Edward puts up his right hand to protest and Faith pushes it back into his lap.

"What you need is help, Edward. We're lucky; that can be arranged." Her own voice is flat, broken. "Swear to me you won't use anymore. Not once. That you'll be sober. We'll get help, and you'll stay sober."

He closes his eyes without answering. How lonely she has grown with him. They've become foreigners. The kind thrown together at an airport in a far-off land, two passengers bumped from the last flight home.

SIXTEEN

Faith awakens from the kind of sleep where one forgets both anguish and bliss, an Ambien-induced stupor, and realizes she's overslept. Piecing together yesterday's drama with Edward, she remembers why she's in the guest room for the first time in their marriage. She tosses off the duvet cover and fumbles for her iPhone.

"Touchstone Hill. This is Brenda." An authoritative tone at the other end. "Hello?" A hesitation. "Hello?"

Faith hangs up, deciding instead to sneak into her own bedroom, avoiding Edward, throw on some clothes, and head west.

You have arrived at your destination, drones the GPS through the sound of dogged rain against the windshield. Winding paths and mission-style architecture make Touchstone Hill look more like the grounds of an estate than the largest rehab and psychiatric affiliate of South Palm Hospital. As Faith parks at the patient center she thinks of how many times Edward has been their "outstanding recoverer," a lecturer, board member, and fund-raiser.

The rain lets up. A musty smell trickles through the morning air as Faith walks to the entrance. A young man with a pierced left brow and a ring in his nose appears through the glass. Without speaking, he holds the front door open for her, and she enters the terra-cotta-floored lobby. After a second, he lights up a cigarette and heads out. Exhaustion drapes Faith as she stands beneath the Twelve Steps posted on the wall, waiting to announce herself.

A lonely couple avoid eye contact with her, a tacit consent that they are struggling with their visit. Next, their daughter, perhaps sixteen, appears and falls into the mother's arms, swallowing air and weeping. She sports a scoop-back T-shirt; a red rose tattoo covers her back, reminding Faith of a Dolce print dress in crimson, greens, and black. *Jesus*, Faith thinks to herself, *is life still defined in terms of designer fabrics?* Except it's a tattoo; it will be anchored by this girl's shoulder blades for the rest of her life. Tattoos don't completely reverse, that's the dirty truth, according to both Andrea Lattice and Maisy Ballalo, two of the premier cosmetic dermatologists whom many of Faith's clients swear by. How prepossessing this daughter is up close, with or without tattoos. It's the girl's glumness, not drugs, that comes through.

Faith's arm is touched lightly. "Mrs. Harrison?"

Her name spoken in that timbre, like Faith has done something fluky, perhaps eaten cat litter, and everyone knows. "I'm Stephanie Stevens, the daytime director at Touchstone Hill." She adjusts her wire-rimmed glasses and wraps her dry hair, which looks wet, behind her ears.

"Right this way, Mrs. Harrison."

Following Stephanie Stevens down a corridor that is not terra-cotta but a white, harsh tile, uncommonly grout-free, Faith realizes that despite her yearly visits to Touchstone Hill, she's never seen this area. The mother and daughter, locked in a twisted caress, become smaller as Faith moves farther from the waiting room. Stephanie Stevens closes the door to her office. A photograph of twin daughters—they look ten or eleven—posing in front of the clock tower on Worth Avenue, is on the edge of her desk, facing outward. The other photograph is of Stephanie with her husband, most likely, a man about her age, with a shaved head and a confident smile. Shaved heads, although perhaps more an L.A. look—are a favorite of Faith's. Everybody in the pictures looks normal, content.

"Let me get right to the point, Mrs. Harrison. Your husband has been a remarkable supporter of the facility. I'm sure you know this—and only last March he was so highly praised at the black tie at Mar-a-Lago. Since then, he hasn't been the same. Mr. Harrison is five months late on his pledge. A pledge that we are counting on."

Money. Although Faith hasn't stated yet that she's in need of help, that Edward is lapsing and no longer in recovery, she's taken aback. Offended by Stephanie Stevens's side of the conversation.

"I know nothing about it," she says. "Ms. Stevens, I'm here today because—"

"You know we're not a Palm Beach charity. We're in West Palm; we're not for profit. Edward's one hundred thousand dollars—and he's paid twenty thousand—is really important. Maybe Touchstone Hill *feels* lavish, but we need funding; private funding is what we count on. Your husband has been instrumental in the new wing, the long-term inpatient facility. An exciting development."

"I am not aware of that. He hasn't really talked about the new wing at Touchstone Hill. Did you ask him about it?" Faith speaks as if she isn't keenly aware of Edward's recent bailout routine.

"I have asked, our board has, our fund-raising office has. Quite honestly, he promised he would deliver a check within an hour of every call made to him. He was polite and sorry. Then nothing arrives."

Although on some level Faith is getting used to Edward's negligence, this one is shocking. Among the causes the Harrisons have supported, Touchstone Hill has been the most personal for Edward. A place where he was in recovery—committed to sobriety and to "giving back." The irony of this foil will travel—those who write their checks to Touchstone Hill because of Edward's connection will be let down. Offended.

"Well, Stephanie, if I may call you that, let's start with my helping out. Why don't you take a credit card and let me pay something. I could do . . . I could do another twenty." Twenty thousand dollars. She can't afford it; the money has to go toward Edward's shortfall. Today, December 6, Edward is expected to put down two million dollars toward his debt.

To save face, she fishes in her wallet for her own—not joint—AmEx Delta SkyMiles card, which can be paid back over time. Faith almost slaps it on the desk. Stephanie takes it quickly, lest Faith evaporate like her husband. "Thank you. So we'll be current. That part's settled, Mrs. Harrison."

"Faith, call me Faith."

"Faith, there is one more issue. . . ."

One more issue. Jesus, what else could Edward have done while Faith was, apparently, sleepwalking through their life together?

"The board has decided they'll be taking Edward's name, yours and Edward's, off the plaque next week. They've found a new donor, a higher level. That name will replace yours."

"I don't understand. Edward's name is on the plaque for what he has done, not what he is going to do. Look at the east wing of the main building. The dining hall, all through Edward's fund-raising."

"It's not my decision. It's made by the board. There are other donations, as large or larger than Edward's. He's supposed to be here once a week for a lecture he gives . . ."

"He hasn't been coming?" Again, that spinning sensation. A vicious spinning. What can't be.

"Oh my, you don't know a thing, do you?"

"No, not really, Stephanie. I'm the last to know, I suppose."

"Well, my question, since I work with addicts, is about Edward. Is your husband unhealthy? Because his behavior, well, I don't have to tell you . . ."

As unsteady as she is, Faith rises. As cold as she is, her forehead is warm. She feels so not the "lady" she has worked her entire adult life to be. "I agree. I came, I called today because I'm suspicious. I'm worried. My husband needs help, and you start a conversation about pledges and charity. You ask nothing, *nothing* about my husband. You then start a patronizing segue into how he isn't himself. How I must know. Finally. After getting money from me to fix a mess. Do you see how thoroughly twisted this is?" She is roiling.

"Have you spoken with him, have you spoken with any of our staff therapists? The protocol is—"

"I know the goddamn protocol, Stephanie."

"Of course he can come here, we can help him." She reaches for her business cards, lined up in a black metal card holder shaped like a dachshund. "The private number's there."

"I don't need it." Faith walks out.

The conversation has been brief—the mother and knockout daughter remain collapsed on the couch in the waiting area, arms interlaced. Faith avoids them. In her haste to escape from Touchstone Hill, she heads left toward the main reception room. Her Balenciaga ballerina flats tap as she walks to the wall that lists the trustees. Edward as board chair is at the very top. On the twin plaque for major donors, Faith finds Mr. and Mrs. Edward J. Harrison III. An absence of pride—a shameful feeling—washes over. She surveys names of the usual players, Norrics, Dexters, Finleys, along with others from Jupiter, Stuart, Boca. Then an addition: Faith squints, reads it twice, three times. MRS. AND MRS. LUCAS DAMON. Pronto, back in Palm Beach a few weeks and already penetrating the "greater good" system.

From behind the glass wall, Faith sees that mother and daughter still, infinite, in their own bonding session, when she perceives something, someone. Someone she would know anywhere. *Mrs. A.*

Not alone, but with her grandson, Rory, seventeen, tall, fetching. Mrs. A has brought him to Vintage Tales from time to time, where he's patiently waited for her to drop off her consignment. Rory lives in Boston with his mother, whom Faith has met only twice. *My daughter*, Mrs. A says, *is difficult to please. She is on her third husband and I'm sure there will be another divorce*. Mrs. A claims to have raised Rory, who visits a few times a year, to have taught him manners, books, life lessons.

"Mrs. A." Faith catches her redirecting the grandson to the far exit door, hoping no one will see them. She's wearing a rather staid outfit, a pair of khaki pants and a navy cashmere sweater from Brooks, a Van Cleef mother-of-pearl single clover and matching earrings. Ferragamo flats. Her lipstick is bright red—cheery.

"Faith, how are you?" Swiftly Mrs. A begins her once-over of Faith—perhaps to understand why she's there more than to assess her attire. "You do remember my grandson."

Rory, who has not budged from her side, is stuck in a residual drugginess, his shirttails hanging sloppily over his baggy jeans. A few weeks at Touchstone Hill and he'll shake it, become more robust.

"Rory, of course. How have you been?"

A banging on the glass wall that separates the two large

rooms interrupts their conversation. The young girl who was clinging to her mother is clamoring, then waves at Rory, who raises his arm back, delighted to see her.

Mrs. A's lips become a thin line. She puts her hand on Faith's elbow, squeezes.

"Rory, you might want an early breakfast, and I'll meet you there, dear."

"Sure, Grammy." He walks off, half-tall, half-slumped boy-man that he is.

"This is between us, Faith, is it not? Since Touchstone Hill is known for helping troubled teens, minors. I chose it over Hazelden or Sierra Tucson. Even if I run the risk of seeing someone I know." Mrs. A lets go of Faith's arm.

"I understand, Mrs. A. People pass through, they get help, get better. Edward's been on the board, head of the board, for ages. For the same reasons you praise it."

"Ah, yes, isn't that why you're here today?"

"Well, I'm off to Vintage Tales, Mrs. A. No worries, I won't breathe a word."

"We should speak this afternoon, Faith dear," Mrs. A says in an ultra-silky timbre. "I mean, here you are, when my impression is you have, might I guess, a lot of balls in play."

Faith freezes, tries out a charming look, a Palm Beach smile. "A busy time of year at Vintage Tales."

"To say the least," Mrs. A sighs. "After the DAR committee meeting at my house this afternoon, we'll talk. It should finish by three."

"I can do that, Mrs. A." Faith leans down since Mrs. A is not as tall as she used to be, to exchange air-kisses.

SEVENTEEN

Babble wafts through Mrs. A's posh beige-and-white living room. Women collect their iPad minis, Hermès Kelly bags, Fendi peekaboos, Diorevers in lemon and peach as well as fundamental black. Some, including the latest models, sold and resold at Vintage Tales. Mostly it's an insular crew of second and third wives in their early forties, married to men destined to die within five to ten years. Others are Mrs. A's peers and a few thirtysomethings, on starter marriages, willing to be on committees and to purchase tables. Faith welcomes their vogue wardrobes and support for the Arts and Media Ball.

Everyone files toward Mrs. A's front door. Smatterings of conversation bounce off the surfaces—Faith listens carefully, as if she's never heard it before. *Backflips for husbands, food was poison, spitting hors d'oeuvres into a napkin, a dreadful dress, children under four, face too tight, the best work ever, stomach flu, missed Kravis concert and the trunk show at Neiman's, Aspen this year . . .*

"There you are!" Mrs. A greets Faith. "Please sit on the veranda—they're dispersing. I've explained to everyone that with your diligence for the Arts and Media gala, you didn't have an hour to spare for our meeting today."

She points with her chin and Faith moves quickly outside the coterie of women. Sitting on a Janus et Cie chair, Faith looks across the lush gardens at Mrs. A's views. Situated at a narrow strip of the island, she faces both the Intracoastal and the ocean. The water slaps against the bulkhead. Tonny, Mrs. A's housekeeper, comes to pour iced tea from a crystal pitcher into two highball glasses.

Mrs. A plunks herself down, ankles crossed, back straight, as if she's a guest in *Upstairs, Downstairs*. The color of the waterway reminds Faith of the bayside in Kendalton at high tide.

"Today the weather is a ten out of ten. I love Palm Beach early in the season. I haven't been to Boston when it's cold in over twenty years. Not so much as a three-day visit," Mrs. A says.

"Most people do it that way, don't they?" Faith says.

"Real Palm Beachers," Mrs. A says. "We're too caught up in what's ahead—theatrics and surprises to not be around."

"I was admiring the water, waiting for you," Faith says. Although a breeze has started up, she's sweaty.

Mrs. A checks that her oversprayed flaxen hair hasn't dared blow in the wind. Her daily blend of powder and foundation, ground to order at Adriana's on Via Flora, cakes slightly at the corners of her mouth.

"I took you under my wing a long time ago, Faith. I knew you were pretty, clever, very young, and such good company."

Kicking off her custom-made Italian sandals, Mrs. A stretches her feet. A few black flies blow over from the west. She gives them a withering look and they turn east to the ocean.

"I'm very grateful, Mrs. A. I can't imagine how it would have been without you."

"Rita Damon says I'm a trendsetter." Mrs. A laughs. "Imagine how true it must be if she'll give me that."

"I met you through Rita. Don't you remember? In 1990. You were written up—*The Daily Sheet* and *On Worth*, philanthropist and diva. Lucas whispered even his mother was jealous," Faith says.

"If you call me your mentor, I'd say you've learned well. Still, one is as good as her last mistake. What has happened, Faith—with you, and what's going on with Margot and Lucas at Touchstone Hill? Are they unseating Edward?"

"Edward is in trouble." There, finally, the truth goes into the ether, toward Mrs. A. Beneath Faith's eyes the skin feels bruised, her face pounded. Her posture is off, her shoulders constricting into a knot.

"Well, let's be frank. Around Palm Beach, people are talking about Edward. Wives are the last to know, plenty of times. If Edward has done something wrong and you love him, there's nothing like his actions to kill that love."

Mrs. A's two goldendoodles come running toward her. She kneels down and takes biscuits from the pockets of her Akris cotton dress. Both dogs drool excitedly.

"The word is that Edward's resigning from charity

boards whenever a check is due. We know what that means." Mrs. A rises, then sits again. The dogs come to her, heads on her lap, their pink tongues lolling on her pale blue dress. She pushes them away. "Women who stand by their men are either poor and have nowhere to go, or they're in denial. The worst scenario is when they're in love with their husbands; that woman is plain stupid. Faith, tell me you aren't in love with Edward after what's going on."

Faith's fear spreads through her chest. "Mrs. A, I promised Edward . . ."

"You live in Palm Beach, Faith, where husbands are discarded and a better model found instantly. If the potential husband, the next husband, belongs to someone else at the time, so be it. Occasionally the wife is in love with the one she nabs."

Faith squirms. *Lucas.* Are they both thinking of him? "I could never do that, never."

"Really?" Mrs. A claps and the dogs come running to her.

"Well, it isn't my plan." Lucas at the pier, how they fit together. Next she smacks it away, an untoward thought.

"No, of course not, Faith. It's that life in Palm Beach can be peculiar—or more dramatic—than those stories your daughter adds to purses and bangles."

"I wish none of this had happened. I keep trying to be a fixer," Faith says. "Edward, he has to do the right thing. For Patsy and for you. I'm not as worried about other clients since they're in High Dune funds. But you and Patsy . . . what Edward has done with our money is what he has done with yours."

"I remember. I specifically asked Edward to hook me in

to his personal funds, investments. Patsy did it because I did it. I doubt she knows yet."

"I reminded Edward right away, when I found out, about you and Patsy."

"I'm sure you did—what power do you have, Faith? Still, Edward has a million dollars of my money. Five hundred of Patsy's. We did whatever bundle he was promising that had a high return. Neither of us could recite one investment in the bundle, could you?"

"Mrs. A, I feel awful about it. I've lost sleep over this; I want to repay you, I want the money to be returned."

"I know it has nothing to do with you. I've been reflecting on the year, how the market has been. I've already called my accountant, who is ever so wise. I can't speak for Patsy. I know I'll take the losses as a tax write-off. I assume she will too; I bet she'll find it helpful. As would any other wealthy client."

"I'm so sorry you ever trusted—"

"Not ideal, not a tragedy, my dear." Mrs. A's dogs place their heads at her feet, their tongues still going out. "Faith, I'm worried about *you*. You can't lose your place. Who knows how Edward will come out on the other side. Do you remember the Dales?"

"I don't," Faith says.

"No?" Mrs. A. sniffs. "They were quite a couple. Maybe it was before you arrived in Palm Beach. Could it be that many years?"

"I never met them, Mrs. A."

"Poor Pamela, fell for her husband's problems—they say he used heroin. She believed he was redeemable. She orchestrated whatever he needed, begged him to stop, waited for him. . . . Then she found him in the shower. . . .

He had . . ." She's out to warn Faith. Her voice is rousing, cogent.

"I want to support Edward." In contrast, Faith sounds punctured.

"Aren't you listening—you *have* to protect yourself." Mrs. A waves her right arm as if she's pushing away exhaust fumes from a truck. Reaching into her pocket, the one that held no dog biscuits, she takes out two business cards. The wind kicks up again and the cards almost blow away when Mrs. A practically mashes them into her hand.

"You'll need a very good lawyer, Faith."

"A lawyer, what kind of lawyer? Edward won't declare bankruptcy." Is she in denial, is it as obvious as Mrs. A makes it seem?

"Faith, *please.* A divorce lawyer. Straightaway. What you had is over. Don't let Edward drag you down, don't be responsible for his problems, his debt."

Could it have come to this? Edward at the center of her brain—the night they met, the dawn that Katherine was born, beside her at every gala, skiing black diamonds, dinners at the Palm in East Hampton, winning member guest golf tournaments at the Harbor Club, spooning her the night long, whispering, *I love you, Faith. I need you.*

A dread deep lodges within Faith, like the tide has come and washed her meticulously crafted sandcastle into the sea. Combined with her respect for Mrs. A's plan—her incisive points, her concern, her wisdom. Anything can be taken, what still stands can be lost. What matters until it doesn't.

"Women lawyers, both of them—and not in town. One in South Beach whom I know, and a Lauderdale contact provided the other; she's in Boca. If you need anything else . . ."

"I can't divorce him."

"Can't or won't?" Mrs. A asks. "I don't believe you understand the ramifications."

Faith stands up, dizzily takes a step. "Mrs. A, I'm not ready to call a—"

"Fine, for this moment," Mrs. A says. "I'd like you to understand your rights, understand the situation. You should call as soon as you leave my terrace."

The little dogs sense the tension and Faith's imminent departure. They start yapping gleefully that she'll be leaving.

"You'll keep me posted, I'm sure." Mrs. A walks to Faith and hugs her, Palm Beach–style, which means they hardly touch.

EIGHTEEN

Perchance it's the early light—not yet eight o'clock—that makes the Publix supermarket in Lake Worth seem enormous when Faith pulls up the next morning. A pseudo-modern, white-painted behemoth with blush-and-aqua trim, it fills the entire square block. How unlike the Publix on Bradley Place in Palm Beach, with its columned entrance and elegant beige-and-white exterior. A destination for shoppers wearing Stubbs and Wootton moccasins and soft shades of cashmere sweaters—since the store is as cold as a Sub-Zero freezer. Even Mrs. A, spotted browsing for hydrangeas or roses, subscribes to food shopping at Publix in town as another form of showing up. No one loads a cart—their housekeepers do the heavy grocery lugging. On the occasion when Faith stops by for a few mangos or a pound of cherries, she has run into Patsy and Cecelia, Rita Damon, and plenty of clients.

As Faith walks inside, a group of vets in surfer shorts and sporting tattoos—devil dogs, anchors, or eagle designs, are gathering. Moving with purpose toward the peace lilies and African violets for Vintage Tales, she notices two of the men following her. Or is it a coincidence and they too need flowers?

"Hey, miss," the first man says. He takes off his baseball cap, which reads MIAMI DOLPHINS, revealing his shaved head. Somewhere between an L.A. and local effect—definitely not a common Palm Beach style.

"Yeah, miss, we just wanna ask a quick question," the second man says. His streaky blond hair is in a man bun. She's mesmerized by the breadth and width of his right bicep, tattooed in the American flag.

"We just wanna know if your car—y'know, we saw yer sedan, yer Mercedes—if you ever want it detailed?" He points with his left hand, and she's struck by the tattoo on that bicep too—a nautical marine rendering in black ink. "Miss, missus?"

He adjusts his aviator Ray-Bans—imitations, most likely. She knows this kind of face—sympathetic, rugged, overly tanned. Like the boys she left in the Pines who grew into local men. Had he lived, Jimmy would have been among them. People without money, without choices. She counts the four miles from Palm Beach to this chasm.

"My car," Faith says. "Well . . ."

"Yep, it's a beauty," the first man says. He too has that rough physical charm. Were they both in the marines—deployed and now home?

"We can wash and vacuum it, real nice. It's a family

business. My bro and I . . . we could keep yer car in good shape." He has a tremor when he pushes a magnetic business card with a picture of a wine-colored sedan toward her. "Here ya go, in case ya need us." They're young, maybe thirty-five, and both wear wedding bands. She imagines their small children at home, wives who waited for them to return from Iraq.

"Thank you, thank you." Faith smiles, ready to slip the card into her hot-pink Prada book bag (one that she'll add to the pink and peach casual bag section at the shop by midday). "How great, and I'll be in touch."

She *should* help these men because no one she knows would, including Edward. Edward, in any of his multifarious roles—sober, successful, drugged, failing and in debt—might claim them too ordinary and from another realm. A threat to civility. Katherine might feel the same. But not Diana—she and Faith know better.

Starbucks, Lake Avenue, Lake Worth. A wise choice of venue since no one Faith knows is in line for iced macchiatos. She assumes the same applies to Henry Rochester, who asked that they meet at eight-thirty. When those who work are in transit to their offices and those who play golf or tennis are already in their games. Besides, no one from town will walk in. Unless they're incognito. Faith thinks of her hour with Lucas on the public beach; they might have chosen this instead. Isn't everything a risk? Although there's a glare filtering in, Faith chooses a table by the window while Henry orders. Particles of dust spin around the chairs.

Little children—toddlers, preschoolers—are winding around the tables, aggravating adults who don't admire them or sigh at their cuteness. Small boys just avoid knocking down coffee cups with a few girls in on the gig. Faith counts seven mothers—no nannies—too engrossed in complaints and disclosures to pay much attention to their own kids. How untroubled they are—oddly calm and friendly. No one is an islander—Faith doesn't recognize a woman among them. They're dressed well enough— J. Crew flats, Tory Burch bags, Lacoste polo shirts. What would they buy at Vintage Tales—beyond costume jewelry or inlaid-wood picture frames? Isn't that the idea— more customers, buying high and low? Georgian paste flower necklaces for less than two hundred dollars versus Miriam Haskell versions that sell for more than a thousand, at least.

"Here we go." Henry proffers Faith a white cardboard cup with her name written above the Starbucks insignia of the twin-tailed mermaid. He is decked out in his custom-made Raimondo suit and shirt, tieless.

"Not quite like the Starbucks on the Avenue." Faith sips her flat white.

Henry takes the lid off his cup of green tea.

"No, the Starbucks in the Esplanade doesn't feel like a Starbucks. Those deep leather chairs, the decor," Henry says. His eyes have been a Superman blue for years. Faith long suspected he wears tinted lenses.

"Allison urged me to meet you, and of course I agreed."

"Did she?" She waits, sips more of her flat white.

"But I told her I'm not so sanguine I can help."

Sanguine. Henry earned his MBA at Harvard, and

Edward always claims the clients like it. Appreciate it. Allison too has a degree from the "B-school"—not that she has worked for the past fifteen years. Before that she had a beauty brand startup that consumed her and then sold to Avon.

For the first time in years that unsettling sense engulfs Faith. How she felt when Lucas brought her to Palm Beach and Rita Damon found her lacking, not a pedigree. Self-doubt creeps up her spine. Henry is waiting for her to speak.

"I've never really paid attention to Edward's business," Faith says. "Now I have to."

"I can talk about High Dune, but I'd say it's that you need to know about Edward." He puts on his sunglasses. Ray-Ban black Wayfarer frames that filter out the UVA light.

"What happened, Henry? Please tell me."

"It happened over time. I didn't notice at first, and I think it took you even longer to realize the problem. I've known for a year about it—the extent of it. Edward was making awful decisions. Mostly for your family, his holdings—and a few choice clients. I told him to stop, I warned him. I said I couldn't do much more, and then I did more anyway. Edward's been my friend a long time."

"Why didn't anyone tell me? Tell me anything?" Faith asks.

"The reason Allison wanted me to meet you is so you understand. I don't know if you've gone to an attorney, sought advice, counsel."

"I haven't," Faith says.

Henry takes a deep breath, bends his arms behind his neck. "If you're counting on information that the Edward we knew would convey, he's another Edward altogether today."

"What went so wrong? How could this have—"

"My opinion? Edward stopped gauging investments. He made some unwise decisions—he and I no longer had the same perspective. I told him the ten million he put into the condo complex and hotel on that ersatz lake in Vero Beach was wrong. The place is overbuilt, the market's gone soft. He would be absent for meetings, not in control. Edward and I had a few conversations about it, and we disagreed."

"I never heard about Vero Beach," Faith says.

"Not only real estate—there were emerging markets that were too skittish, I didn't like them. He wanted to take big positions, they became a black hole. I forced him out of High Dune for cause. Did you know that?"

"For cause?"

"High Dune didn't guarantee anything Edward invested in. I knew not to do that. But the company is being scrutinized nonetheless; he's hurt us by investing recklessly."

Edward harming his beloved company—it's too much for her to fathom.

"We'll survive, we'll weather the storm." Henry tilts back in his chair, contemplating what he has endured.

"He owes money to these phantom people," Faith says. "Who are they?"

"He owes thirty million. To investors who lost, mostly. Twenty million might get him off the hook."

"We're frantically trying to sell things," Faith says. Like an aura before a migraine, a flashing image of Edward, young, suave, aspiring, waves across her brain.

"I know that Edward has been trying to pay off the creditors; it's hopeless. He should file for bankruptcy." Henry impatiently glances at his Vacheron Constantin watch. "I'd suggested it when things first started. He wouldn't—he was adamant."

"He doesn't want to. He's too proud." Perpetual seasons of Edward walking Faith into every party in town—no one dared *not* include them. The house dangles before her as their most valuable asset. "Don't people borrow against their homes or sell them?" She rubs her forehead. "We'll sell the house."

"If you declare bankruptcy maybe you can hold on to the house." Henry takes a gulp of tea. He's rushed.

"Either way, Henry, we can't afford the house, the lifestyle, anymore."

He doesn't say Edward could be using, he doesn't say Edward's become an impulsive man. The implication hangs between them, polluting the air.

"He said he could pay the debts and could protect you. He didn't want the shame, didn't want you and Katherine to be shamed. It would all go away."

"People find out everything, no matter what; he knows that. Whether you're bankrupt or not in Palm Beach," Faith says. "Wouldn't it have been, I don't know, better? I don't have much time now. I need to make decisions."

"You're free and clear on your shop and the building on the Avenue; Edward put that in yours and Katherine's names, ages ago. I remember. Try to hold on to it. Maybe it's worth eight million. Maybe more."

Eight million, as if it's so little, the way it's viewed in concentric circles of Palm Beach. A place where Edward's losses aren't the most egregious.

"I'm trying. I'm trying to sell everything inside the shop."

"The shop—well, Faith, we're speaking about bigger numbers than a vintage shop could possibly . . ."

"Weird, how it falls away—luncheons, Pilates, parties, kaffeeklatsches, what the allure is or was. I can't walk into Renato's or Bice without people whispering."

"Edward has put you in a terrible bind." Henry squinches his mouth.

A small boy, maybe three years old with curly blond hair, muffin crumbs around his mouth, races toward Faith, brushing against her knee. His mother is there within seconds, gently persuading him away. Other mothers start calling out their children's names, ready to go.

Advice as best he can give it. Lifting his Ghurka chestnut leather attaché case, Henry straightens his shoulders and stands to leave. Once he's gone there won't be another day for a conversation.

"You know there's not much left. It could be nothing is left. Except for Vintage Tales."

Walking along Lake Avenue, the main one-way street that heads east, to the island and the ocean, Faith looks at every storefront. The air smells of suntan oil and damp heat—today will go above eighty-five degrees, rare for mid-December. At the pawnshop, a man in jeans and a T-shirt that reads PRINCESS PAWN, WE LOAN OR SELL is opening up the steel gate. She stops and waits, wanting to see in the window.

"What ya got, lady?" he asks her. "Something to pawn?"

"It depends," Faith says, "on what's inside."

"C'mon in." He motions for her to follow him into the cluttered, if clean enough store. There's a bottle of Windex and a roll of paper towels by the cash register. "We've got computers, jewelry, electronics, cell phones, power tools, motorcycles . . ."

"Motorcycles? Where are they?" Faith looks at the jewelry in the bright glass case. A few gold necklaces and a pair of citrine-and-white-gold hoop earrings are presentable. "You have a lot of merchandise."

"That I do." The man turns on the fluorescent lights. "Motorcycles are out back—whaddya want, a Harley?"

Faith laughs. "No, no, I was just curious. This is all so interesting. . . ." She takes inventory of the purses— Michael Kors, Longchamp, a beat-up Vuitton.

"Sold more than pawned," the man says. "Them pocketbooks. The ladies, they want the money."

"I'm sure they need it," Faith says.

In the next case, cell phones—iPhones, Samsung, old Motorolas—and Nikon cameras are lined up. Behind them are Dell laptops, MacBook Airs, iPads, iPad minis.

"People gotta survive, y'know?" His landline rings and he answers, lighting up a cigarette. He places the portable against his chest.

"Bring me your stuff, ma'am. I bet you have good things to pawn."

"I will. I have to get to work. Another day." She lifts a business card from his plastic tray and waves. When the door to Princess Pawn swings closed, it's the same chime as Faith and Eve had chosen for Vintage Tales.

NINETEEN

Clouds dip low as Faith drives the curvy A1A. Without traffic she'll be on the Avenue in ten minutes. The meeting with Henry was sufficiently miserable that Faith doesn't so much as glance at the cobalt-blue ocean. Nor does she, as usual, admire the mansions that rise, one after another, inviting and formidable at once. She pilots her Mercedes with the determination required to guide a tank into a war zone. When she passes Mar-a-Lago, she realizes that she's missed the Female Leaders breakfast held there earlier this morning. After being asked to sit at three different tables—Cecelia's, Mrs. A's, and Patsy's—and having chosen Mrs. A's (safest) she's *forgotten* the entire event. One that Allison might or might not have mentioned to Henry when he insisted he and

Faith meet today. Unless Allison and her "core" didn't go, instead filling chairs at the Island Court for a Poets' Breakfast. The competing events on any given morning are steep; some seasons Faith has hopped from one to the next to be seen, five or six on the same day. Until now, when she's missed a critical appearance. *She's slipping, seriously slipping.*

Through the etched-glass mirror, Faith sees Katherine, with her matching tales, Diana, with her iPad improvements for the Web site, and Eve, examining a Georgian pearl cluster brooch from an estate in Michigan. Her family, fictive and real. She tiptoes upstairs, hoping no one will notice her.

"Don't you want to wrap up the journal ads?" Eve follows her. "Today's the last day and they go to the printer."

"Do I have to?" Faith is practically stripping into a "uniform" kept in the closet. Louboutin nude slingbacks, a Fendi tan sleeveless dress, fitted in the hips with a slight swing to the skirt. The subtlety of the effect, clothes as costume. An absurdly expensive costume. Faith walks to the mirror. While she appears fresh, stylish to the outside world, her eyes are stone colored and she craves a bath. She thinks of vets at the Lake Worth Publix, of Henry Rochester in his limestone-and-teakwood office, the High Dune logo discreetly placed throughout. Eve sifts through a stack of mail. "I thought before we begin we could clear the Arts and Media pile."

"Clear it? I can't think of it. I'm so behind. I fucking forgot to go to Mar-a-Lago this morning for the—"

"I heard. I know," Eve says. "Mrs. A called. I said you had an emergency root canal and that your text must not have gone through."

"A root canal? Jesus, that could jinx me."

"Oh, please." Eve holds up Margot's signed check for fifty thousand dollars made out to the Arts and Media Ad Journal. "Signed and delivered by a messenger for Margot Damon five minutes ago."

Margot. Gingerly Faith walks to Eve and takes the check, suppressing her instinct to snatch it. "Why not deliver it to the executive offices or to Stenton?"

"That's quite a message. So you'll resign—too tired and poor to do another minute of the Arts and Media suck-up game. Too much an outcast to survive the suck-up game. Even I get that's why the check is here," Eve says.

Diana comes in. "Faith, I ran an online ad for sixties Swedish and Danish designs for necklaces, bracelets— what we'd decided. There's tons of responses already. It's very cool. . . ."

"What client will buy Scandinavian silver jewelry?" Eve asks.

"Younger women. Maybe mothers-in-law for their daughters-in-law—to please them, for Christmas," Diana answers. "They're good pieces."

Katherine appears behind Diana, anxious to speak.

"So, Mom, there's this feminist novel by the least-read of the Brontë sisters, Anne. *The Tenant of Wildfell Hall*—about a young widow who comes to an empty mansion. Everyone talks about her . . . it turns out she's not widowed. She's escaped, dumped her husband, who drinks and debauches. In the end she falls in love with a sublime man."

"A happy ending," Eve says.

"Hey, when it was published, in Victorian times, it was shocking. I can tag the mid-nineteenth-century rose-gold earrings and necklace with it. The set that's real, not costume," Katherine says.

"Not costume? Eve, how are we pricing that?" Faith asks.

"Well, I'm not sure. It's just in and already so much interest . . ." Eve says.

"Expensive," Diana says. "Maybe eight thousand for both together, and we can't break up the suite. I have a buyer in mind."

"Plus the story, it makes it important," Katherine says.

"If not exactly uplifting," Eve says.

Smoothing out her blue print cotton Oscar day dress, Priscilla comes into the office. Her honey brown hair is gathered in a knot—a sedate enough look that Faith knows she was at the Mar-a-Lago breakfast.

"I'm listening. I like the Anne Brontë novel. I know it's dismal, but you root for her," Priscilla says. She carries a small plain shopping bag. "I was an English major. Anne Brontë was overlooked; her sisters were the ones described as brave and romantic writers. I *love* this Victorian jewelry. I bet Walter would want me to have it."

"Priscilla, you get it—comprehend it! See, Mom?"

"Oh, I do. Meanwhile, I've brought less fascinating wares." Priscilla fans four Hermès hinged bracelets and three Clic HH bangles, and places them on the desk. "Who wouldn't wear a few at a time—right?" While neither unique nor coveted, owned already by almost every client, they do sell steadily.

Pleased with Priscilla, Katherine picks up the first

three bracelets. "Do you by chance have any period pieces? Like through a great-aunt, an ex's mother? I'd like to write a really impressive tale for you."

"How nice that would be." Priscilla is genuinely pleased. She floats toward the two Alexander McQueen bags, one in leopard pony hair, the other a skull-and-crossbones clutch. "Do you think these are too young?"

The landline rings, and while not set at a high volume, it's strident, invasive. "Vintage Tales," Eve answers in her pearliest voice. The one that mimics Faith's cultivated tone and inflection.

"Yes, she is." A pause. "One moment, please." Eve puts the call on hold, the pearly voice turns matter-of-fact. "Faith? Inez needs you to come home."

The room muddies. Faith takes the cordless receiver from Eve. "Okay, Inez. I'm on my way."

"Is everything okay?" Priscilla scans the room, checking out the latest Guccis and Leibers scattered onto the Hans Wegner credenza.

"Diana, you might want to be downstairs," Eve says. "It's almost ten. And I'll come too."

"Is it Edward?" Priscilla asks. "I've heard he's playing tennis and golf the day long. Doesn't he have to be at High Dune, Faith? Isn't it the end of the fiscal year or something?" She's poking around the inside of a white leather Gucci hobo. "This would be useful."

"Is it Dad?"

"He isn't feeling well," Faith says. "That's all."

"Dad's home?"

"He could have that twenty-four-hour bug my roommate has," Diana says.

"He never gets those bugs, right, Mom? Maybe I'd

better come with you." Katherine looks around as if she's planning to fly out the door.

"No, Katherine, thanks. I'm fine. I'll run home and see what Inez wants. It might be the pool company with the new part, I don't know. I'll be back."

Inez is mournful when Faith arrives. The kitchen, the entire house, has a sense of despair, hopelessness. Almost like a gathering scent or a germ, it moves toward her, billowing out of control. The library is quiet, Edward's desk chair is creepily empty. This time the bathroom door is completely closed, and she pushes it open too late. Instead of Edward snorting cocaine, he's wiping up, the act completed. Didn't he hear her, doesn't he know she's there? Again the dilated pupils, his runny nose. He turns to her in his terry-cloth Frette bathrobe.

"What the fuck, Faith? Don't you have a shop to oversee?"

"Inez called, she said you weren't yourself."

"Well, if that were true a half hour ago, I'm on my third line. Another hit." He's incredibly high. He speaks in a confident, detached tone.

"Edward, please. Stop this."

"Lighten up, relax."

"I can't forgive this, Edward," Faith says.

"Try your best."

A chilling conviction, the ugly tone he uses. He smells like a dirty auditorium at a pep rally—like those they have in the Pines at the regional high schools. Sweaty, shiny bodies too close to one another.

"I'm doing my best. You're the user, the one who lost our money. You need help."

"You find help, Faith." He snorts and breathes in. "Go ahead."

Faith imagines the ambulance whisking Edward off to the ER, then to Touchstone Hill. Is Touchstone Hill strong enough to fight her husband's demons?

"Edward, I beg you, please stop. You need help, nothing is that dire. Please, don't do this. . . ."

"You're my wife and you're on my arm, wherever we go." Edward speaks quickly, excitedly. "Every charity event, every fucking private party. Just want you to know that your friend Stenton Fields called. Chasing me down, for chrissake."

The light is too bright in the bathroom; Edward's skin is jaundiced. Faith backs out. "Edward, let's sit down, talk this out, like we always do, always have."

He moves ahead of her into the library and begins to patrol the length of the room.

"Sure, Faith. And first let me bring you up to speed. Since I never wrote the check for two hundred and fifty thousand and you only coughed up forty grand—the amount Stenton mentioned in his call—you're officially—"

"What call?"

"Stenton called my cell. I dunno, maybe an hour or so ago." Edward marches to the very end of the cherry-paneled bookcase, twists, and marches to the other side.

"What did he say?" Faith asks, although she already knows.

"What did he say? Hell, Faith, let me tell you."

Edward is animated, springy—he wants to chat about

it. "He called to say you *have* to relinquish your title as sole chair. I suppose you've hit rock bottom with me." He shrugs an exaggerated shrug. "There goes the sole chair." He does a little jig, pauses. "Unless you want to keep up appearances, which is what everyone lives for around Palm Beach. Then you can be a *co-chair.*"

Co-chair. Finally and at last, it is pointless. For the interminable effort to achieve the title, she can't recall what it ever meant. Faith watches her overly animated, completely drugged-out husband as he moves incessantly, babbling on.

"Understood, Faith?"

"Yes, I get it. I just wish I hadn't given him that forty thousand. We need it, Edward." To say nothing of the twenty thousand to keep Edward in good graces at Touchstone Hill. Where he ought to be inpatient.

"Forty thousand dollars wouldn't get my pants dry-cleaned. I'm in really deep, my love." His face is slackened, the handsomeness drained out. "Oh, and Stenton mentioned Margot Damon now that she's barreled back into Palm Beach. I thought you'd want someone else."

"I don't care, Edward, I don't care. What is more ironic than your taking me down with you while women will try to decimate me? What could be shittier?"

"You'll figure it out—you always do." Edward remains on his stomp around the library.

"You know how I feel, Edward? Like you left me on the curb and a bus came along."

"Ah, Faith . . ." Edward pauses theatrically, holds his arms out for an embrace. "I wouldn't do that to you."

"I'm going to call for help."

"Are you? What sort of help? 'Cause the two million

that was due two days ago, that has to be paid. That's the sort of help I'll take." Edward backs into his chair and waves her away. "Two million by tomorrow, and then another two million. And then . . ."

He was like this once before, twirling around, practically tripping on his own feet. Twenty-four years ago, she found him, manic, high, and then he passed out in the bedroom of the apartment they shared, five miles north of Worth Avenue. She was frightened and had never seen anyone in Edward's condition. Instead of calling an ambulance, she hauled him into his Volvo. Gunning the motor, she raced across the Southern Boulevard Bridge, straight to South Palm Hospital. Afterward, she explained they wouldn't get married and raise a family unless he swore on his life to never use again. He promised, he made a solemn vow.

"Mrs. Harrison? Is everything good, fine?" Inez hovers at the door, doing that tense patting of her head, stroking her meager bun.

"Just dandy," Edward says. His arms move fast, he seems giddy.

"No, you need to detox, to stop using," Faith says. "Please get in the car and go to Touchstone Hill."

"No, that's not happening. I'm not leaving. I'm waiting for news, investment bulletins, Faith."

"I'll call nine-one-one and order an ambulance. I'm too worried you'll be using again."

"Faith, Faith, tomorrow morning, after I hear about the two million, I'll go with you to Touchstone Hill. I'll sign up. I'll do outpatient."

"Mrs. Harrison, I'm with Mr. Harrison. You can go back to work."

"One condition, Faith." Edward jiggles his hand flimsily.

"What is it?" Hearing another word is unbearable. She has to walk out of their library.

"Katherine must not know. I'll clean up, we'll pay the debts, but she *must never* know."

"Oh, Edward, it's much too late. How could I promise you that?"

TWENTY

The air is infected with fear, and Faith's heart beats unevenly as she pulls up at Vintage Tales twenty minutes later. Edward's request hammering in her head, what Katherine mustn't know—that her father has plowed through their money, that he's snorting cocaine. Combined with Faith's request, a few days to mull over her own reveal, to disclose Diana. Who would put her beloved daughter through that much?

Dampness leaks through the front door of the shop, as if the dehumidifier has collapsed. In the oval mirror in the entryway, Faith reflects pale and distressed. She pushes her hair off her face, inhales, tries a phony smile.

"How's Dad? He isn't texting back, you're not texting back? When did you both become unmodern?" Katherine is calmly attaching a tale to a Judith Leiber Fabergé egg minaudière. "Mom, high-end, see? I know you've been obsessed with selling the most overpriced things lately. I thought I'd recycle 'Rapunzel.'"

"Faith, we've got four people bidding on that black crocodile Chanel bag!" Diana announces.

Eve holds out an ice water. "This is the first reprieve we've had."

"Might I borrow Katherine and Diana—for a few minutes?" That she's still in the same clothes—that it's still the same day, not even late afternoon—isn't credible. Like being in one of those films, *Groundhog Day* or *Date Night*, where the inciting incident blares and blares at the featured actors. "We'll go into the office."

"During peak hours? Are you sure Dad's okay?" Katherine asks.

"Oh, he is. He is," Faith lies.

"Well, while you were gone, it's been madness—till two minutes ago. We sold three Lady Diors," Eve says. "There's only one left."

"Did you?" Faith adds it up—fifteen thousand dollars. If only they keep going—hour by hour.

"The yellow snakeskin, that brown python, and the hot-pink lambskin," Diana reads from her iPad.

"A straight split," Eve says. "Consigned, not an estate. Then we sold costume Chanel earrings, the ones with the double C's from the eighties, the Cavalli blue-and-green enamel bangle, the Versace Medusa earrings, the Vuitton 'V' ring . . ." Eve says.

Another two thousand—from an estate, with a better return for the shop. "Any fine jewelry?" Faith is adding as she goes.

"We did, the last round of buyers—no one we know—

bought the real stuff. You were right, Faith, it sells. The Chopard watch, the sporty one, and the Temple St. Clair starfish earrings."

More math: another five thousand. "The Roberto Coin woven link bracelets—did the woman come in?" Faith asks.

"She bought one," Diana says.

"With 'Rumpelstiltskin' attached as the story," Katherine says. "I dashed it off—had no idea we'd sell that quickly. It really works—the bracelet is *so* gold. I played up the part about a young woman spinning straw into gold and played down the wicked imp and his magic. . . . Y'know, how she narrowly escapes the consequences."

"Well, that was clever." Eve watches Faith. "Since I doubt any buyer wants to read about a goddamn elf demanding someone's firstborn child."

Faith smiles although she'd like to vomit. "Girls? Let's go upstairs while it's quiet."

Katherine and Diana are ahead of her, winding their shapely, thin bodies up the stairs.

". . . even Rhys was dancing—most times he's reluctant," Katherine says.

"No! He's quite the dancer," Diana says.

"His cousin too. Cute, right? I bet he likes you."

"No, that's not true," Diana says. "He's sort of cute, though."

"For tonight, for the Clements' party, we're doing Joie dresses. We could borrow the *Anna Karenina* earrings, maybe the Scarlett O'Hara necklace," Katherine says.

"Those haven't sold?" Faith asks. Not that they'd bring in as much as other pieces, but everything must sell, must earn money.

"Well, they're about to sell to the same customer, someone young, who likes drama," Diana says.

"No way," Katherine says.

Diana checks her phone. "She texted a few minutes ago to hold them for pickup, so we can't be borrowers."

The girls—what Faith has come to call them—remain swanlike as they stand by the desk. "We need to talk."

"About what? These other fussy women are coming back. They're on the Avenue after two painful hours downstairs without figuring out what to buy. Plus someone Diana knows from South Beach said she'd come in," Katherine says. "I have like three tales to attach and one to whip up."

"Your mother wants to say something," Diana says.

"She does? How do you know?" Katherine is on her iPad mini, tapping away.

"I do. I'll need your attention," Faith says. "I wish we were in the library at home, not the office."

"Ew. Not a good sign." Katherine looks up. "That's where you and Dad took me when I was missing an A on my report card in ninth grade. I got a B-plus. In Algebra. Remember?"

"A B-plus?" Diana asks.

"I know. The pressure was on," Katherine says.

"Please, sit down," Faith says.

The "girls" sit side by side. Faith walks to the stereo system and turns the music off upstairs as "It Must Have Been Love" by Roxette is beginning.

"What I'm about to say is very important. It's something

that no one knows . . . something that I've kept to myself for years—decades."

Diana faces out, toward the window. Katherine stares at Faith.

"Mom, what are you talking about? You have a secret?" Katherine snickers. "Sure, a big, dark secret, yeah? Diana, she's not usually so gripping—honest."

Diana turns back to Katherine. "I believe you."

Faith faces them, standing. "I've always lived in fear of being found out, every day of my life."

"Jesus, Mom, when did you get like this? You're scaring me." Katherine says.

"I know it's time to tell you; it's been time ever since Diana walked into Vintage Tales."

"Diana—what about her?" Katherine raises her voice—she's speaking fast. "Mom, you're *really* freaking me out. Why is Diana part of your broadcast—seriously?"

"Katherine, you and Diana, you get along . . . feel connected."

Diana nods. "We are connected."

"Yeah, we're close for having just met. So?" Katherine says.

Faith paces the small area, two by two.

"Sit with us, Faith." Diana walks to the Egg chair, tugs it out of the corner.

Faith almost collapses into it; a sense of dread engulfs her. "Thirty years ago, I did something . . ."

"What could you have done thirty years ago? You were sixteen," Katherine says.

"I was. And I left home—ran away, left my mother and grandmother."

Downstairs the chimes ring once, twice, as customers

come in and out of Vintage Tales. Voices, noises, enthusiastic hellos, travel upward.

"The woman who gave me a ride, drove us through this blinding rain, kept asking, 'Does your mother know you're out in this weather? Where are you going? How old are you?' I lied about everything, the beginning of my lies."

"What was the woman like?" Diana asks.

"'What was the woman like?' Diana, my mother has never acted crazy before—has never acted like this—and you're asking her about the woman?" Katherine says.

"No, it's okay. This woman, she had a profound effect upon me. She was, I dunno, driving the getaway car, so to speak." Faith clears her throat. "I didn't think about it that night—I was too young and too afraid. Since then, I remember her as kind, worn. She seemed proud of her house and tired of her life—maybe that's why she invited me in. I'd never been away from home. She had a lavender Laura Ashley bedspread on a skinny twin bed, a scratchy tan rug, a gold bar of Dial soap in the bathroom. I cried all night long . . . .about what I'd done, how I missed home."

"Home, where was home? You told me, told Dad and me, that you're from outside of Philadelphia. You worked in Philadelphia before you came to Palm Beach."

"I did work in Philadelphia, and the woman who picked me up that night, her name was Nan, she helped me. She was from Cherry Hill, on the New Jersey side of Philadelphia. But I didn't get there till that night. The truth is, I'm from Kendalton."

"Kendalton? What's that?" Katherine says. "I don't believe you, Mom. You're acting out of your mind."

"There's more to it, there's more to my secret, Katherine."

Katherine jumps up. "What's going on? Why do you keep looking at my mother, Diana?"

Diana says softly, "It's about us, your mom and me."

"What are you *talking* about?" Katherine shouts, utterly furious. Her world being moved around for Diana, for Faith.

"Faith, can I speak? To Katherine?" Diana asks.

"What the fuck? Can you speak to me, what does that mean?" Katherine asks.

"Sure, go ahead," Faith says. Diana's avowal has to be every bit as upsetting as her own—for each of them.

"I was raised in Chatsworth, about twenty miles northwest of Kendalton," Diana says. "I was adopted when I was a few days old. My parents were wonderful. My father died when I graduated college, and my mother died a few months ago—I think I told you that."

"Diana was born on September 1, 1984—that's the other part of my secret, Katherine. She's my daughter. Her birth father died in a car crash before she was born. I put her up for adoption—thirty years ago."

Katherine walks to the window, sobbing. "I don't get it . . . I mean . . . what you're saying, what you did . . . Mom, you *knew* when you talked with Diana, right?"

"Wait a second. *I* sought your mother out, *I* came to find her," Diana says. "I told her who I am."

Katherine remains looking out at the Avenue below. "How could you, how could you not tell me, tell Dad? He doesn't know, does he?"

"No, he doesn't. I wanted to tell him so many times—for years. Finally I planned to the night of the kickoff Rose Ball. But Dad had his own news, some problems with High Dune, and I couldn't. Then he met you, Diana, and was taken with you, pleased that you and Katherine were spending time together. I thought, now's the time to tell him and Katherine. Then Edward became very worried—is very worried—about his work, and he's not been himself. I didn't want to lay this on him."

"I don't believe you. Dad's fine. You just don't want to admit or apologize to anyone for what you've done," Katherine says.

"That's not true. I concede what I've done . . . I admit my successes and my failures. Still, I think let's wait a few weeks, then speak with him. The three of us—let's keep this to ourselves, adjust to it, see how Dad is then," Faith suggests.

"Why should I promise you anything?" Katherine asks. "You've pretended my whole life to be someone else. Hey, you might have told me I had a big sister. I was always talking about wanting one. Since I was four. Now I have to figure out how we're alike, how we're different, how we were without each other . . . what you did, Mom . . that's the real kicker, what you did."

Diana comes to Katherine's side, attempts a jumbled hug. Katherine freezes without stepping away.

"What matters is that we are together, Diana—that your adoptive mother left that note and you came to Palm Beach. For you, Katherine, how one day, out of nowhere, you have your half sister. We're together today, and for years I dreamed of it. I did nothing—I was wrong, such a coward. It felt too thorny, too complicated."

"So we can't really hate you," Diana says.

"I'm not sure . . . maybe hate what she's done?" Katherine says. "I mean, how do I trust you, Diana, when you didn't let me know, you became my friend—was that a ruse? Was it real and about me, or about my mom? *Our mom*?

"I met you and liked you, Katherine. We got along, that's what happened. When you said your mother owned Vintage Tales, I thought it was a sign. I couldn't quite believe how lucky it was. You're my sister!"

"What about having a kid at sixteen, Mom? No one got abortions in the boondocks? Remember how worried you were about me in high school? Now I know why."

"No one got abortions, no one believed in them. It was a backwater, Katherine. You're from Palm Beach, you've been raised with privilege and beauty. This was rugged, no one had money, a lot of kids didn't go to college," Faith says.

"Such another world, even today," Diana adds. "I was hell-bent on escape myself."

"Oh my God, Diana. Will you live with us now? Maybe you're too old, but you're . . . family. I don't know. And you're from some form of Appalachia. This is Palm Beach . . ."

"I'm not sure. I know I'll work at Vintage Tales and get to see you and Faith most days. That's the reward for me."

"I pray you can forgive me, Katherine. I pray you can forgive me, Diana. Please, forgive me."

In the suspended moment while Faith waits for an answer, she feels Jimmy die again and her baby being taken from her.

Then she walks to Katherine at the window and motions to Diana. The three of them together, Faith in the middle. She places her arms around each of their waists. Katherine puts her head on Faith's shoulder and Diana does the same.

TWENTY-ONE

Time slows down for Faith when she and Edward pull into the parking lot at Touchstone Hill together. She is on speaker with Lara Mercer, canceling at six o'clock for her sit-down dinner that starts in an hour.

"My husband *has* to have the flu." Faith is persuasive. "I'd *never* forgive myself if your other guests caught it. High fever, chills. I'm concerned he's dehydrated."

"Are you certain, Faith? You could come by yourself, so I'll only have one hole at my table," Lara says. "A party at Justine's requires a long lead."

Faith pauses, looks at her husband, whose head is lolling against the "silk beige" leather passenger seat of her Mercedes.

A hole in her table at Justine's. Is she fucking kidding?

"Oh, you're too generous, Lara. Believe me, I'd leave Edward and be there if I only could. But then *I* might be contaminated. I'm awfully sorry. I know we'll be missing a wonderful night."

After she hangs up, her stomach starts flipping uneasily. She reaches past Edward for her cardigan and bag from the backseat. Together they open the trunk and take Edward's T. Anthony duffel out. Faith adjusts it over her shoulder.

"Gimme . . ." Edward slurs. "I can . . ."

"No, Edward, I'm fine. You seem weak. Thank you."

Turkey hawks, ravens, and parrots swoop down, a few inches short of landing on the roof. She half expects Edward to scare them away; the usual Edward would. With Faith leading, they walk through the electronic double doors of the inpatient wing and angle toward an antiseptic check-in desk. In a matter of seconds Stephanie Stevens appears, finessing Faith's out-of-body experience.

"Faith?" She looks at Edward. "Please, right this way."

Air-conditioning blasts at them as they travel down a quietly lit corridor to a private room. Stephanie opens the door. "I'll send someone to help you get settled. The evening director of inpatient, Dr. Brisbaine, will stop by shortly. I stayed after hours to greet you. And to wish you the best." Stephanie avoids Edward's glazed, exhausted eyes.

Footsteps. Faith would recognize them anywhere. Katherine arrives, her lace-up high-heeled sandals echoing on the tile floor. Rhys catches up, puts his arm around her. They are very young—Katherine is the age Faith was when she and Edward became a couple. She ought to warn her daughter how the years fly by and what is carefully constructed gets trampled on. There's no magic wand of reassurance, no just reward. She might praise Rhys, how he is with Katherine tonight. Faith could be emphatic, saying don't let him go, not now, not later.

"Mom?" Katherine advances toward Faith, who is outside of Edward's room, waiting for her. "Is this a joke? A nightmarish joke? First there's Diana, the discovered, exquisite Diana. Wasn't that three hours ago? *Then Dad at Touchstone Hill?* Oh, and when I left the shop, Eve told me we have to keep up with these frantic, hugely expensive sales. Apparently *you* want to? What is that about?" There's a nonchalance about her, yet she's in tears. Rhys waits, several feet away, concerned, baffled. As if the Katherine he has chosen and understands is being replaced with a beleaguered young woman. Every aspect of it put upon her.

"How unfair this is for you, sweetie," Faith says. "I didn't want you to know about Dad's relapse, I wanted him to stop, stop on his own. Today I knew he couldn't. He's fallen back on an old, dark habit. . . ."

"That's not who my father is. My father is in recovery . . . he's resisted for years."

"Katherine, Dad hasn't used in decades. So the hope is that at Touchstone Hill—"

"At Touchstone Hill, his pet charity, he'll detox?"

"That's right." Faith sighs. "He's a good man, a really good man."

Having invested in Edward for her entire adult life, she is exhausted by the past weeks. Perhaps the entire past year. While she was looking in the other direction, feigning that Edward wasn't slipping from her, he was. Worse, her daughter is devastated. Faith despises what Edward's quagmire is doing to Katherine. Hasn't she, Faith, done enough wrong?

"He's a secret drug addict and you're a secret liar. You're both liars, both full of shit." Katherine is crying.

Rhys, faltering, moves toward her. "Katherine?"

She sniffles unbecomingly. "Rhys, I'm sorry, you should go. I'll stay here with my mother. I want to see my father. I have to see him. Where is he?"

"In his room." Faith points to the door closest to them. "Talking with Dr. Brisbaine."

"Who? I mean, do we have to wait—is he being treated?"

"Treated? Not quite yet." Faith too wants a quick fix for Edward's using. "He's getting settled."

A tall man holding a chart with a stethoscope around his neck, fortyish, a green hippo-print Hermès tie beneath his white hospital coat, comes out of Edward's room.

"Are you Faith Harrison? I believe we've met at Touchstone Hill fund-raisers in the past. I'm Dr. Brisbaine. Keith Brisbaine."

He offers Faith a reassuring handshake, reserved for wives who bring their husbands in while they're high as a kite. "I've been chatting with . . ." Dr. Brisbaine turns to Katherine. "With your father . . . You must be Katherine. Your father has been talking about you. He's aggrieved that you'll see his decline, how he has become. Very quickly, apparently."

"You mean since a few days ago? I dropped by to borrow a dress from my mother and saw him. Then he was at her office a day later and he was okay." Katherine is grim.

Faith wishes she could console Katherine as she did when she was eight. Instead she's helpless; there's no secret sauce, no panacea. How dare Edward put Katherine through this—with Rhys at her side, apprehending, getting another impression of Edward altogether. Nothing reminiscent of a consummate Palm Beach man-about-town.

"I believe, Katherine, that Dr. Brisbaine is describing a process. First how Dad's . . . gone downhill . . . and now, at Touchstone Hill, he's on the path to recovery. He'll need to get well and whole again."

"Thank you, Mom, I'll ask Dr. Brisbaine myself. Knowing I'm not the one who pushed him to drugs."

"Katherine." Rhys takes her wrist and she yanks it back. "Your mother isn't—"

"How do you know, Rhys, what do you know?" She spins toward Dr. Brisbaine. "May I go see my father, please?"

"This isn't ordinarily permitted, although I can arrange it. He'll appear languid. He's coming down from the drug," Dr. Brisbaine says.

"The drug?" Katherine asks.

"Cocaine."

"Cocaine?" Katherine is incredulous. "Dad uses cocaine?"

"He does, that's why he's come to us for inpatient care," Dr. Brisbaine says. "We're going to work getting him off it."

"Is my father okay—isn't cocaine bad for your heart? I read this book by Abraham Verghese where one of the characters has a heart condition from cocaine." She is speaking quickly.

"A primary loss of a strong heart can be from cocaine

use. Your father knows that. Your mother"—Dr. Brisbaine looks at Faith—"is also aware of your father's health, since he used earlier in his life. And then was in recovery for many years."

"I know that. But I don't understand. Does my dad have a heart problem or not?"

"Will you follow me, Katherine? We'll leave your mother and your boyfriend behind. Your father is asking for you."

In the discreet visitors' area, two women are whispering. The only other woman, who looks much younger, holds her fingers to her forehead, quite alone. Rhys sits beside Faith. He gives her a rueful smile and studies his iPhone.

"Katherine said to me, when we got here tonight, that if Edward were himself, he'd be on the golf course a lot this time of year—at least for the back nine."

"I know. Except he hasn't been himself for months. He's been sort of sliding out of reach," Faith says.

Sitting at dinner hour in an inpatient rehab facility makes Faith feels slimy and hopeless. She looks around the room as Katherine comes in and sits on the other side of Rhys. She digs around in her book bag until she finds an eyeglass case and a container for contact lenses. Adeptly, Rhys takes out the lenses and puts on his glasses.

"'Sliding away'? Now you tell us?" She looks stricken. "Dad's asking for you. I don't know why."

"I'm sorry, Katherine, I can't tell you how very sorry. About every—"

"He wants you to come in," Katherine says.

Faith rises, stretches her neck. "We need to get him better. That's the point." Faith should stop, she isn't helping matters.

Katherine looks around. "I was born at South Palm Babies Hospital. Down the street."

"You were. And you were a patient once in this building when your appendix burst. The day before we were going to New York for Easter week—you were in ninth grade."

"No, tenth grade," Katherine says. "It was horrible. People brought me copies of *Madeline*."

"Weren't you born in South Palm, Rhys?" Faith asks.

"No, I was born in Munich, when my dad worked at the bank and—"

"Mom, do you remember the day I was born?"

"Of course, sweetie. Every minute of it."

Faith is alone with Edward. He sits in a chair by the window. His hair, usually combed back meticulously, is in clumps and falls onto his forehead. His chest is rising and falling rhythmically while Faith struggles to get enough air. He hasn't been tranquil in a long while, perhaps since last season.

He opens his eyes. "Faith, you've stayed awhile."

"Katherine sent me in. I've been thinking, since you're in a private room we can be honest. Your old habit came really close to destroying you."

"Faith, I'm going to become sober, stay sober," Edward sits up straighter.

"I hope so, Edward, I wish for that. By Palm Beach

standards, you're young—an amoeba. You've got to live a healthy life. I have a feeling you should be in recovery awhile. If it were outpatient, like you suggested earlier today—was it only today? I doubt it would work. Touchstone Hill is too glossy, with wealthy repeat offenders."

"I want Touchstone Hill; I identify with the place. They helped me once."

"I get that. I don't think it will work for you unless you commit to this wing, inpatient, end-of-the-road rehab for as many months as it takes. That means very few visits with us. One or two visitors over a six-month period. No phone calls or e-mails, texting. Stephanie Stevens has explained it all."

Edward fumbles with the lamp until he turns it on.

"Please don't be offended by the idea," Faith says. "It's been such a tough path with . . ."

Katherine and Rhys come to the doorway.

"Mom, do you want me to stay with you tonight so you aren't sad?"

"Katherine, that's very kind," Edward says softly.

"It is, sweetie. I'm all right. You should go to your apartment or go with Rhys. I'll stay with Dad."

"You can't sleep in the room, I asked," Katherine says. "I thought maybe I would . . ."

"I know. So I'll stay in the waiting room."

"Don't worry, Katherine. I'll send your mother home," Edward says.

"Can I have one more moment alone with Dad?" Faith asks.

They pull the door almost closed.

She bends over, her voice nearer to Edward. "I don't want you to be stressed. I blame stress for this, a big part of it. I'll figure out the deficits—how to schedule repayment, how to sell in order to have a payout."

"Where will you find the kind of money I need?"

"I'll grow Vintage Tales into a more commercial operation, online, open another shop or two in South Florida. Sell our house. I'm going to clean up every part of our sloppy lives, as long as you come back clean. In recovery. I want my husband back. Katherine wants her father back."

Under the watery lamplight, Edward looks less yellow-greenish than before.

TWENTY-TWO

Shoppers move in hordes, evocative of a rambling mall rather than a stroll on Worth Avenue. Mostly women roam from Via to Via, swathed in the cocoon of Palm Beach. Their shopping bags rustle in the wind from the east. With the season in full throttle, they are impervious, happy. With eleven days to go on Edward's payments, Faith's ambition feels more central than ever before.

Eve is dazzling Nadia Sherman when Faith gets to Vintage Tales. Spinning the latest items, accentuating the value of selling real jewels, the lure of Birkins in calf and exotic skins. She's pushing a set of Christofle picture frames, a limited-edition Waterford decanter, Limoges butter plates.

"Faith, hello!" Nadia is more sprightly than when they

first met. Could that possibly have been only two weeks ago? "I've returned to what I call 'the Bergdorf of resale shops.' Why is it that your shop doesn't *smell* like some of those resale shops—y'know, with sickly mothballed old clothes that gag you?"

"We don't sell clothes." Katherine rises from the desk where she's frantically matching her tales. "And my mother's deranged about keeping the shop fresh. Right, Eve?"

"Of course, Faith's very diligent." Eve turns to Nadia. "In fairness, I've been to resale shops that are very clean— where their Dior, Alaïa, and Marni dresses match our purses and scarves. We do sell scarves, shawls—Hermès, Chanel, Loro Piana."

"I have plenty of secondhand dresses in my closet," Nadia says. "What you have at Vintage Tales are luxury *necessities.* I love how it's curated, how things are displayed." She walks toward Diana, who is placing Trifari costume brooches from the forties and fifties in the armoire. Nadia puts on her reading glasses to examine a cherry tree blossom brooch, a seashell brooch, a starfish pin, and a grapevine pin. "These are amazing!"

She moves to the next grouping and picks up a Buccellati picture frame. "And more housewares?"

"Not housewares," Eve says. "More luxury necessities, to quote you."

"Yes, sure. Does it ever feel like it's from someone's house in a rampage? You know, your life changes and you scrounge for what to unload. A fire sale."

"A fire sale? Absolutely not," Eve says.

Katherine and Diana, in their fitted jeans and open-toed suede booties, concentrate on their tasks. Not exactly a palpable tension, yet they haven't gone out together any evening since Faith's disclosure.

"Let's go upstairs, Nadia," Faith says. "I'm sure you don't have much free time in season."

"Déjà vu," Nadia says, crossing her legs and settling into the Estrella sofa, like she did the last time. "Sitting here again."

Yet she seems more piercing, more rushed. Why not, who can say how it's been for Nadia? What counts is for Faith to promote her shop while shape-shifting, if not quelling dirt that Nadia has dug up along the path.

"Well, when we last met I was hoping to do a piece about you and your husband. I'm sure you recall. A profile of the two of you, a working Palm Beach society couple. Sounds like an oxymoron."

"I do recall. I have a thought, Nadia." Faith digresses. "What if I talk about my shop, what I bring to the community, mixed with the new trinkets, baubles, and purses being sold?"

"All good, and God knows your shop is fabulous." Nadia wiggles her toes in her Stuart Weitzman metallic ankle-strap sandals, sighs. "Just not compelling, intriguing enough. I'm not even sure if the Harrisons as a golden Palm Beach couple would be enough. I was hoping your husband would come today, since this interview was *scheduled*."

"Oh, would that he could—you know husbands." Faith's voice crackles, her lips are stuck to her front teeth when she dishes up her Palm Beach smile.

"Maybe we could call High Dune, put him on speaker, Faith?"

"Be my guest. I doubt you'll get through to him. I myself have trouble getting in touch." The hoax makes her anxious; the room is stuffy, blurring.

"I've heard he's left High Dune—so is it true?" Nadia wiggles her toes more, admiring them while she waits for Faith to respond.

Faith doesn't speak. More blurriness.

The chimes of the front door, familiar and unfamiliar voices floating upward. Next footsteps—anyone who manifests in Faith's office will be welcome—encouraged to sit down, break up the interview. Katherine comes, with Diana. "Mom, we thought . . . we think you should come downstairs now."

"Why is that?" Nadia asks.

"Someone's here. Asking for you, Faith. A private seller," Diana says.

"Is this unexpected?" Nadia asks.

"Very unexpected." Katherine is looking at Diana when she speaks. "She says she has two Birkins and one Kelly bag. She chose Vintage Tales over getting them to a 1stDibs vendor."

Diana nods. "She bets you can sell them 'in a jiffy.'" She and Katherine exchange another glance. "Eve said you should wrap up your interview."

Faith feels calmer; escape is within reach. "You know, Nadia, when you write me up, please mention that Eve, Eve Crane, my dearest friend, runs the show. She's imperious. Totally."

Nadia frets over her iPhone, turning off the recording device. Most likely annoyed, unwilling to reveal it.

"You're used to filling in, right?" Katherine asks. "Because when I adapt my tales to earrings, a bag, a shawl, parts works, and the parts that don't quite fit I make fit."

"I'll write it as I see it, I always do." Nadia is ready to leave. She tosses her Fendi Zucca canvas bag—one that's too dark and heavy for Palm Beach on a very sunny day—over her shoulder.

"Let's see what my editor makes of this. My impression is that features, profiles, matter. Reporters get their stories however they can." Nadia bobs her head, first toward Faith, then Diana and Katherine. "Wow, what a trilogy. Mind if I get a picture, unposed, to have with my notes?"

"Well, we're not at our best," Faith says.

"C'mon, Faith, you look fabulous." Diana situates herself to Faith's left and Katherine files in on the right. "A candid or two is fine."

"There's no private seller," Eve says five minutes later. "I can't stand that Nadia—I had to get her out of here."

"You saved the day," Faith says. "Thank you so much. Who knows what she'll write."

"You can't control her anyway, even if she sits there and records you," Eve says.

Faith folds Hermès scarves, including four of her own that she's about to tag and sell. Eve assesses twelve Georg Jensen silver soup spoons—just in from a divorcée who lives in Clearwater. Her collection includes three Ebel watches, two Cartier tank watches, and one Rolex. All circa 1985.

"I'm the one who has to cover up, pretend. I'm the pretender," Faith says.

"I'm an Edward fan. I worry about him, hope he's getting better," Eve says.

"I remember the night you and I met him at the Royal Room at the Colony hotel. The piano player that night, playing Broadway tunes. We were at the bar; Edward asked if I could dance the tango. I was about to tell the truth and you said I did a mean tango, Eve, remember?"

"I liked him for you. You said he wasn't your type. Then he was, and now?"

"I'm faithful; it has to do with my name," Faith says.

"That's sweet, loyal of you. What'll you do? Don't tell me you still love him?" Eve asks.

"I don't know," Faith says.

"Maybe you wish you did."

Dreamless. That's what her life has become, Faith realizes an hour after she leaves the shop. She pulls up to the Ritz-Carlton in Fort Lauderdale, parking on the far side of the main entrance, avoiding the valet. By the ocean, south of Palm Beach, the Florida Gold Coast is pacifying. Not her turf, the charm is untainted.

"A mysterious lender—Lauderdale? How creepy." Faith was dubious when Eve got the call two days ago at Vintage Tales.

"You can't ask Edward about it—we can't disturb him," Eve had said. "You need the money; maybe this was in the works before Touchstone Hill. . . ."

Worth a try would be Faith's justification. The lender and Faith are meant to meet at one o'clock. A smell of verbena and white jasmine, fine hotel scents, waft toward her as she filters through the massive lobby. Beyond the in-door seating sections, Faith spots the pool area and afternoon sun slanting across the ocean. How she wishes she could flop herself onto a lounge chair, or better yet, go to the spa for a signature spa treatment, with sea salts in the remedy.

Eve has made a reservation in Faith's name at Osteria Bruno, the hotel restaurant. Straightening her Cushnie et Ochs lemon-colored sheath, Faith walks inside. She clings to the idea that she's on hiatus, one where a meal will result in less debt for Edward. The silken, overly tall hostess, chatting away about Faith being the first to arrive, leads Faith to her table, a window table overlooking the A1A and a view of the water.

Seated, Faith opens her compact and pats her nose, puts on lip gloss.

Absurd how free she is; not a soul in this place would know her or her latest drama.

"And here we are!" The hostess returns to the table. Because she's over six feet tall in her platform sandals, Faith misses a glimpse of the guest for a second. Until the hostess backs up, and at a clip returns to her station. Lucas, in his Palm Beach best, Trillion shirt and khakis, scrubbed to perfection, smiles. He's tanner, tauter than when they last met, as if he's been preparing for this.

"Lucas?" Instantly a rash begins at her neckline. "What are you doing in Lauderdale? How is it that . . . ?"

"Hello, Faith." The sunlight from the window shows off his forearms, his wrists.

Faith jumps up. "I'm meeting someone, Lucas. For Edward. A lender. What are you doing here?"

Lucas laughs. " I know, so far from the beaten path . . ."

"Well, yes. I mean I've only been to this hotel for weddings, charity events. . . . Who are you meeting?"

He places his hands on her shoulders. *"I'm your lender.* I called your shop."

Faith cranes her head to see more ocean and sparkling sand. "That isn't funny. We should be careful, in case we both know the lender."

"Faith, it's fine." As if she's precious, Lucas clasps her to him. "Isn't this what you need? What you want? I swear I'm the lender."

She laughs at his persistent joke. "C'mon, stop it."

Her meeting won't take but an hour. Afterward she imagines herself with Lucas in a bedroom suite overlooking the turquoise shoreline. His mouth on hers, his dark eyes, more stirring today than the night they met, searching for her. Or they'd skip the hotel room that pigeonholes their feelings into some predictable tryst. Instead there would be furtive kisses in a cabana on the beach or a dusty corner of the empty grand ballroom. Anywhere to be near Lucas, to foster what exists without time or place. Like the fable that Katherine favors and Eve keeps nixing—about the hawk and the goldfish who fall in love and have nowhere to coexist. *Who wants that downer?* Eve quipped only last week.

"I could be delusional, but when I'm with you I think we look the same as the day we came to Palm Beach together," Lucas says.

"The day you bought me a Pucci dress in yellows and pinks. On the Avenue. And showed me around the shops— the Vias, the flower beds."

"What a dress," Lucas says.

"I loved it so much, I thought that was it, everything would be fine."

It wasn't fine, and her life since Lucas left her happened in slow motion. There was the devastation and disbelief, the broken heart. Each step forward was in reaction to his action, a survival mode after she was forsaken. Resuscitation.

"Faith, listen to me, come with . . ." Lucas says.

A thickness fills the room. Unexpected memories barrage her. Edward tossing a beach ball to a four-year-old Katherine in Nantucket, a family ski trip to Aspen, his first terrific run at High Dune and a celebration dinner at Chez Jean Pierre. Enough missionary-style married sex to feel she counted. Respect and dignity stamped across their collective passport.

Faith shakes her head. "I built a whole life without you, Lucas."

"Let me sit down for a moment," Lucas says. "Let me at least explain why I called Vintage Tales for this lunch."

"I should go." Faith doesn't move.

Hastily he sits, butters a seven-grain roll on his bread plate, and takes a bite. "I'm starving. How about you?"

Outside the guests are milling about the pool deck. Women in skimpy bikinis, maillots, little children in water wings jump off the small diving board.

"I'm not very hungry," she says. The years she's hated him, missed him, loved him. Triumphed over every bit of it.

"I have something for you." He gives her a check.

Before Faith reads it, he says, "Made out to Vintage

Tales. For you, to save your shop. By now everyone knows about Edward. I thought this could help preserve things."

"I can't accept it."

"You need serious money, don't you?" Lucas looks expectant.

"Lucas, this is for a *half million* dollars. Besides, as I get deeper into it, I'm managing, sorting it out."

"Well, it's my investment, my loan, however you want it to be, for your future, your franchise—or whatever you want to make of it. No strings attached, Faith. I promise."

"No strings attached," she repeats, looking at the amount on the check. "That's tempting."

"I have always loved you, Faith. Tell me you'll think about it? We shouldn't be apart," Lucas says.

At this juncture, Mrs. A would recommend Faith go for it—start the next chapter with Lucas, an obvious Palm Beach option. Including the check he has brought along. Instead she imagines Edward. Margot. The dread of being caught. Next she pictures day-to-day life with Lucas. The two of them arguing over a broken garage door, the tugs of adult children, unborn grandchildren. Commiserating over arthritic body parts. Old age. Beyond that, *he* set her on this course, untrustworthy guide that he was.

"You know, this isn't a good idea," Faith says. "To be honest, Lucas, my life is complicated. I've done enough damage."

"I owe you." He taps his finger on the check, which Faith has put in the middle of the table.

He does owe her. "I can't do this," she whispers. "I really can't."

Finally, she's crying. Becoming tears, not the ghastly

ones from the day Lucas left her and she cried interminably—bordering on hysteria. "Here, take it."

When Faith tears up the check, Lucas stands up abruptly. She watches him leave; his gait is the same— partly sprinting—as it was the first night they met in Rittenhouse Square. Another life ago.

TWENTY-THREE

Twilight. Rhys steers Faith's Mercedes to the front of the car line at the Breakers. Katherine twists around in the passenger seat to face Faith and Diana.

"Dad loves these ultra–Palm Beach parties. He always looks so regal—almost military—the way he stands," she says.

"Was your dad in the military?" Diana asks.

Katherine waits a beat. "Was he, Mom?"

"No, never," Faith says. "Katherine, you know that."

"Who knows what I know," Katherine says. "My father just does a dapper, dignified thing, right, Mom?"

"True, he does," Faith agrees.

"Here, Diana." Katherine passes her the phone. "Look

at this picture of my parents from last season, for the same event. The Arts and Media Ball."

Diana holds it up. "A year ago? Wow. You and Edward look like royalty."

"Ah, yes." Faith unbuckles her seat belt, squinting at the screen. "I love that photo."

Edward was healthy then, wasn't he? How confident Faith appears, standing in a black Givenchy cocktail dress with three-quarter sleeves and a flouncy hem. She carries a Saint Laurent black satin clutch, on her right arm she wears a Cartier "C" bracelet, on her left arm a Buccellati Bukhara gold watch with a face like a flower (sold yesterday to an unknown buyer). She squints again, unable to see what earrings she's wearing, nor does she recall. She starts to enlarge the image.

"Mom? We have to go," Katherine says. Faith returns the iPhone.

"Ready?" Rhys asks. A valet is at Faith's door and at Katherine's. Rhys jumps out, straightens his bow tie, then opens Diana's door. "Ladies, shall we?"

About to walk into an outstanding party of Faith's own invention—her own magic potion—she watches guests pile into the lobby and onto the piazza for the reception. Orange, red, and gold lanterns fight the starless sky that presses in. Spotlights shine on the beach—the waves slam against the seawall. Women assess one another—fine jewels and costume, short and long dresses, ball gowns. Calculating every designer on the Avenue and in the Vias.

"The makeup and hair," Diana says. "From the swept-up, to the crazy beehives, the tiaras."

"It's always like that—big hair," Katherine says. "Check out the shoes tonight."

The three of them study the array of heels—pumps, platforms, stilettos. "Crippling, practically every pair," Faith says.

"That's uncool." Eva emerges from the shadows.

"But true," Faith says, looking around at the evening bags and clutches, most identifiably sold or bought at Vintage Tales. "Eve, see, there are the silk Chanels." Faith lifts her hand to point, and Eve pulls down her arm. "And that lizard clutch where we couldn't find the provenance."

"Faith! Let's be discreet," Eve says.

"My mother, until tonight, kept a sale a secret no matter what," Katherine says to Diana. "Maybe because you and Eve are with us, she has this desire to be more outspoken, oddly. . . ."

"Katherine, don't be ridiculous. No one can hear us over the din. I'm only speaking to my family." Faith looks directly at Katherine and Rhys, Eve and Diana.

Katherine steps back, takes inventory. "Rhys, are those your friends from Cornell, only in for the week?"

"Go ahead, Katherine, Diana too. Mingle. I'm fine." Faith waves them away. Katherine, like a dancer in her Sachin & Babi fluttery black dress, leads Rhys. Diana, blithe and diaphanous in Katherine's short Milly cocktail dress and chandelier earrings from Vintage Tales, is ready to explore.

"They look so pretty," Eve says.

"It wasn't easy getting Katherine to loan Diana a dress," Faith says. "I begged her."

"Ah, they'll settle down, Faith," Eve says. "They were fast and furious friends when they met. . . ."

"You see it all, Eve," Faith says.

"I *know* it all," Eve says, and laughs.

Faith peers out at the frantic crowd. Clients, society, celebrities, enemies, journalists. The varying amounts of perfume and toilet water synthesize into one noxious brew that settles rather than lifts into the night air. Up close, the Nolands, Pierres, Martins, and Clarises half smile at her, pseudo-genuflect, and speed date away. Coupledom, a major flavor of the evening, creates a frenzy of movement in pairs. *Hello, Faith, how are you, Faith?* they say. What is missing is the next logical greeting: *We must get something on the calendar. You are stunning, Faith.* Why should they reach out to her—everyone in Palm Beach has been buzzing with Faith's fate: *Demoted from sole chair of the Arts and Media Ball to no chair, not so much as a co-chair.*

Above the sounds of the lead singer of De Santo, singing "Fly Me to the Moon," Faith hears what's being said. *He had no judgment, probably lied to everyone . . . who could believe it . . . guts to show up.* How dare they trash her?

"Faith dear," Mrs. A is pure gloss. Draped in a wine-colored gown and wrap, she carries a Valentino clutch (the same one Faith sold to Kerilla de Sants today). Her David Webb onyx-and-diamond necklace glitters in the overhead lights.

"Mrs. A." Faith dutifully leans in to her for an air-kiss. "You look lovely."

"As do you, my dear," Mrs. A says. "You are perfection. Besides, one should only worry when they *stop* talking about you; gossip is flattering."

"Really? I feel like it's the inverse effect," Faith sighs. "I never imagined being the topic of it."

Mrs. A sniffs. "Your gown. Marchesa—is that it? I didn't know they did royal blue this year. The embroidered overlay . . . and strapless."

"I bought it when I was the chair. I'm wearing it anyway. A bit tight around my ribs."

"To the outside world, it's a showstopper, my dear." Mrs. A puts her hand on Faith's elbow. "Let's move across."

Palatial gardens stretch before them. Mrs. A leads Faith in a circuitous route toward the throng of guests situated to the west. They pass Margot and Lucas Damon huddled with Allison and Henry Rochester at the oyster station.

"Ah, to win by default and then share oysters—Colville Bays and Olympias—like they're the spoils of war." Mrs. A follows Faith's gaze. "Be brave, Faith. Take a deep breath."

"Everything is different now." Faith exhales; her dress tightens.

"I don't know. You're not dead yet, are you?"

Admiring one another, pseudo-hugging, air-kissing, guests begin their stampede to the Circle Ballroom. As Faith glides by the quasi–receiving line where Allison and Henry, Margot and Lucas are greeters, Margot reaches out to Faith.

"What a terrific night," Margot says,

"Yes, it's a hit," Allison says, attempting generosity.

"Everyone can be proud of this night," Lucas says, while averting his eyes from Faith altogether. Can she blame him? As if they signed a pact, she too looks out at the crush of patrons.

"It is quite a party," Henry says. "I'd say we're at over three hundred."

"Allison, Margot!" Ryana Delce, event planner, teeters in her platforms. On her cell, she texts wildly, searching the room. "Press pictures now. There's no other time that works," Ryana orders. "Co-chairs, flanked by the men? Yes?"

Allison and Margot put their arms around each other's waists while their husbands frame them. Pictures are taken while accompanying journalists wait to get a few quotes. *The Daily Sheet, Palm Beach Post, The South Florida Times, Palm Beach Confidential, On the Avenue.*

As the flashes go off, Ryana looks over her shoulder. "Faith? You are Faith Harrison, aren't you? Allison wanted me to tell you . . . I did seat you with your family and your staff. Wasn't that it? Toward the middle of the room."

A deluge of guests pushes forward. Katherine and Rhys approach.

"Let's wait here a few minutes, Faith," Rhys suggests. "Until more people are seated." He puts his arm around Katherine.

"Wise idea." Eve comes into view, holding on to Diana's elbow. The two of them flank Faith.

Ryana squiggles by in her skintight Herve black bandage dress. "Who is that dreadful woman?" Eve asks.

"Someone who cares about taffeta tablecloths and analyzes the pros and cons of deep eggplant jacquard," Katherine says.

"Obviously," Diana says. She turns toward Faith. "I'm proud to be here with you tonight."

Spellbinding, magical, enchanting, guests remark as they move in a gaggle toward their tables. "Brown-Eyed Girl" is being sung by a female singer. Holding the mike close to her mouth, she gestures to the crowd with her other hand. "C'mon, everybody, even in Palm Beach we've got some brown-eyed girls."

The band wraps up their last stanza. There's a clearing of the dance floor as Stenton Fields taps the microphone. A welcome speech to be followed by Allison, who has, apparently, elbowed Margot out for the honor of speaker. At the podium, Allison delivers Faith's rhetoric—what she gleaned at Vintage Tales yesterday. Afterward she was grateful enough to buy a Chanel pearl choker, circa 1985, and a chartreuse satin Gucci evening bag, circa 1950. "I'll wear them to the ball," she promised. "They'll be perfect with my gown—it's bottle green, a column, sleek." She has kept her word, which matters somehow to Faith.

Guests clap enthusiastically when Allison explains how their mission enriches people's lives. Outreach, schools, retirement communities, throughout the county.

"Mostly I'd like to thank Faith Harrison for what she began as chair of the Arts and Media Ball. Of the five million dollars raised for this evening, four point seven was in place when she stepped down ten days ago. We are so pleased. Pleased by her hard work—her dedication and vision."

A burst of applause followed by Allison's practiced closing lines and more applause. Tables break up. Some gravitate toward the dance floor, others to the bar. The band begins "Livin' on a Prayer."

Air. Faith needs it enough to head for the vast, turn-of-the-century lobby with its coffered ceilings and the courtyard facing the ocean. Fanning herself with the *Arts and Media Journal*, she looks around for Eve. Katherine comes to where Faith stands.

"How about we not talk about whatever just happened in there. Allison's conscience, I suppose . . ." Faith keeps fanning herself.

"Are we supposed to pretend we're in a palace the entire night?" Katherine asks. Eve and Diana show up.

"It's the Venetian grandeur," Eve answers. "But there's no majesty here." Faith would say more, spill all her feelings, that it's Palm Beach in the twenty-first century and those who paid a thousand dollars a plate feel entitled. That she's ready to leave the Arts and Media Ball.

"Y'know, Rhys and I wouldn't mind cutting out early," Katherine says.

"I was wishing we could," Faith says. "What about it, Diana—you've never been to a black tie in Palm Beach, at the Breakers. When I was your age . . . I wanted to show up at every one."

"I'm ready to go. Where should we go? Someplace fun," Diana says. "Katherine, should we do that dive bar in West Palm?"

"Which one?" Eve asks. "Do you mean Jay Jay's?"

The rooftop bar at Jay Jay's, overlooking Clematis Street, rocks. The DJ plays "Take a Walk on the Wild Side," people are drinking or dancing, filling every inch of the place. Rhys sort of guides them to a table, where Katherine passes around the list of craft beer.

"We're a little overdressed," Faith says. "Aren't we the only ones not in a short dress or short shorts?"

"Hey, Rhys is in black tie," Katherine says.

"I left the bow tie in the car," Rhys points out.

"If we were dressed like everyone else, we'd still stand out." Eve motions for a server. "We'll order some fish and chips. Lobster clubs, what else?"

"This is so much fun!" Diana says.

"I wish Dad were here," Katherine says.

"Me too," Faith says. "I miss him."

"Can he come to a place like this . . . afterward?" Katherine asks.

"I think so," Faith says. "If he's totally committed to sobriety."

"I once had a boyfriend, for three years, who was in recovery," Diana says. "At first we didn't go anywhere unless it was dry. It took a while, but after about a year, we'd go anywhere. He had made the commitment."

"Where is he?" Eve asks. "What happened?"

"I'm not sure. I wonder about it . . . a lost chance . . ." Diana says.

"You could find out easily where he is, Diana," Katherine says.

"Maybe she doesn't want to." Eve is flailing at any server within the vicinity of their table. "Isn't that what it's about?"

Katherine and Rhys are locked in a glance, as if waiting to speak.

"Sweetie, is everything okay?" Faith asks. "Relatively

okay, since we blew the Arts and Media Ball and Dad's away and we can't call him for what, like two more weeks?"

"I wish we could call him tonight, Mom," Katherine says.

"We can write him tomorrow from the shop," Faith suggests.

"Actually, Rhys and I, we have some news, that's why I wish I could call Dad tonight."

"News?" Faith isn't certain she can handle any more news. Of any kind. At least until she's out of her uncomfortable gown and has taken out her contact lenses.

"You'll be happy, I think, I hope so." Katherine leans into Rhys. He's smiling.

"You'll be pleased, Faith," he says.

"Do tell." Eve stops trying to flag a server and focuses on Katherine. The DJ begins a round of Bruce Springsteen. "Born to Run" is blasting through the bar. People move in clusters onto the dance floor. The smell of beer and wine and sweat filters through the slight breeze.

"Mom, listen to this! I got an e-mail while we were at the Breakers. I'm accepted at Columbia for the fall! For my MFA!" Katherine brandishes her phone. "Read the e-mail—it's incredible. It's amazing!" She shows her iPhone to Faith.

"Oh, Katherine, it is wonderful!" Faith says as she reads. "Unbelievable!"

"Are you truly happy for me? Honestly, Eve, is she?" Katherine asks.

Eve takes the phone from Faith, gives it to Katherine, smiles. "She is. It's not easy . . . we know that. Your mother would want you at Vintage Tales *forever*. And I'd say she's thrilled for you. We all are."

"We are impressed!" Diana says. "It's about your talent . . . your writing."

"There's more news," Rhys says. "Katherine and I, we're both moving to New York in the fall."

"Rhys is going to try something in the city. He hasn't decided what yet, and we're going to live together, be together!" Katherine is sincerely happy, bubbly, decided.

"Oh, I'm delighted!" Faith says. "What wonderful news!"

A pair adventuring out beyond the fiefdom of Palm Beach. Katherine's acceptance—an act of hope, proof of wings.

"The first good news to come in a while." Eve starts waving her arm again. "Let's get champagne . . . whatever they serve. To celebrate."

"A two-year program, isn't it?" Faith asks. "I'm able to manage. Once Dad is back we'll come to visit. We love the museums, ballet—"

"Diana, you'll be at Vintage Tales, won't you?" Katherine asks.

"I promise." Diana smiles. "I was thinking about it when I was getting dressed for tonight. How since I've met you, each of you, everything is better."

Diana takes Faith's wrist and tugs her to a standing position. Katherine, Rhys, and Eve stand. They dance together, an impromptu jig. A family of their own making.

TWENTY-FOUR

"Twelve million dollars, that's the listing price."
Peggy Ann Letts of the Bailey Group drums her
Bulgari gold pen against her Louis Vuitton knapsack. "Furnished—as if it were done yesterday." She
pauses. "Just look at the light . . . early-morning light that
only gets better in different rooms as the day goes on."

"What if they don't want the furniture?" Faith asks.

"The furniture is exquisite, you'll sell it elsewhere.
You'll keep some of it. The art . . ."

"The art I'm selling. Katherine and I have been re-
searching . . ."

"Well, some buyers might want to purchase a painting.
Others won't want so much as a side chair."

Peggy Ann's tone is self-assured. Her buyers must love
it. Savvy and smooth in her beige sleeveless dress and

pearls, auburn hair, fortyish, she seems above the glut of brokers who sell only waterfront properties, preferably with dual views. As bittersweet as it is to list the house, Faith is steady. Hasn't it been in the offing since the night of the Rose Ball at the Shelteere?

In the short time since the two women have met and walked through Faith's house, Peggy Ann has described her penchant for black-diamond skiing and the trapeze. Antidotes to her stressful days. Yoga, Pilates, or the Lake Trail won't work; too many client sightings occur.

"I'm confident the house will sell fast. Especially in season. Everyone is inspired and yearns to own a home." Peggy Ann holds out her manicured right hand to shake Faith's. "How nice that we've been introduced by Mrs. A."

"I follow Mrs. A's advice," Faith says.

"She's a source. I'm glad we're both listening to her." She opens her knapsack and takes out her iPhone. "Let's see if Mrs. A called. I'd left her a message that I'm pairing up."

"Pairing up?"

"Pairing up, yeah, it works. So Margot Damon joined the firm—she's been with the Bailey Group for years . . . worked at our office in Marin County, when she was in San Francisco. I'll bring this listing to her and she'll bring the Lestat listing to me. You do know their house is going on the market too?"

"Leslie Lestat's house is two streets south," Faith says. "It's a beauty, a Regency, decorated in those lemon-yellow couches and white chairs, the glass, the pale wood tables."

"Another impeccable home. The ocean views, almost blustery half the time. You're more protected here. . . .

Truthfully, Faith, a buyer for a Regency isn't a Sims Wyeth candidate. I don't have to tell you." Peggy Ann checks her iPhone again. "No word from Mrs. A. She doesn't really text much. I'll tell Margot that I've done the appraisal and paperwork. We have buyers in mind already." Peggy Ann pauses in front of the mirror in the foyer. "You don't mind about Margot, do you?"

"Not at all. I'm counting on both of you." Faith smiles.

Twelve million dollars: a larger amount than Faith expected—perhaps more than Edward had pledged against their house to his creditors. Besides, any joy that existed within these walls has been contaminated—and vaporized. Not that it stops her from taking pictures of each room with her iPad mini—remembering life when she was naive, uninformed.

Inez is in the squeaky-clean laundry room, folding towels. "Mrs. Harrison. I didn't know you were selling the house. Your *home*."

"What is it really, Inez, but a perfect box? A place to house yourself, your husband and child. One you get to make beautiful—an ivory and off-white interior, wisteria and hedges outside."

"It's your home." Her touching loyalty.

"It has to be sold. Soon."

Faith is beside the far wall. Inez takes the sheets from the dryer and starts smoothing them. "You know you'll always work for me, come with me, Inez."

"I'll always want to work for you, Mrs. Harrison."

"I'm glad of that. I have made some inquiries for Albert,

Inez. Since he'll want something as substantial as here. Unless Edward, Mr. Harrison, makes an impressive come- back, it's best he find a job elsewhere. I've spoken with Patsy and Mrs. A. They both want to interview him. He can choose, which is a great thing. . . ."

"Thank you, Mrs. Harrison." Inez keeps folding the sheets. "But what about Vintage Tales?"

"I hope to keep it. That's my plan. I'm sure women will be cordial in the shop and exclude me from the rest. I don't mind, honestly, I don't."

"Mrs. Harrison, you should keep this life—go to par- ties and clubs. The charity events. You work so hard. You look so pretty in your dresses. How you walk in high heels . . ."

"I appreciate that, but I'm fine." Faith means it. "What- ever happens, Inez, I hope you'll come along. You know, like Ruth and Naomi in the desert."

Inez stands straighter. "I hope to, Mrs. Harrison."

"Isn't it true that we majorly worked our glutes and legs on the bikes this morning?" Katherine asks Diana.

"Totally. Arms and shoulders too," Diana says. "Very efficient."

"Body fat, that's what they measure at the Breakers, in the fitness center," Priscilla, who has just arrived with Patsy, says. "We did an Ananda yoga class there this morn- ing. You know how it gets hectic. The cycling classes, on the terrace—mobbed at seven A.M."

"You used to come to those, on occasion, didn't you, Faith?" Patsy, dressed in her classic Lacoste tennis whites, asks as she walks around, fingering the newest, in-demand purses.

"I did, but it's been utter chaos at the shop. I know I should be doing more . . . doing *something,*" Faith says.

"Mom, you would like what we did at Eve's gym, at Sunrise Point!" Katherine turns toward Eve. "We'll all go!"

"Where were you, Katherine?" Patsy asks.

"At the class in Eve's gym at Sunrise Point. I'd call it a great twenty-minute workout. A virtuous way to begin your day," Diana says.

"Well, thank God the workouts are finished. Here we are shopping. For Christmas gifts, not only for ourselves," Priscilla says, decidedly jolly. Walter's divorce was finalized yesterday morning, and her entire affect is different. Dressed in Bohemian chic, a linen maxi dress and red-framed progressives, she's a breezier version of herself.

Patsy lifts up a gold mesh purse with a black onyx flower in the center. "Is this chain made of seed pearls?"

"Yes, it is," Eve answers. "We love that bag. Very special indeed. A winner, right, Faith?"

Patsy studies it and looks away, as if she's pondering why she's at Vintage Tales at all.

"I'm in the mood to shop," Priscilla says. "I could start with that bag, Patsy, if you're not going to take it—and it's one of a kind. Or I could get it for Walter's daughter maybe. . . ."

"We have some interesting new clutches." Eve's buff patent slingbacks, copies of Manolos, click loudly on the marble floor. Walking to the shelf where she's displayed four beaded bags, painted or feathered, flowered or jeweled, she holds up one with an aqua-and-deep-blue mermaid motif. "How about this?"

Priscilla swoops toward the purse. "Fabulous. So unique . . . that mermaid . . . is she glued on? The bag, it's almost whimsical, it reminds me of something my aunt Beatrice had. She took me to London, we traveled the globe together."

"Priscilla, you did not travel the globe," Patsy says. "That's a fabrication."

"No, I did. When I was young and Aunt Beatrice was still wealthy. We were in London and Paris." Priscilla sounds wounded.

"Do we know the designer? Who has the guts to buy someone we don't know?" Patsy says. "And they're not expensive enough. You should charge more, Faith, the way you do for couture bags. You could use the proceeds, right?"

"I found the collection," Diana says.

"Online, that's where it's from." Katherine looks up from the tale she is scribbling on the small pad she carries. "From out of state?"

"Faith, how are you being treated? Is it a form of the widow's walk?" Patsy asks.

"Widow's walk?" Eve bristles.

"Patsy!" Priscilla is clutching the bag with the mermaid attached. "Please!" She twists toward Faith. "It's not that bad, Faith, don't listen to her. To anyone."

Eve raises her eyebrows. Priscilla turns to Katherine. "I'd like a tale for this bag. Can I make a request?"

Katherine, at the window, looks down at the Avenue, as if she doesn't hear Priscilla.

"Katherine?" Priscilla comes close to Katherine, dares speak into her ear. "Would you do a synopsis of 'The Little Mermaid' for me? I'm not talking about the Disney version.

I remember the real story, written by Hans Christian Andersen. If I buy this bag . . ." She turns to Eve. "How much is it?"

"One thousand eight hundred dollars."

"Really?" Priscilla holds the purse up to the light. "Patsy said this batch costs less than the usual. Didn't you say they're about six hundred dollars?"

"This collection is varied," Diana says. "The bag you've chosen is one thousand eight hundred."

"I'll take it." Priscilla wields an American Express Black card. "Walter will be pleased."

Patsy frowns at Priscilla. "Are you sure, Priscilla? This isn't Fendi or Prada from twenty years ago."

"I'm sure," Priscilla says. "What do I care who the designer is. That isn't the only standard. I love the bag."

Faith comes to the register and stands behind Eve as she writes up the purchase. "See, I already have Walter's card and his last name is on everything." Priscilla signs with a flourish.

No one says anything; Eve gives her the receipt.

"I'd like 'The Little Mermaid,' Katherine, for the story, because she falls for a prince who can't even see her good deeds and she saves him, remember? Then she wants to leave the sea, leave where she's from and what she knows, to live near the prince. She manages to get legs and it never feels okay. When she walks, it's as if she's stepping on knives," Priscilla says.

"Still, she dances for the prince," Katherine says. "He's in love with her, then he marries someone else, because he doesn't even recognize, or remember, who the Little Mermaid is. That she's the one who saved his life, in the ocean."

Eve looks at Faith. "Honestly, isn't that too tragic?"

"Not only tragic, a primer. She has the chance to live. If she'll kill him on his wedding night, she can survive." Priscilla holds the evening bag close to her.

"She can't do it—that's what I remember," Diana says.

"Oh, Christ, another dreary one." Eve still watches Faith. "I'm happy with the Disney film. Here, Priscilla, let me wrap it up." She almost plies it out of Priscilla's grasp. The seafoam-green and ice-blue tissue papers rustle when she begins.

"I never wanted Katherine to know the Andersen version," Faith says. "These fairy tales are morose, foreboding. Let's skip a tale, Priscilla, or find another."

"I always wanted to do that tale, but to contour it to a bag or a pair of earrings is a challenge." Katherine smiles at Priscilla. "I'll write something up."

"Exactly! Let's have the tale, and I'll hope for the best on my wedding night," Priscilla says.

An hour later Faith stands alone in the middle of the upstairs office, a crazy salad of shipping boxes filled with jewelry boxes, assorted-size purses surrounding her. Shawls are piled on her desk. Katherine comes in.

"You're a good sport, sweetie," Faith says.

"Adapting a story—that's easy. What upsets me is what's been said about Dad. That he could be disgraced."

"I don't want you hurt or pitied, that too. People will talk about Diana as soon as it gets out. Countless talks about our money, about our secrets," Faith says.

"I don't care, I really don't. I'm sort of relieved. We have Vintage Tales—we have each other," Katherine says. "You know, Mom, I liked Diana before I learned anything."

"Me too," Faith says. "From the minute she walked into the house."

"Will you divorce Dad? That's what everyone says."

"Everyone? How can they know what I don't know?" Faith says. "Seriously, Katherine."

"Will you divorce him?"

"I don't want to. I want him to be sober. I'd like him back, sober, in life again," Faith says.

"Well, you don't have to worry about 'The Little Mermaid'—the true story or what people say, as far as I'm concerned. I'm leaving Palm Beach with Rhys. Not some prince who won't know who I am one day. You know, I truly love him. That's the good news for today."

"You've no idea," Faith says.

"Remember when I was little and I'd beg you to let me come to Vintage Tales after school, to skip tennis and ballet, every after-school program you thought I should do, so I could be with you? Remember Dad would stop by and sometimes we did an early dinner at the Grill? Dad and I would play charades, and you never wanted to. Dad figured out every charade I thought up. I liked it and I didn't. Do you think he let me guess his charades and acted like I was right when I wasn't? I'd say a blowfish and he'd say yes. Maybe it wasn't that. . . ." Katherine begins to cry quietly. "The way I miss Dad, I can't stand what's happened. When will it end?"

"I don't know. I honestly don't." Faith puts her arm around Katherine.

"Mom—how do *you* miss him?"

No one has asked her, not Eve, not Mrs. A, not Inez, the pivotal question.

"Without him life is strange. Not the lack of parties or dinners or clubs, invitations. What I miss is Dad. His jokes, especially the one about the three women who get to heaven and one of them has to get her hair done. He taught me how to play bridge and tennis, how to balance a checkbook. I miss being beside him. You know, Katherine, he always thought what I did with Vintage Tales had merit, added something to the Avenue."

"Dad believes in you."

"I know. I wish he were here."

TWENTY-FIVE

argot Damon and Allison Rochester?" Eve asks. "Not wise to miss a lunch they invite you to. Especially that crowd."

"She's waiting, asking if you're coming. I put her on hold," Diana says.

"It's true, Mom. It's nice that you've been asked," Katherine adds. She's splashed water on her face and seems calmer since they've come downstairs.

"Could be good for business to show up," Eve says.

"After the Arts and Media Ball? Is there no mercy? Say I'm not feeling well."

"Go while you're still invited," Eve advises.

"Mom, go for an hour," Katherine says as she spins around in the lime green Swan chair. "You haven't gotten one reminder for a party, those engraved, laser-cut, Lucite numbers. You used to save them, put them on your desk."

"Okay. Diana, please say yes. I'll get changed."

Again Katherine spins around. "What about Cleopatra-inspired jewelry—this gold-link-and-turquoise necklace?"

"That'll sell to someone younger," Eve says. "Price it at three fifty."

"Maybe four fifty or five hundred?" Diana says. "Aren't we going for broke?"

Prompt and refined, Faith moves through the dark wood bar area at Ta-boo. Shoppers sit on stools, facing bottles of Jack Daniel's, Grey Goose, tea mixers, shopping bags from Saks, Pucci, Gucci, Chanel, Vintage Tales placed at their feet. A trace of black bean chili, fried calamari, and pizza mixes in the air as Faith heads to Margot's table. She half smiles at clients, quasi-friends, friends of friends. Heavily ringed fingers of thin hands, young hands, old hands, wave half-heartedly. Several tables of four or five, ornamental and ornamented, are there to be seen. Women hold glasses of Pinot Grigio or Virgin Marys and chat softly. Some chew on the celery sticks. Although inaudible in the din of the restaurant, Faith knows too well the repetition, the tenor of their conversation, the tone of their attire, from day jewels to wardrobe—Kors, Akris, Stella McCartney, Céline—coolly selected. She takes a swift, covert inventory of the designer bag lineup—Kelly bags, Birkins, Bottega Intrecciatos, medium versions only. Burrata and tomatoes, grilled salmon, chicken Caesars are being carried by the waitstaff on oversized trays.

Faith does her best, moving on to where Allison and Margot are at the front table in the room with the fireplace. Allison stands up; her green-and-yellow Cavalli swirly print clings to her hips. "Faith, Ah'm glad you've come."

"I hardly get here. But I love the menu," Margot, seated, says. "There should be more lunches on the Avenue."

The table feels too intimate; Faith's worry is heightened. She feels ill, a stomach bug, a migraine headache, something. She straightens her Erdem print, deep blues, fuchsia, and gold, and taps her Jimmy Choos, black suede and crystal-beaded sandals. *How far does infallible get you?* Faith has wondered lately.

"Together at Ta-boo." She smiles weakly.

Odd how little she cares whether she's at a club or a restaurant, nor does the guest list mean much to her. For the first time that Faith recalls, there is scant reassurance in how many Vintage Tales clients paper the room—what has predictably elevated her spirits. Instead there's an edge to it—as if she's treading water in the Rochesters' chlorine-free pool, centered in their luxuriant backyard. Or she's in a tennis game, at match point. "I've left everyone to fend at Vintage Tales."

"We have news," Margot says. "I would have called or had Peggy Ann call. Then Allison suggested we have a quick lunch."

"News?" Faith's mind fills with what can go awry. Plumbing, heating, A/C, the pool has algae, the closets are a disappointment. The asking price too high.

"Yesterday I showed your home to a young family. A young wife, mother, with a little girl, I believe. The husband is a banker, and they're moving, half the year to begin, to Palm Beach from Philadelphia. They were quite taken with the house, the gardens, the views." Margot stirs her latte.

A young wife and mother. "How old is the little girl?" Faith asks.

"Hmm. Perhaps she's three or four? A darling little girl," Margot says.

"Ah remember Katherine at that age in your house, Faith," Allison says.

"They love the house," Margot says. "This morning they made an offer, Faith, for your asking price—which means they want to preempt. They want it very much, I must say. They're offering twelve million."

"That's amazing," Faith says. "In less than a week?"

"You see, Faith, we should all be sittin' together for your news," Allison says.

"And we are," Faith says. She's about to accept Margot's offer when Nadia Sherman from *Palm Beach Confidential*, appearing slightly sun damaged, her dark hair loosely braided, heads toward their table.

"Faith, always a pleasure. Allison, Margot." Nadia is beaming. "I'm not sure you've heard, but I did get that feature in. What was supposed to be a lead story about the Harrisons, their philanthropy, their Palm Beach essence, your shop. The focus kept changing. . . ." She pauses.

"Excuse me, Nadia," Allison says. "Ah believe we're having a very private lunch at this table."

Nadia raises her voice. "Please, don't let me interfere, Allison. I only came because I noticed Faith and thought I'd give you a heads-up on my piece. A Palm Beach story that goes beyond money."

"This seems like some feeble attempt to presell your feature, Nadia," Margot says.

"Faith is an amazing businesswoman. Her shop makes us sane, makes us happy," Allison says. "Ah'm not sure what you're after. Faith isn't on trial, is she?"

"My article runs in four days. It's called 'Scandal.'"

"Nadia, this won't work, Ah'm sorry," Allison says.

"Maybe it won't work for you, Allison," Nadia says. "Still, since I noticed the three of you together, I thought I'd mention the content."

Allison and Margot look away as if they're bored while Faith tries the same approach.

"Just that it's the truth about Faith Harrison, Palm Beach wife, entrepreneur, mother, and fraud. What she did long before you met her . . . I've got photos of—"

"You should get the fuck out," Allison says.

"Who wouldn't want to know this?" Nadia asks.

"Please go. Now," Margot says.

As Nadia moves away, Faith feels that old fear again and pushes it down. "I'm sorry, Allison, Margot. That was uncalled-for."

"If you didn't come out and socialize, they'd talk about you anyway, right, Faith?" Allison asks.

"But look at this." Margot points toward Katherine and Diana, standing beside the headwaiter, waving.

"What are they doing?" Faith says. Their bodies are mostly in shadow, their faces are illuminated in the dining room's windowless glow.

"Ah bet they came to save you," Allison says.

"I was born to have daughters," Margot says. "I've thought that every day raising my sons, those damn basketball games and soccer practices. Football season. I wanted to go shopping and share sweaters with a daughter."

"Thank you, Margot," Faith says.

Although she's only five feet away, a text comes in from Katherine. *Knowledge comes, but wisdom lingers. — Tennyson. Your rescue crew is here.*

"Wow, that was fast," Eve says. "You weren't gone an hour."

"Fast and furious," Faith says. "Almost slipped and fell."

"We moved at a marathon speed—couldn't wait to be back," Diana says.

"Yeah, Mom in her teetering heels doing this frantic walk/run from Ta-boo to Via Amore."

Eve is wrapping a seventies pink-and-black butterfly-print Pucci scarf in gray tissue paper. She carefully places it in one of their heavy cream-colored calligraphed shopping bags. "We're busy," she says quietly, eyeing where Cecelia stands, in front of Faith's gilded mirror. "Cecelia has come to collect her Christmas gifts."

Faith nods. "Well, we're back. The girls are poised and ready."

Quickly, out of habit, Faith watches her shoppers encircling a pair of rhinestone button earrings, a faux pearl choker with a zirconia clasp, a Sidney Garber peridot-and-gold ring, a Ferragamo leopard scarf.

Cecelia looks at Faith in the reflection. "Your daughter and Rhys! You must have some say, Faith. Even in your circumstances, perhaps more so due to your circumstances, wouldn't you prefer to have an engaged daughter?"

"She's really current," Diana says. "She's *young*."

"And Rhys has applications in to the B-schools in New York," Katherine adds. "Can you stop talking like I'm not in the room?"

"B-schools?" Cecelia asks. "Doesn't he already work in a business?"

"We might want to live in New York for a few years. Experience winter," Katherine says.

Cecelia puts her bags down as if Katherine has announced an awful plan, terrible news. "Faith, are you okay with that?" Cecelia asks. "I mean, Palm Beach is Katherine's home."

Palm Beach. Home. Faith shrugs. "What more could I want for my daughter than that she sees the world? She and Rhys should make their own decisions."

"Call me of the *Mad Men* era, but I wouldn't allow my daughter such a plan." Cecelia looks stricken. "Seriously, Faith, is this the best you can do?"

Faith can't recall why she ever liked Cecelia. Did she ever?

"That's okay, Cecelia, you're not Katherine's mother," Eve says.

By late afternoon Faith sits in her upstairs office, calculating payments for Edward's debts on her iPad. Homes in London and Aspen—sold for less than expected—and now a Palm Beach sale bring her to a grand total of fifteen million. With nine days to go, she's five million dollars short. Below on the Via she sees Mrs. A and two women, each ash blond, each with a cashmere cardigan tossed over her shoulder—one is the faintest shade of blush, one is sage, the other is lemon. A threesome walking toward Vintage Tales. Before Faith is on the first floor, Mrs. A's voice cheeps through the shop.

"What is there to do but go on Worth Avenue when that damn wind whips up from the east? We couldn't sit by the pool. Laetitia and Violet, my childhood friends. They're new to Palm Beach, renting in town for the season."

"Is there a way to open the armoire with the Saint Laurent and Bulgari clutches?" Violet asks. "Laetitia and I, we collect evening bags."

"Then you've come to the right place." Diana scampers toward the armoire with a Palm Beach smile.

"Shall we, Faith?" Mrs. A motions toward the staircase.

Upstairs, Faith watches her place a Neiman Marcus shopping bag on the desk. "How refreshing to have Katherine and Diana's company."

"It's distracting. A respite of sorts," Faith says. "The girls like the hunt for product, the tales."

"The girls," Mrs. A says.

"My girls," Faith says.

"How brave you are."

"Am I?" Faith pauses. "Anyway, about selling paste, costume, in truth, I'd rather sell high-end."

"Why share a three-hundred-dollar sale when you can share a three-thousand-dollar sale?" Mrs. A starts emptying out her shopping bag, lining up three small bags, each wrapped in an original Judith Leiber pouch.

"Mrs. A, you are my most loyal client. I don't think we should sell your bags for a while. You've brought so many in lately."

"After this, we'll take a break, I agree," Mrs. A says. "But you have to admit, I have quite a collection. Is 'Cinderella' too prosaic? Naturally it is. But people forget how important the fairy godmother is."

"True," Faith says. "Still, in my recent cynicism, neither fairy tale resonates for me—too generic."

"Really? Aren't they rife with symbolism?" Mrs. A sighs. "Well, this is the cache. In excellent condition, the edges and corners are perfect."

"This is exciting, Mrs. A. Let's look," Faith says.

"I have to fly. Violet and Laetitia, my Boston friends, are probably finished buying up your scarves and a few clutches downstairs. We have to get makeup at Saks, pressed powder for our jowls. We're off to Mar-a-Lago tonight with nine other widows, to trade fears of decrepitude," Mrs. A says as she stands up.

"Shouldn't we go over the value for consigning? We should view the bags together. Vintage Leiber, especially if it's signed, is popular. Priscilla could have Walter buy them up by tomorrow."

They both laugh.

"Before any interruptions, go through each purse very carefully. Check the lining. Open each and every one. I know you would do that. The little gold combs are inside. Authentic Leiber, to get top dollar. By the way, these aren't to consign. You take the proceeds. Put whatever money comes in toward the new shop. Delray, Lauderdale."

"You have been so kind to me. I don't know how—" Faith says.

Holding up her hand, Mrs. A says, "Go ahead and leave this life behind, but keep your shop on the Avenue. That's all I ask."

Mrs. A gives Faith an awkward hug that lasts several seconds.

After Mrs. A leaves, Faith uncovers the minaudières. The first is a Pierre French bulldog made of Austrian crystals. A noteworthy model, possibly used once or never. Faith opens the clasp and runs her fingers across the gold leather lining and the signature, JUDITH LEIBER, NEW YORK. The second minaudière is a vintage box made of Swarovski crystals, circa 1985. A small gold key and Mrs. A's calling card, which reads ALICIA AINSWORTH, are placed inside. Both in immaculate condition and quite distinctive. Despite Mrs. A's penchant for buying, then selling, only to buy and sell again, wouldn't she want to keep these two limited editions? Carefully Faith places the calling card on her desk.

The third minaudière is an owl head, circa 1990, with purple crystal eyes—the most exorbitant of the three. Again, in mint condition, as if never used, not taken to one party. A black leather ring box from Graff and a few sheets of paper fill the interior. Faith unfolds the first and reads the GIA report. *Round, brilliant fancy vivid yellow diamond. Flawless, twenty carats.* Next, the appraisal: three million dollars.

Opening the box, Faith holds the cocktail ring, so luminescent that it seems alive, to the light.

TWENTY-SIX

The Touchstone Hill campus is a labyrinth that Faith never anticipated having to finesse. Although she knows full well the lecture hall and public areas, she is uncertain where Edward will be before noon. She walks along the manicured path from one Mission-style building to the next, wondering how she doesn't know the names of each. Surely Edward knew long before he went inpatient every donor of standing, every board member who wrote the largest checks and made Touchstone Hill into the high-caliber facility it is. The place to cure her husband and send him home recovered. Her heart is beating quickly—she is both ready to see Edward and dreading it.

"Faith, Faith!" He calls her name and waves from the first building that rises on an embankment. She squints and reads the name, engraved on a stone plaque above the door: MATTHEWS HALL. He saunters toward her, his skin rosier, shoulders broader, clean-shaven. A sanitized version of her husband. His crisp demeanor is misleading; Faith almost forgets what happened that brought him here. His black-rimmed Ray-Bans and deep green polo shirt are deceptive. She briefly believes he's leaving a board meeting and she's merely picking him up unexpectedly. Maybe his Bentley has broken down, feasibly he rode out with another board member and he has remained longer to address a few kinks in the Touchstone Hill system.

By the time Edward has caught up to Faith and is initiating their embrace, what really happened is playing in her mind. Her husband has gone inpatient—it can't be erased or annihilated. A minor infraction compared to her ceaseless worries about what he'll do when he returns home, and if he'll remain sober.

"Faith." He says her name for the third time. The wind blows, Florida-style, kicking around pollen and dry grasses. He holds her close, like they're young and in love, dating while others on the quad are lonely and disenfranchised. He could be her college boyfriend, the one she would walk with to class, students envying their deep connection, their transcendent love.

"There you are!" he says merrily.

"Edward, I can't believe it. You look healthy. . . . You seem so . . ." Faith says merrily.

He puts his mouth on hers. She opens hers, not sure how wide it should be. She hasn't kissed him this way in ages; she learned to live without it. Without him. He starts with such fervor that he doesn't quite notice she's fish-kissing, open mouth, slight pucker—minnows could make their way down her throat. She stops. He puts his hand beneath her La Petite Robe wrap dress, which she intentionally chose for the cheery print. She puts it back at his side. "I seem so what?" he asks.

"I don't know, so robust."

"I hope I do," Edward says. They walk along the paved path toward the inpatient residences. "I couldn't wait to see you."

He's too relaxed, too scoured and unburdened. As if it's a country club, not a rehab center.

"Aren't you happy to be together?" Edward asks. They are near enough to the salt marshes that ospreys orbit the trees and a few egrets are visible in the distance.

Faith stops walking. "To be honest? I am, but I'm worried, Edward. The cares of the world have been removed for you. You're away—at a place somewhere between summer camp and college—or some kind of getaway for adults who screw up. Meanwhile I'm out in the world, cleaning up your mess. Including a credit plan here"

"Faith, please . . . it isn't quite as you describe it. . . . You've gotten my letters, haven't you? My apology . . . my profound apology."

Edward steers them toward the walkway that leads deeper into the complex. Other inpatients join family members. They stroll past a small brook and deliberately planted wildflowers like they're in the Bois de Boulogne in Paris.

"Yes, I've gotten them. Have you gotten mine?" she asks.

They're standing in bright sunlight, and he's more hairy than she remembers. Slight hairs on the lobes of his ears. She could send one of those nose and ear hair electric clippers, but it might be confiscated. Contraband. His smile is better than she remembers, more inviting. *Handsome husband*—Mrs. A's constant chant.

"I've gotten every letter, Faith. From you and from Katherine. Rhys sends postcards. On occasion."

"That's sweet of him."

"Eve too. Comic book postcards."

"I'm sure." Faith waits. "The letters must mean something, without being able to speak by phone, text, no Internet."

"I know, the lack of communication, it's not easy. Although it has made me introspective. I think a lot about what I've done, why I did it, things we need to talk about when I get back."

He leads her to a line of wooden benches. Behind them the thick trees sway in the breeze, reminding her of their trip to Prague and the public park they found there. Edward points to the only bench that's shaded and they sit together.

"Wow, Katherine could find or cook up a tale for us— about the old couple who has been estranged and then are reunited," Faith says.

"Wouldn't that be *The Odyssey*?"

"Is the journey that arduous?" Faith asks.

He nods. "Everyone is trying to be human again to varying degrees, depending how far we've fallen down, how long we were using or drinking. It's very tough, more difficult than I can describe."

If only he knew what she's been through. The lawyer hired to help negotiate a settlement, the amount Faith has cobbled together to pay what she can and strike a deal on the rest. A payout. It could take the rest of their lives.

"We can't speak for two minutes about what's going on with your finances?"

Edward shakes his head. "Against the rules. No stress, no . . ."

"No responsibility," Faith says very quietly. He is with her, filling the space, and he's not. If she touches the base of his neck, behind his ears, he might disintegrate.

"Sorry, what did you say?"

If it has to be unspoken, it can't mean her husband doesn't remember what he has done, what Faith must do to save them. Edward looks at the babbling brook and surrounding rosebushes, his face preternaturally calm. She waits. After a few minutes she asks, "What are the people like, Edward?"

"Nice, very nice. We have a softball game on Tuesdays and Thursdays at five. There's tennis—I play with a guy named George—and an aerobics class every morning. We have group sessions where we get to be friendly, understand each other." His contentment unnerves her, how pleased he is with his social life.

"I meant what are their stories? Why are they here?"

"They're varied. A lot of professionals. Men and women of every age, wanting to shake their habit, be clean." Edward speaks with precision. Faith has the urge to put her thumb and forefinger to his lips when they move, to feel the skin. Doesn't he have any questions—about Katherine, Vintage Tales, how she herself is faring?

"I'd like to report on Katherine, her life, her news."

"No talk about family either, unless the member is

visiting. Katherine will tell me when she comes in two weeks. I only need to know that she's well. I'm trying to stay sober, to become strong again. We have to keep it light."

"Well, she's good. Katherine is good," Faith says. She'll follow rules that have a shot at delivering Edward back to her. "I'm steadfast, supportive. I joined Nar-Alon. I go twice a week at night to meetings in Lantana. I've met some women, everyone is cordial. First-name basis, of course."

"I didn't know you joined, that's great. Just great." His face lights up. "I'll be stronger when I come home knowing this. I'll do daily meetings."

"We'll be moving, Edward, before you return, to—"

Edward puts his hand to Faith's mouth. "Shhh. Faith, don't tell me yet. I'm not ready to know."

The interior halls of the main inpatient building are painted a lifeless blue, the floors are a medium wood, and the lighting is nuanced. The subdued effect washes over Faith and Edward when they return to his residence a half hour later. Staff members move from room to room, doors open and close quietly as patients head to lunch. Lysol spray, Crisp Linen, envelops the entire wing. Faith waits outside Edward's door while he retrieves a sweater and then quickly reappears.

"Do you know what I've been taught at Touchstone Hill, Faith?" Edward asks as they walk toward the exit. For a midday meal, so ordinary an occurrence, so unclear what is ahead. "Not to make false promises. Not to make promises at all."

"Edward, I'm out there, doing my damnedest . . ."

"I have gratitude for that," he says. Spoken like a true recovering addict, a specific jargon, a necessary brainwashing. "I'm counting the days until I return."

"I'm counting them if you are sober, if you're coming home to me whole, Edward."

TWENTY-SEVEN

A six-day countdown until the meeting with the creditors begins. Reminding Faith of a wedding anniversary or Katherine's birthday once she hit the double digits. Except with a sordid aftertaste, a reflux. She hits the gas pedal and drives thirty-five in a twenty-five-mile-an-hour zone—cause for a ticket, not a warning, if stopped. Sun filters in and out of the clouds along Royal Palm Way. As she parks she can't recall the last time she was at High Dune—or what the occasion was. Perhaps when she worked with Gregoire ten years ago, decorating Edward's office for full impact. Bygone, another existence.

The longtime office manager, Joy, mid-fifties, polite, mild, ushers Faith into Edward's empty office and does a once-over. It could be Faith's eyeliner is smudged or her DVF wrap dress, a favorite, has been stained with pomodoro sauce. Faith refastens the hair clips holding her hair up and blows her nose.

"Is there anything I can get you?" Joy asks. "Would you care for something to drink, Perrier, a latte?"

"No, thank you. I'm okay, Joy," Faith answers. "I'm just looking around."

A bamboo charcoal air freshener is in the corner, something Edward would dislike. Joy follows Faith's gaze.

"No one has really been in here for a few weeks. I mentioned that when I called you. Now Henry has someone he'd like in this office." She stands very close.

"That's reasonable." Faith walks toward the midcentury Nakashima armchairs and Edward's sleek white marble desk. The light seems unnatural—even with the slatted blinds closed, the room feels both peaceful and deserted.

"Henry will be right in," Joy says as she reaches the door. She stares at Faith again, pauses. "I worked with Edward for thirteen years. That's how long I've been at High Dune. He was very good to me, very nice. Always."

"I know," Faith says. "I believe that."

Holding his hand out as if they're acquaintances who have run into each other at an oral surgeon's, Henry comes in. Again the Raimondo suit and shirt, the uniform that Edward also sported.

"Faith, you are a trooper."

"Hi, Henry. I don't know about that. I've come to empty Edward's desk." She puts on her progressives, looks at the shelves and cabinets beneath. "Who knows what I'll find—default letters, evidence of more loans. Could there be more obligations, more secrets?"

"I doubt it. Edward cleared out his files. I thought you

were here for what he didn't collect—books, photographs. His tennis trophies from Longreens."

A lineup of novels, John Irving, William Styron, John Updike, remain, along with history books, Stephen Ambrose, Joseph Ellis, Ron Chernow. A photograph of Faith, Edward, and Katherine in front of the Pierre Hotel, New York City, Thanksgiving, ten years earlier.

"Where are the trophies and the other pictures?"

"I asked Joy to have them bubble wrapped. She'll bring them to you along with anything else that's around."

Edward's office, ex-office, is a fortress. An abandonned corner room. She walks to his desk. "I spoke with the legal department at Touchstone Hill about coming today."

"So did we. Obviously, we wanted clearance. Full disclosure."

Full disclosure. Faith shakes her head. The sadness of it is biting.

"I wanted to tell you how much I regret what happened. I know you've been a good business partner to Edward," Faith says.

"We had a good run, a great run," Henry says. "It must be a nightmare for you, since I know how it's been for us. That someone, that Edward, could have gotten into this mess. I hear from Allison that Margot and Peggy Ann already have a buyer for your house. That'll raise cash. Are you freezing your membership at Longreens and the Harbor Club? Does Mar-a-Lago allow that?"

"I'm resigning, not freezing memberships. Every club, including Justine's. I figure you've heard already, or Allison has. Gossip is like a windstorm in the women's locker rooms. First whisperings, then judgments whipping up, from locker to locker. Clients ask why I'm not waiting to make big decisions for a year—isn't that the idea with widows and divorcées?"

"Ironically, the Edward we miss would be pleased with you," Henry says.

"I hope so. Anyway, I'm tired of pretending. I tried to, right after I found out. Then I became too monomaniacal about finding money to keep it up."

"What's your plan?" He coughs and clears his throat. "Are you ready to negotiate his debts in six days' time? I'm aware who's waiting for their money."

"I know too. I've contacted your lawyer, the one you suggested. I've taken charge."

"Good. Rob's excellent. He's seen it all." Henry seems remarkably relieved.

She conjures up a Palm Beach smile. "I brought a tale from Katherine that feels more like a parable or a sentimental gushy thing. She's been trying to attach it to a few colorful Gucci wallets. But it doesn't fit. *Le Petit Prince* by Saint-Exupéry. You know it, right?"

"I don't." Henry is getting impatient.

"I'll be quick. The Little Prince who came to Earth from a tiny planet was moral but naive. Here's what Katherine wrote." Faith unrolls the parchment paper. "'The Little Prince—Wisdom at a Price.' At first the prince didn't value his rose, he was insensitive as to why or how to love her. He left her behind—she was demanding and annoying. Then he saw beds of roses on Earth and realized his was special. Too late he gleaned the secrets of life and tried to return to her.'"

"I'm not sure I see the connection."

"Well, it's about loyalty, how mixed that gets. How lonely the Little Prince was without his rose. How hard it is to get a second chance after a serious mistake." Faith tucks the paper back into the envelope and passes it to Henry.

"The connection, the fable, won't ever work for an object, a thing sold in a shop; it's about people. About what's true."

"So can you pay Edward's debts?"

"I'm working on it. I'm hopeful," Faith says.

Heading south on I-95, Eve blasts the Grateful Dead. The songs fill her Durango, almost bouncing against the windows.

"I like brokers who meet you after six," Faith shouts over the music.

"I like brokers who aren't full of shit. You'll see, she's narrowed it down already, she won't waste your time."

"Did you clock the distance?" Faith asks.

"Twenty miles. Less than a half hour." Eve takes the exit for Atlantic Avenue.

Faith looks past Eve and out her window. "I'll miss dusk over the ocean."

"Hey, the view's free. Just get in your car and head east. Not everyone lives on the water. Not everyone who doesn't live on the water misses out on sunrises and sunsets."

Denise Laforte, Eve's friend, is waiting inside the first house with a slim folder in her hand. She opens the front door and shakes Faith's hand vigorously.

"Hello, hello. I'm so happy Eve introduced us. Eve"— Denise turns to her—"thank you."

Perhaps Denise is a Delray version of Peggy Ann

Letts—the ambition bubbling up, her pumps bonking on the off-white tile floors. She wears the Theory shift dress in black and medium-heeled nude classic pumps—they could be anyone's from Tahari to Cole Haan. In the ceiling light, the five shades of blonde—popcorn to butterscotch—show through her hair.

"We have three houses to see. I thought we'd begin here since the price is right; the house was renovated last year. I'd call it move-in condition. Spacious for not the most square footage of the three—the vaulted ceilings make the difference."

Faith looks up at the heavy bronze chandelier in the center of the double-height ceiling. "How many square feet, Denise? Oh, wait, I know, this one is two thousand square feet and small pets are allowed."

"Do you have a small animal?" Denise asks.

"I don't," Faith says. "I'm only citing the descriptions of each house."

"Well, then you know there's an eat-in kitchen with plenty of cabinet space. You'll notice the contemporary finishes. The white cabinets and quartz-like material used for the counters."

Eve is ahead of them, already by the screened-in patio. "Look, Faith, this works—almost like having another room."

"There's a two-car garage, and three bedrooms are off to the right." Denise is still peppy, but Faith senses she too has had an enervating day. "The bedrooms, Faith? This way."

Eve and Faith follow her the short distance to the bedroom "wing."

"A single-level home, with a patio for entertaining and

a darling backyard." Denise keeps the rhetoric going. "There's a master bedroom with an interior bathroom." She guides Faith and Eve. "And the two bedrooms with a shared bathroom."

An unexpected freshness comes through. Faith opens the closet door in the master bedroom, calculates what other parts of her wardrobe she'll sell to the RealReal. Dinner dresses, cocktail dresses, platforms, stilettos, a Burberry raincoat, a Prada spring coat in loden green. Gloves and scarves will be sold at her shop. Elsewhere she'll sell ski clothes, ski equipment, the kayak, the solid-silver Jensen vase and pitcher. She will winnow her belongings for the closet space of her new life.

"And no carpeting," Faith notices. "That's the selling point for me."

"Torn up and gone," Denise says. "I've rented this house for the last five years. It's very fresh; there's been only one tenant since the renovation."

A text comes in for Faith when the bell rings.

"Oh, excuse me." Faith opens the front door. "My daughters are here for a walk-through."

Katherine and Diana tumble into the small house. Since closing up Vintage Tales, they've changed into yoga pants and Puma sneakers. In contrast to Denise's footsteps, theirs patter across the bare flooring—prima ballerinas on stage in toe shoes.

"Why, your daughters must be about my daughters' age," Denise says as soon as introductions are over. "Early twenties, almost thirty?"

"Close," Eve says, looking out into the night from the floor-to-ceiling window in the living room.

"Mom, after you and Eve left we sold two Chloé bags

and a Birkin came in." Katherine is stretching as she speaks.

Denise smiles an obligatory smile. "The washer/dryer unit is in the utility room." Her shoes rat-a-tat as she leads them to the back door.

"Wow, that's efficient." Diana says. "Katherine, did you see how they've put it into the corner of this little space?"

"Sweet." Katherine looks around. "Small, but then lots of openness."

"There are three bedrooms, I've shown Eve and your mother. Would you like to see?"

"Yes, a bedroom for each of you," Faith says. "That's what I asked when Denise and I spoke. Rent is an issue, size is an issue—those are negotiable—but three bedrooms, that has to be."

"That's fine," Katherine says. "Except I'm with Rhys most nights. Then I'll be in New York by early August, a few weeks before school starts. We're looking on the Upper West Side, near Columbia."

"My lease in West Palm ends in two weeks," Diana says. "I have good friends in Delray, so it's a matter of shopping around and getting some leads on an apartment."

"I don't want you to be hasty, Faith," Denise says. "While this has its charm and the price is right, there is the one home, about a mile from here, that I suggest we drive to. We can pile into my car. The square footage is much more; there are five bedrooms and four baths. Then I have an apartment in a gated community, on a very quiet street. What works with that is the gym and pool."

"You know I love the gym at my place," Eve says. "We've talked about the amenities and the—"

"I'm sure they're a step up, and I'm sure they're more

luxurious. I like this place; it's simple and clean, and three thousand a month sounds about right to me. What do you think, girls?"

Mostly Eve and Katherine are processing Faith's decision, adjusting to the disparity between what was and what is. Diana walks the length of the living room, stops at the sliding glass door to stare at the December night. "It's comfortable, it's easy," she says.

"Faith, don't you think we should go with Denise, especially to look in the gated community?" Eve asks. "A step up, the price is still affordable. You don't need to be so extreme."

"With a fake lake? Some phony water canal, is that it? Not necessary. I understand what I'm doing," Faith says. She opens the file that Denise handed to her twenty minutes ago. "A one-year lease. Time goes quickly."

"Where will we find furniture?" Katherine asks.

"We'll find furniture," Eve says. "I know exactly how."

"I'd keep it fairly spare," Denise says. "To enhance the rooms. Its a trick of the eye."

TWENTY-EIGHT

W e have to pay in cash," Diana says, leading the way through the winding D&R Indoor Market the next morning at nine o'clock. "I told you that, right?"

"Eve told me." Faith looks around. "What a place. The scope of it."

"Thank God we wore sneakers and yoga pants." Katherine is on Diana's heels, tugging at Faith to follow. "The air-conditioning is a freeze-out."

"Plus we're on concrete floors." Diana moves as if she's speed walking for her workout.

"Wait, wait a second . . . let's see." Faith stops in front of a stall. The sign reads PASHMINAS $12, written on a large framed mirror in white chalk. "Look at how cleverly this is displayed. I doubt they're real pashmina—the term gets used so loosely. Not from some mountain goat in Kashmir for twelve dollars."

"Does anyone wear pashminas?" Katherine asks. "Remember when you had them in Vintage Tales in those blues and greens, those crazy pink shades? I was in third grade."

"Since it's about to be 2015, I'd say no one wears them like they did in 2000. Yet they're being sold. Some are really beautiful—so soft, and the colors," Diana says. "Katherine, you could do a tale about their history. Weren't they part of a wealthy woman's dowry in Nepal and India, centuries ago?"

"We'd need a romantic angle. Maybe some princess whose family no longer has wealth and she hasn't any pashminas."

"That's amusing," Faith says. They all laugh. "Seriously, we could try to resurrect the trend."

"No, you're supposed to give them up and make room in your closet. Especially since there isn't much closet space in the rental house," Katherine says.

Again they laugh. Faith walks up to the stall to feel the fabric. "Stiff," she whispers to the girls.

"Let's go!" Diana says. "Eve said to be quick."

Together they move through what is known as a Middle Eastern bazaar. An enclosed space filled with zealous sellers, the atmosphere frenzied, the mission obvious. Costume jewelry, fine jewelry, assorted rugs—Moroccan, contemporary, Southwestern—hats, toys, kickboards, surfboards.

"We thought you'd like it," Katherine says. "The furniture is at the other end. Diana and I sort of chose a few things. Kind of scouted for you."

"I thank both of you—it's a tight schedule. But these sellers, the funky booths, the more sophisticated ones, are fabulous."

Faith points to old steamer trunks and suitcases stacked up at one stall, mismatched dinner plates and pressed-glass pitchers placed in a large wicker basket at the next.

"They're stunning. I remember similar things from the mid-eighties, when my mother and I did the flea markets in South Jersey. We were outside, on crabgrass with unin-spired vendors, hell-bent on making money. No one sell-ing had any imagination. We just put out the goods and waited to make a sale."

"Before Jimmy?" Diana asks.

Katherine stops, waits.

Faith hesitates, watches Katherine. "Before and during Jimmy."

"I wish we had pictures," Diana says.

"Tell us, Mom," Katherine says. "We want to imagine you back then. With your mother."

Faith shakes her head. "I'm sorry, I haven't any pic-tures. How it was, well, they were summer fairs. We did it for three summers in a row. I remember each season they blasted songs by Sting, you know, 'Every Breath You Take.'"

"Sting. Sometimes you sound more like a big sister than a mother," Diana says.

"That's because she's a young mother, for both of us," Katherine says.

"I don't feel very young lately," Faith says. "Being here,

though, today, I remember those meadows, those merchants."

"What did you sell?" Diana asks.

"Whatever we could. Place mats, sheets, shampoo. Magnifying mirrors. Fake pearl bracelets, and I mean *fake*. They cost a dollar each. The last year I found these old evening bags, tossed in the trash. Some were mesh, a few were velvet. My mother and I painted flowers on the plain ones or glued on plastic shells. For the mesh ones we attached brooches. They became these crazy, whimsical little bags—very popular."

"You did not!" Diana says. "Is that your precursor to Vintage Tales?"

"I suppose," Faith says. "You know, I was thinking we could look for some vintage evening bags here—maybe Whiting and Davis bags—and decorate them. Go to an art store, get costume jewelry, and embellish them. Sell online or as an inexpensive item at the shop. We'll add appliqué—leaves or sunflowers—beaded handles, crystal handles."

Katherine blinks twice at Diana, who blinks back.

"Is it too corny?" Faith asks. "I guess so."

"It's not that," Katherine says. "Diana, show her."

Diana opens a small brown shopping bag and holds up a Whiting & Davis bag in black mesh.

"How weird that you're talking about this. Katherine and I bought this from a woman on the other side of the floor. She said it's from the twenties, Art Deco. She has others too, fifties versions, sixties. We were going to surprise you."

Faith almost cries, stops herself. She reaches out to

Diana and Katherine for an embrace. "So perfect, of course."

They hold on to one another. Faith imagines how it would have been on each occasion—birthdays, holidays, graduations—of the many lost years. "Thank you. I love it."

Diana leads once more. ". . . to the furniture. We have to get back to Palm Beach; Eve texted they're super busy at the shop."

"Look at this—the distressed dressers," Katherine says. "For the bedrooms. They're natural wood."

"That orange couch and the chaise in that plum faux leather." Diana points. "We found these for you, ahead of time."

"Let's get them," Faith says. "We could decorate the entire rental house, except for the beds, in twenty minutes!"

"Good." Diana walks to the couch and takes a tape measure out of her book bag. "The couch fits perfectly. Just what Katherine thought. What about that three-piece bistro set for the kitchen?"

Faith sits on one of the delicate wrought-iron chairs that has been sanded and grit-sand blocked to be an antiqued finish. She reads the price tag. "Two hundred dollars. This is like a garage sale."

Katherine plops down on the couch and Diana does the same. With the sharp fluorescent light overhead for the indoor stalls, they strongly resemble each other. Beyond that, some sort of gestalt that they share. *Sisters.*

Diana takes a tortoise-shell hair clip from her knapsack and clips up her hair.

"Do you have an extra one?" Katherine asks. "Out of nowhere it's hot."

"Take it." Diana offers Katherine her clip and starts scrounging around for another. She finds a scrunchie. "I'll use this."

The seller, a woman in her late fifties drinking a Diet Coke, is friendly. "Your daughters have good taste. The couch, the breakfast set, they're top quality. We deliver."

"Thank you." Faith smiles. "They really do have an eye; wherever they go, they'll select well. . . . I love what you have out on the floor."

"And the white writing desk." Katherine points. "Distressed wood, Mom. It's ninety-nine dollars."

"We'll take it all." Faith starts unrolling hundred-dollar bills.

The girls settle against the couch together while Faith writes the delivery address.

"I'll text Eve and tell her we're heading back," Diana says.

Katherine looks at her phone. "When can we tell Dad about the house?"

"Both homes," Diana says. "A signed contract and a lease."

"I'm writing him a letter tonight, and I'll say things are moving along. We're not supposed to write much more. Very upbeat, light information," Faith says.

"I wish we could FaceTime or text. I'd settle for an e-mail or phone call. That's how far away Dad seems."

Katherine looks around the indoor market, conceivably noticing the amount of Sheetrock on the walls and how close the stalls are to one another. "Do you know what today is? It's the winter solstice. Isn't this your favorite time of year, Mom?"

"For a long time it's been like that," Faith says.

With three days left to pay Edward's debts, Faith texts her attorney. *I'm about ready, please set up the meeting.*

TWENTY-NINE

South Florida in late July becomes a tropical climate. Faith adjusts to the spotty rain showers and unrelenting humidity, thunderstorms followed by sunbursts.

Having not been here in the summer beyond a day or two en route to other destinations, the ninety-degree temperatures, with a real feel of one hundred, astound her. Worth Avenue is unfrequented, left behind by snowbirds and locals alike. Yet for those who stay, there are enticements. The intensity of season is gone, summer sales are rampant, nighttime cools down—outdoor dining at Renato's or Bice is a treat. Although Eve has always managed Vintage Tales during the summer doldrums, Faith now joins the merchants left in town.

Perhaps today is the worst scorcher, Faith thinks when

she parks on the Avenue and winds through Via Amore to the shop. She finds Katherine standing at the printer in the upstairs office.

"I'm stockpiling tales," Katherine says. Like her mother, she wears the thinnest cotton dress from Island and thongs. "I thought if I printed them out, it'd be easier for you and Eve. Diana will look on her phone or the iPad. This way they're in front of you when inventory comes in. You can text me if you're not sure about a match."

"Katherine, you're not leaving for at least a week," Faith says.

"I want it complete for you, and you'll want a lot of stories, fables."

Placing the stack on the desk, she recites, "We have *Breakfast at Tiffany's*, *The Doctor's Dilemma*—you know, the Shaw play—and *Pygmalion*, also Shaw. Artemis—the myth about the Hellenic goddess, a protector of young girls—*Women in Love* by D. H. Lawrence, Lilith. A poem by Neruda, Cosette and Marius from *Les Misérables* . . . My motto is there's always another tale to attach."

"I promise we'll do our best while you're at Columbia, Katherine. We'll send pictures and you'll write up the tales as the items come in."

"For amazing new things," Katherine says. "Diana is so good at high/low merchandising. Paste, precious stones, crazy amounts of bags. Our latest—those embellished and adorned little mesh ones."

Faith walks to the thermostat and checks the temperature. "Is it too warm?"

"No, it's fine. Maybe you're nervous. I can go with you to Touchstone Hill, help with the drive, Mom."

"Thank you. I appreciate the offer. I told Dad I'd come

alone. I'll bring him up to date on the ride back." Faith holds Katherine tight. "He'll be great. He'll be his old self."

"How are you so sure, Mom?" Katherine says.

The concern, the fear, the threat that he won't be. "These last six months have been intense. I haven't had a chance to process . . ." Faith says.

"That's absurd," Eve says, coming up the stairs. "You've processed everything, sat at the desk, working, weeping. Don't judge quickly. See what stuff he's made of when he gets home. You've fought hard for him, and today's the reward, a fresh start."

Faith waits at the stairs, marveling at the Via and Worth Avenue. "It has to be like that."

Although they've been in together for most of the day, Faith remains uneasy, unable to settle in. As she drives, an awkwardness persists. Edward tips somewhat in the passenger seat. His navy polo shirt is faded, the Ralph Lauren insignia crumpled from too harsh a wash cycle at Touchstone Hill. He looks around, admiring Atlantic Avenue, the main street in Delray, when Faith pulls up.

"The street is jumping after seven o'clock," she says as they park parallel to Vintage Tales II in her white Jeep Cherokee. Moving back and forth, reverse and drive, Faith sandwiches them between a Hyundai SUV and a Pontiac sedan.

"You like driving this, don't you?"

"I really do. I leased it five months ago, as soon as I sold the Mercedes. Katherine and Diana weighed in on the choice."

She turns off the engine as Mick Jagger finishes singing the last stanza of "Wild Horses." "I even like the local FM station."

"Here we are, Delray Beach, 'a village by the sea.' Isn't that what they call it?" Edward asks.

"Well, take a good look, because our house is inland, beyond Military Trail. Let's go into the new shop and then—"

Edward puts his hand on Faith's knee. "Let's go to the house first, Faith, and you'll show me what you've done. What Katherine and Inez are up to, the decor, the goods, the better price point at the recent shop. I know it's fantastic. After we're at the house and have some time alone together—we'll do it then."

Alone together. How long she has missed him—before he left for rehab, before he actually lost their money and his career. For how long was Edward absent? Weren't the signs there—hasn't it been more than a year since he was himself? At least in his appearance, the man who sits with her, temperate, agreeable, reminds her of when Katherine was in kindergarten.

"Sure, that's fine." Faith turns to him.

Edward is breaking out in a sweat, not the kind he's gotten when playing tennis on a humid morning, but beads that gather in a row beneath his hairline.

"Are you okay?"

"I'm okay," Edward says. "A little lightheaded. The excitement of coming back, of being with you."

She loops toward him and kisses his cheek. He's

clammy. "Edward, I don't know, are you sure you're all right?"

"Anxiety," he laughs, and the color seems to return to his face. "Coming back sober. I'm fine, Faith."

"I know, I have the same anxiety," she says.

Opening the glove compartment, Edward finds a packet of tissues and pats his forehead. "I knew I'd find these."

"Always," she says. "Ready?"

"I am, especially since you confessed you're on edge too."

He is better. She backs the SUV out of the tight spot. They head west.

A few palm trees frame their tidy backyard. Faith switches on the ceiling fan and sits beside Edward on the screened-in porch.

"I bought the table and chairs at a flea market. The love seat is from Ikea," Faith says.

"It's great, there's a homey feel to it," Edward says.

"The house is compact and only slightly charming." Faith puts her forefinger and thumb in the air to show an inch.

"I like small spaces. I always have," Edward says.

"You like small spaces, how could I know?" The two of them smile.

"I can help too, fix things up. You said you wanted to find shades for the bedrooms, and I'll install them."

"You install shades?" Faith is surprised.

"I have done it. I've plunged toilets, I've even changed lightbulbs. I'm handy. I'll plant a vegetable garden too, a row of zinnias for you. Maybe wild roses; they're durable, pretty . . ."

Faith doesn't speak. After a moment he says, "I am committed to sobriety, Faith."

"I have your letters, your repeated promise. Doesn't everyone in rehab have to write that same form, that apology letter?" she asks.

"I suppose on some level. I sent one to you and one to Katherine. I asked for your forgiveness and hers for different wrongs. Some overlap, but essentially I failed you. I left you with my shambles."

"And at first I was shocked, then angry. Then in survival mode, which was effective." Faith looks out at their waterless view. Crabgrass mixed with old sod creates an ersatz sense of a lawn. Haphazard bushes scattered to the sides form a boundary.

"When I came to visit you that day, I wasn't sure how we'd do, if we'd make it. In the months since then . . . I missed you. I missed you by the end," she says.

"Why did you stick by me, Faith? Plenty of guys at Touchstone Hill weren't going to be welcomed back."

"You're worth it, that's why." She hesitates. "Still . . ."

"I'll have to figure things out, Faith."

"I've gotten by on my own. I've had to."

He puts his arms around her, tries to kiss her again. She tucks her head in to his shoulder. His hair smells like apple cider.

"This is where we talk about having each other, how I want it to be enough. How what we've been through isn't a deal breaker and makes us stronger," he says.

Several black flies flap against the screen, pushing hard to get inside. Faith faces Edward, assembles her courage.

"The night at the Shelteere, at the Rose Ball, I wanted to tell you something, Edward."

His stare, his eyes on her.

"Something I should have told you before we were married." She sighs. "Something that happened years ago. When I was sixteen, I—"

"I already know, Faith."

"No, you don't. You can't possibly know what I did and then didn't do. I have been carrying this around . . ."

"Katherine and Rhys visited. I sat with Katherine, the two of us, and I learned about Diana."

"Katherine? How could she do that? We were told, instructed, to only chat about superficial things with you—the weather, sports, comedy cable series."

"After I'd been there three months, she asked for permission to talk about a 'serious family matter.' Somehow she was allowed to do it. She wanted me to know ahead of my coming home, to not be upset when I first got back. She also wanted me to know that she's okay with it. That she accepts it—so I would be okay too, so I could understand."

The porch swirls around her, the heat rises. Faith tilts to hold her husband. His chest is broad again, the skin on his wrists is smooth, no longer tan. "I do understand, Faith."

He takes a note from his pocket. "While I was away, I read constantly. The library was impressive—Katherine liked it too. After she left that day, I did a little research. I guess I selected a tale—for you."

"For me?" Faith sits upright.

Edward nods. "Read it aloud."

Faith squints, begins in what's left of the daylight.

DEMETER AND PERSEPHONE

Demeter searches endlessly for her beloved daughter, Persephone, who was abducted into the underworld by Hades. Goddess of corn and harvest, Demeter is grief-stricken. She halts the seasons and living things die. A threat of extinction of life looms large, and Zeus sends Hermes below to fetch Persephone. But she's already eaten a few pomegranate seeds and is thus bound to Hades and the underworld for four months a year. "Please give me my daughter," Demeter beseeches Hades. "And when she is with me, I promise spring and summer." Hades complies and there is lightness on earth. When Persephone is beneath, in Demeter's sadness, earth endures autumn and winter. It is Demeter's fierce wish to be reunited with her daughter that makes this myth so poignant.

"Truly, Edward. I love this." She holds the paper to her heart.

"Good. I'm so glad."

He moves a bit nearer to her. They watch green herons and palm warblers hover over the yard.

"Do you remember the brown pelicans along the Intracoastal?" Faith asks.

"Of course. At night sometimes it's like I hear them, by our house. Our old house."

"Me too. I do too." She jumps up. "I'll make us iced tea—mint iced tea. And then we should think about dinner."

Faith returns, places the tray on the bamboo sideboard. "You will love the sunsets here, Edward, they're exquisite."

She walks to the screen. "Our new birds have landed. Did you notice?"

He doesn't answer. Faith turns around. "Edward?"

His head is lolling to one side. In what is left of daylight his eyes appear open. As if he sees nothing, hears nothing.

"Edward!" She rushes to him and kneels down. The setting sun casts him in light, then shadows.

The night moves in.

ACKNOWLEDGMENTS

I am grateful to those who stood by me: Alice Martell, wise, faithful agent; Jennifer Weis, patient, instinctive editor; Jennifer Enderlin and Sally Richardson, publishers, for their ongoing encouragement. Others at St. Martin's include Dori Weintraub, Sylvan Creekmore, Paul Hochman, and Bethany Reis. Early advisers: Sarah McElwain, George Bear, James Parry, and Jonathan Stone. Family and friends: Brondi Borer, Helene Barre, Thomas Moore III, Katinka Matson, Jane Shapiro, Meredith Bernstein, Helen Metzger, Judy H. Shapiro, Mark L. Shapiro, Suzanne Murphy, Kara Ivancich, Tina Chen, Sandra Leitner, Jane Gordon, Kim Weiss, and Patti Abramson.

For her incisive edits and discerning eye, Alexandra Shelley. Meryl Moss, longtime publicist, who suggested the locale; Linda Berley, savvy guide to this barrier island; Gregory Ivancich for his boat knowledge; Jeffrey Singer, cofounder of Circa, for his skill in precious stones. My father and late mother, staunch cheerleaders, who introduced me to Palm Beach and together never missed a winter season. My daughters, Jennie and Elizabeth, muses always. My son, Michael, and son-in-law, Max. Howard Ressler, intrepid, constant.

ABOUT THE AUTHOR

James Maher

Susannah Marren is the author of *Between the Tides* and the pseudonym for Susan Shapiro Barash, who has written thirteen nonfiction books, including *Tripping the Prom Queen* and *Toxic Friends*. She lives in New York City and teaches gender studies in the Writing Department at Marymount Manhattan College.